To the left, a man was standing alone

He was staring at her with single-minded concentration. It wasn't simple curiosity in his gaze, and the quality of it locked her in place. For a weird moment she thought she was falling over the balustrade right into his arms.

Even now his eyes didn't let go. In fact, the connection grew stronger. They might have been illicit lovers or sworn enemies, so strong was the focus each had on the other. A shiver passed through her; it was as though no man had ever looked at her before. She wanted to move away, but the hypnotic nature of his gaze blocked her every attempt.

Was he sizing her up and finding her wanting? Why should that be? She felt dizzy, as though not enough oxygen was getting to her brain. It was clear she had to do something to break the deadlock.

She closed her eyes tightly. When she opened them again, the man was gone. She was shocked by the impact a stranger had had on her, especially when neither had spoken a word. Who was he? She didn't know him and had no desire to. Her intuition told her he would be dangerous.

Dear Reader,

The Horseman completes my four-book series entitled
MEN OF THE OUTBACK. I do hope you've kept with
me so far, as the stories are linked not only in their setting,
the Northern Territory, the remotest and wildest part of the
continent, but also by the lives of the interlinked families
who call this fascinating place home. If you're one of my
longtime readers you'll know "family" is a recurring theme
in my books. (And if you're not, a big welcome to you!)

I like to portray family with the petals and the thorns.
Families anywhere in the world don't differ all that widely.
They have secrets, running feuds and personal histories
that often contain more than a grain of fiction. As I have
frequently written, the sort of family you grow up in affects
you throughout your life, sometimes to the very end. The
strong and resilient will break free; others are doomed to carry
the conflict forward into succeeding generations. I'm sure
many of you can name a family—perhaps even from your own
street—that runs the risk of being called dysfunctional. But I
like to bring balance to such families by writing of hopes and
dreams, and to introduce heroes and heroines who focus their
energies on making a bright future for themselves and those
they love.

My warmest wishes to you all. Happy reading!

Margaret Way

THE HORSEMAN
Margaret Way

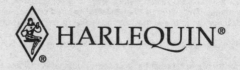

HARLEQUIN®

TORONTO • NEW YORK • LONDON
AMSTERDAM • PARIS • SYDNEY • HAMBURG
STOCKHOLM • ATHENS • TOKYO • MILAN • MADRID
PRAGUE • WARSAW • BUDAPEST • AUCKLAND

ISBN-13: 978-0-373-71363-9
ISBN-10:   0-373-71363-0

THE HORSEMAN

Copyright © 2006 by Margaret Way Pty Ltd.

This edition published by arrangement with Harlequin Books S.A.

® and TM are trademarks of the publisher. Trademarks indicated with ® are registered in the United States Patent and Trademark Office, the Canadian Trade Marks Office and in other countries.

www.eHarlequin.com

Printed in U.S.A.

ABOUT THE AUTHOR

Margaret Way was born and bred in the river city of Brisbane, Australia. Said to be able to read at three, she hasn't had her head out of a book since. When she wasn't reading she was playing the piano. She turned to writing when she was unable to practice while her infant son slept. She sold that first book–which she wrote longhand–and has gone on to publish over eighty books with Harlequin.

Books by Margaret Way

HARLEQUIN SUPERROMANCE

762–THE AUSTRALIAN HEIRESS
966–THE CATTLE BARON
1039–SECRETS OF THE OUTBACK
1111–SARAH'S BABY*
1183–HOME TO EDEN*
1328–THE CATTLEMAN**

HARLEQUIN ROMANCE

3891–THE CATTLE BARON'S BRIDE**
3895–HER OUTBACK PROTECTOR**

*Koomera Crossing
**Men of the Outback

CHAPTER ONE

The Moreland Mansion
Darwin
Northern Territory
Australia

CECILE MORELAND sat in front of her dressing table making final adjustments to her bridesmaid's headdress, a garland of silk flowers and foliage scattered with sparkling crystals. Excitement, like a swarm of butterflies, fluttered in her stomach. She wondered how much more excited Sandra was for this was Sandra's day of days, the day she and Daniel were to be married.

The weather was perfect. No bride could have asked for more. Cobalt skies of perfect clarity, a light cooling breeze off the harbor, the mansion's extensive gardens coaxed to perfection, ablaze with flower beds that dripped gorgeous blossoms. Brilliantly colored parrots, chittering and chattering as if they, too, were caught up in the excitement, flashed through the great shade trees that formed a canopy over the long drive, from the massive wrought-iron gates at the entrance up to the house. Everywhere smelled of flowers and cut grass. It was absolutely intoxicating.

Cecile swallowed a rush of emotion she couldn't afford

to indulge; she was all made up and just about ready to join Sandra and the other bridesmaids, but she was still experiencing an overwhelming sense of gratitude and amazement. Daniel, who had grown to manhood with his origins uncertain, had been discovered to be a Moreland; in fact, her first cousin. It was especially hard to believe, because it was less than a year since she had become aware of his existence, let alone that he was part of her family.

They shared a grandfather, Joel Moreland, known throughout the Territory as the Man with the Midas Touch. Daniel, it turned out, was the son of her uncle Jared, who had been killed as a young man in a freak accident at the Alice Springs annual rodeo when Daniel was still in his mother's womb. Whether Jared had been aware of the pregnancy no one would ever know, but the consensus of opinion was, Jared would never have let the mother of his child disappear from his life; it was alien to his nature. Now, Daniel and Sandra's meeting was a wonderful example of synchronicity, the connections that govern human life. Cecile felt moved by that thought. If ever two people deserved to be happy, it was those two.

Softly humming Mendelssohn's "Wedding March" beneath her breath, Cecile rose from the small gilded chair, satisfied with the positioning of her headdress. She smoothed the lovely floor-length skirt of her strapless silk and satin gown, happy in the knowledge it suited her beautifully. The lustrous material was the color of a silver-gray South Sea pearl that under lights, appeared to be shot through with rays of color from her headdress, a mix of pinks, yellows, lilacs and amethyst with accents of palest green. The maid of honor, Melinda, Sandra's friend from her university days, would be wearing an intense shade of pink, the other two bridesmaids, Eva and Denise, sunshine-yellow and a complementary deep lilac respectively. Sandra had taken her inspiration from the exquisite pastel plumage of one of her favorite birds of the Red Centre. This was the elusive Princess Alexandra parrot, named in honor of the Danish princess Alexandra who later became consort to Edward VII of England. Sandra, herself, had been christened Alexandra Mary after her Scottish great-great-grandmother, so it was easy to see the connection. The garlands they all wore on their heads took their theme from the infinite varieties of wildflowers that cloaked Sandra's desert home after the rains. The five of them had settled on their outfits over one very happy get-acquainted weekend on Moondai, the historic station Sandra had inherited from her late grandfather, Rigby Kingston. All four bridesmaids were brunettes, which made a striking contrast with the buttercup blondness of the bride, Cecile thought. She felt honored that Sandra had chosen her to be part of the bridal party. After all, she was a newcomer to Sandra's life, but their rapport, established before the big engagement party on Moondai, had been instant, which is about as gratifying as it gets.

Cecile drifted onto the balcony to look over the extensive gardens, ten acres in all. Huge white marquees with pink pelmets and tassels had been erected in the grounds: one for the banquet; another to house drinks of all kinds, from French champagne to Coca-Cola; the third for the lavish selection of desserts and coffee. Hundreds of circular white tables and chairs, their backs adorned with huge ivory satin bows, had been set out on the lush green lawn, which swept down to a delightful spring-fed lake that glittered under the tropical sun. Ever since she could remember the lake had been home to a pair of black swans called Apollo and Daphne. Though she recalled how Daphne, initially trying to escape Apollo's attentions, had turned herself into a tree, the two had mated for life.

The surrounds of the small lake were densely planted with continuously flowering white arum lilies and gorgeous Japanese iris, the water and the boggy conditions ideal for both plants. The actual ceremony would take place not far from the lake in a sheltered glade where countless heads of blue hydrangea were in big showy bloom. The glade had been a favorite haunt of hers as a child, mainly because of the large pentagonal-shaped summer house with its exotic pagoda-like roof. Under that magical roof Daniel and Sandra would be married.

When she was younger—Cecile was now twenty-six and the despair of her mother, who thought twenty-six high time she was married off and carrying her first child—she had thought the glade was where she would like to be married. Stuart, her fiancé, didn't care for that idea at all. He wanted a big cathedral wedding with lots of pomp in their hometown of Melbourne. Stuart was big on pomp and the symbols of success: the grand house; stable of luxury cars; beautiful wife; two perfect kids, boy first, then girl; rich in-laws highly respected in society. A lot to ask for and obviously not yet attained, but she had said yes to his proposal almost a year before. Why, then, was she having difficulty naming a wedding date? Both Stuart and her mother had been pressing her of late to do so—she didn't blame them—but still she couldn't bring herself to commit. She was beginning to realize there was something profoundly significant in that, though she continued to berate herself for her intransigence as though intransigence were a dirty word. She was *certain* Stuart loved her. She loved him. She *did,* didn't she? Why this awful doubt? Why *now?* Their architect-designed house in Melbourne was already undergoing construction. The exclusive site was a gift from her parents. She and Stuart had known one another for years and years. Their families approved, especially her mother, who continued to try very hard to dictate her only child's every move.

Thinking of her mother, Cecile gave an involuntary sigh. Her mother wasn't a happy woman. She was a good woman who had tried all her married life to be the perfect wife. She fussed over her husband who was, in fact, a distant Moreland kinsman, so she'd never had to change her name. She was a tireless worker for charity. She kept a beautiful house and a legendary garden. For decades she had devoted herself to endless dinner parties run like military maneuvers to further her husband's business and social status. Cecile's father was now CEO of Moreland Minerals, a position he held for more than fifteen years. It was confidently expected he would one day take over from her grandfather as chairman. Her mother *should* have been happy, achieving so much. Instead she was a rather driven woman, taking pride but no joy in her accomplishments. Cecile knew for a sad fact that her father had sought physical and mental balm in the occasional discreet affair. For years she had been terrified her mother would find out, but eventually she realized her mother would never question her father until the day she died. Instead, she had made an art form of blocking out any unpleasantness. Her mother's headstone might well read: *Here lies a woman who never delved too deeply.*

Cecile caught back another sigh as the old troubles and tensions of her childhood and adolescence began to creep over her. It was essential she throw off these unhappy thoughts, indeed obligatory, on this happy day, but they kept invading her mind. It saddened her deeply that there was no crucial spark of love between her parents, no special looks they gave one another as Stuart's parents did. There were no intimate, loving glances indicative of a happy shared life, certainly no private let alone public displays of affection. They were more like colleagues who rubbed along comfortably together. There must have been a spark at the beginning surely? Or had her father—as her razor-tongued great-aunt Bea had occasionally suggested—considered that there were more important considerations in marriage than romantic love? Her father was brilliant at business transactions. Were she and Bea too cynical? On such a day as today it was difficult not to contrast what Daniel and Sandra had with what love was in her parents' marriage. Maybe that *blaze* of love happened only rarely. Maybe her mother wasn't destined ever to know it. Maybe, for all her so-called beauty, she wasn't even the kind of woman who inspired passion. Physical beauty certainly didn't reflect all the manifestations of the psyche. There were far more important traits that allowed one to take that enormous step forward.

It was Daniel and Sandra who had been so blessed. In less than an hour they would exchange their marriage vows. It was truly a love match. A fairy story that offered the promise of living happily ever after. Cecile hoped and prayed that promise would come true. Although Sandra was about to become Mrs. Daniel Moreland, the press was still calling Sandra the Kingston Heiress. Probably that label would stick to her all her life. The couple who had wanted a quiet wedding with only family and close friends had a big society

wedding on their hands. It couldn't be otherwise with the
bridegroom having Joel Moreland for a grandfather. The top
journalist from the nation's leading women's magazine was
numbered among the guests. The hefty fee for sole coverage
of the wedding would go to the charity closest to Sandra's
heart, a foundation doing research into childhood leukemia.
Sandra had once had a little friend called Nicole, who had
lost her life to that cruel disease.

At his death over a year before, Rigby Kingston, Sandra's
grandfather, one of the Territory's most prominent and influ-
ential cattlemen, had shocked the entire Outback by doing
what had never been done before. He had bypassed his son
and his grandson to leave Moondai and the bulk of his estate
to his estranged granddaughter, daughter of his deceased
firstborn son and acknowledged heir, Trevor, who had been
killed when the station Cessna plowed into the purple ranges
that lay at Moondai's back door. That tragedy had marked the
family forever. When Trevor's daughter inherited, many
believed it was Kingston's effort to "make things right."
Moondai would have gone to Trevor had he lived. That his
daughter inherited was seen as reparation for Kingston's
having banished her and her social-butterfly mother shortly
after the tragedy. At that time Sandra had been ten going on
eleven—not the best time to be banished. Sandra had suffered
because of it, but it was apparent to everyone who knew her
that she hadn't broken. Rather, she had grown strong in ad-
versity, a sign of her strength of character. Cecile greatly
admired her for it.

What happened after Sandra arrived on Moondai to take
up her inheritance was the stuff of romantic fiction. Desti-
nies converged when she met Daniel. He had been Rigby

Kingston's overseer at the time of his death, and Kingston's right-hand man. With the future of Moondai at stake, Kingston had left Daniel a substantial legacy to ensure he would remain in place until such time as his granddaughter, Alexandra, could find a suitable replacement to help her run the historic station should Daniel wish to leave. Her uncle and cousin would be no help to her. Something Kingston had clearly taken into account. Neither by their own admission were cattlemen. They had no taste for the job, let alone the talent. Daniel, however, was highly regarded by everyone in the industry. Some thought having the brains and the sheer *authority* to run a vast cattle station had to be in the blood.

And so it had proved. Daniel had grown up in humble circumstances not knowing the identity of his father. His mother, physically and emotionally fragile, had been badly affected. She had gone to her grave never revealing his name. Daniel, not surprisingly, grew to manhood despising the man who had abandoned his vulnerable mother in her time of need. His mother's fate had always rankled him far more than his own rejection at his father's hands. Daniel was tough. But blood, like the truth, will out eventually no matter how long it takes. Daniel in maturity carried the stamp of a Moreland—the looks, the voice, the manner—and the double helix, the DNA that binds blood. A deathbed confession had led to an investigation that in the end established Daniel's identity. Daniel, born posthumously, was the son of Jared Moreland.

It was their grandfather Joel who had acted on that staggering deathbed confession made by his own wife, Frances. Now Daniel had taken his rightful place within the Moreland family. It had come as a further shock to Cecile to discover she and Daniel shared the "family face." Indeed anyone seeing them together could easily mistake them for twins. Both were happy to settle for first cousins, and she had the honor now of being in his bridal party.

Weddings, she reflected, had a miraculous way of bringing everyone together. She rejoiced in the mantle of happiness that had fallen over the Moreland household. Their grandfather Joel was in splendid form. All those long years without his beloved son, Jared! Now the wheel of fortune had turned full circle. It had restored to him his grandson. All the Morelands were gathered here today, happy to share in this joyous occasion. Three hundred guests from around the country and overseas had already arrived. A great many were roaming all over the grounds like butterflies that flew around the great banks of lantana, pink, white and gold.

It had been decided in a family conference that the logistics of holding the wedding at isolated Moondai in the Red Centre were much more difficult than holding the wedding at "Morelands" in Darwin. Sandra had had no objection; the guests could attend and find accommodation. She wanted nothing more than to marry her Daniel. But then, too, Sandra had grown close to Joel Moreland. She knew intuitively that a wedding held at Morelands would have very special meaning for him. Cecile couldn't have been more pleased. Her grandfather was as good and kind and brave a man as one could ever wish to meet. That Daniel shared many of their grandfather's characteristics had made her warm to him at once.

Graceful as a swan in her bridesmaid's regalia, Cecile glided over to the white wrought-iron balustrade, dazzled by the scene in front of her. Everyone looked resplendent in their wedding finery—many a dashing morning suit among the well-dressed men, glamorous gowns, gorgeous hats, the glitter of expensive jewelry. The children, too, were decked out in formal dress, the little girls adorable in silks and taffetas and organzas, with shining hair drifting down their backs, though no one could stop them from darting all over the grounds, calling to one another, ignoring the pleas of their parents as they hid behind billowing bushes of hibiscus, frangipani and oleander. She could remember doing exactly the same thing with her friends at the innumerable functions her grandparents had held in the grounds.

It was a few moments before that special sense of hers told her she was under surveillance. There were no words to explain where that sense came from; it was just *there*. She stayed perfectly still, though she was aware her breath was coming unevenly. Then, not making a business of it, she shifted her gaze slowly…slowly…following the magnetic beam.

To the left of her, a man was standing alone in a little pocket of quiet. He was staring at her with single-minded concentration. It wasn't simple curiosity in his gaze, and the *quality* of it, indeed his whole body language, locked her in place. For a weird moment she thought she was falling…falling…plunging over the balustrade right into his arms.

Wedding hysteria? The delusion of falling lasted no more than a second or two, yet she remained in a state of confusion, steadying herself with one hand on the wrought-iron banister. She was positive he had been staring at her for some time. Indeed he inclined his head in what she interpreted as a sardonic bow to which she found herself giving him the smallest nod in response. It was a graceful but essentially aloof acknowledgment that wouldn't have been amiss in royalty.

Heat burned in her cheeks. Even now his eyes didn't let go. In fact, the connection, which defied interpretation, grew

MARGARET WAY 17

stronger. They might have been illicit lovers or sworn enemies, so strong was the focus each had on the other.

He was impressively tall. As tall as Daniel, which meant well over six feet, with a similar athletic build. He was dressed in a beautifully tailored camel-colored suit, a deep blue shirt with a white collar beneath, and a wide blue silk tie with broad white stripes banded in either black or navy; she couldn't at this distance tell which. A shaft of dappled sunlight was shining directly on his thick, springy hair, picking out blond strands in the dark caramel. She couldn't see the color of his eyes. She thought dark. What she knew for certain was that they were holding her in place while he took his fill of her.

She registered the strong bone structure, the high cheek-bones, fine straight nose, beautifully sculpted jawline. It was a face not easily forgotten. His skin had the dark tan of a man who spent long hours in a hot sun. He looked to be around thirty, thirty-two, no more. She had never seen him before in her life, but she thought she could pick him out of thousands. He exuded power and vitality as though at any moment he could morph into a man of action, striding across the desert or tackling the world's highest mountains.

A shiver passed through her; it was as though no man had ever looked at her before. She wanted to pull away from the balustrade, but the hypnotic quality of his gaze blocked her every attempt to move. It seemed like an age but it could only have been moments. She couldn't believe this was happening. It *shouldn't* be happening, yet she stood there as if she wanted to do nothing other. What was his expression? It wasn't relaxed. It wasn't smiling or even pleasant. For an odd moment she thought his gaze was judgmental. Was he sizing her up and finding her wanting? Why should that be? They were perfect strangers. She felt a little dizzy as though not enough oxygen was getting to her brain. It was clear she had to do something to break the deadlock.

She closed her eyes tightly in an act of defiance, wishing Stuart was by her side. Did she think herself in need of protection?

When she opened them again, the man had moved into the cool green shadows of a feathery poinciana, where he was joined by a trio of attractive young women with their arms interlaced with one another. She could hear their laughing voices as they introduced themselves. One took hold of his sleeve, gazing up into his face, while the others talked excitedly. But then, a man who looked like that would have a steady stream of women beating a path to his side.

At last she felt free to move away from the balustrade. She was shocked by the impact a total stranger had had on her, especially when neither had spoken a word. As she moved back into her bedroom, a ripple of something approaching antagonism passed through her. She made a real effort to control it. Who *was* he? She didn't know him and had no desire to. Her well-honed intuition told her he would be dangerous to know. Perversely she speculated on who he might be. He had to be a guest of Sandra's or someone from Daniel's past. She knew just about everyone on the Moreland side. She couldn't remember a time any man had so caught her attention. Whoever he was, he was a force in his own right.

SANDRA'S HUGE BEDROOM WAS abuzz with excited young women in beautiful gowns, but none more beautiful than the bride, who was executing a dreamy little waltz around the room, her arms raised as if to her groom. Sandra was wearing traditional white, an exquisite high-necked Edwardian style lace-and-silk bodice, with dozens of seed pearls hand-applied, the full-length sleeves a continuation of the bodice lace, pegged down the arm. The tightly fitted sashed waist emphasized the billow of the silk skirt. The style suited her petite frame and the blue and gold of her looks. On her head she wore, set straight on her forehead, a garland similar to her bridesmaids', only her flowers were in shades of ivory and cream with the addition of a short shimmering white tulle veil.

The excitement in the room was palpable. Cecile thought she could reach out and grab a handful out of the perfumed air that had as its top notes a floral bouquet of rose, gardenia and lily of the valley.

Sandra flashed a radiant smile. "Ceci, you look wonderful!"

Cecile hurried to her, hugging her with real affection. "I couldn't possibly rival you. You're as lovely as a tea rose." Cecile could feel tears rise to her eyes.

"Don't you dare cry!" Sandra warned, not very far away from bursting into emotional tears herself.

Cecile bit her lip, calling to the other bridesmaids in warm tones, "You look great, too!"

"It's the wedding of the year, my dear," Denise answered, with a flourish of her skirt.

"Ladies, please!" The hairstylist who had been employed to do their hair clapped his hands to get their attention, but that proved impossible. For Sandra's mother, Pamela, looking as glamorous as a film star in a short-skirted Chanel suit and a sexy fascinator on her blond head, chose that moment to walk into the room carrying the beautifully wrapped gifts from Sandra to her bridesmaids. She presented one to each young woman in turn while they exclaimed in delight.

Melinda lost the least time pulling off the elegant wrapping. What she saw made her suck in her breath. "Oooooh!" Slowly she withdrew from the jeweler's box a rope of freshwater pearls fashioned into a choker with a large central clasp of deep pink tourmaline. "Sandy, is this for me?" Her voice wobbled in a mix of awe and delight.

"No one else!" Sandra smiled. "As you can see—" she looked at each of her bridesmaids in turn "—each clasp was chosen to coordinate with your gowns. Pink tourmaline for Melinda, topaz for Eva, amethyst for Denise, pave diamonds for Cecile."

"How absolutely gorgeous, and so generous!" Denise rushed to the long pier mirror to put on her choker. Once fastened, she stared at herself wide-eyed as the big central amethyst caught the light.

"I'm going to treasure this all my life!" Eva was poring over her gift, her fingers caressing the lustrous rope of pearls.

"Here, let me help you put it on," the hairstylist offered, thrilled he had been chosen for what was a big society wedding, one that would get national coverage.

Denise moved away from the mirror to allow Cecile her turn. Beautiful before, the choker with its sunburst of pave diamonds complemented Cecile's gown dramatically and drew attention to the silver shimmer of her eyes.

"Perfect!" Sandra murmured in satisfaction, smiling at Cecile's shoulder.

"Heavens, don't blind us, Cecile!" Denise joked, wishing she could look like Cecile Moreland if only for one day. "Hey,

Sandy," she addressed the bride, "you've got to have something old now, something borrowed, something new…"

"And something *blue,*" Melinda chimed in.

Sandra waved her magnificent sapphire-and-diamond engagement ring in the air. "Here's the blue. Mama—" she pointed to her youthful-looking mother "—supplied the something old, but that's a closely guarded secret."

"A very fancy garter, I bet," Denise giggled.

"*Nooo,* Denise," Pamela dragged out the word humorously, "not a garter. So are we all ready?" Pamela picked up her daughter's exquisite trailing bouquet and passed it to her. "You look beautiful, darling. I'm so proud of you." Pamela hugged her daughter one last time. "We're going to get through this splendidly. That means no tears to ruin your makeup. All right, girls, the bridegroom, his attendants and hundreds of guests await!"

Laughing happily, they moved in succession out of Sandra's bedroom, excitement alone lending them all a special loveliness. Weddings spread their own magic, Cecile thought. This was a day when nothing could go wrong. Or nothing would *dare* go wrong. So why did she feel something already had?

CHAPTER TWO

THE CEREMONY WAS one of high emotion. Family and guests were infused with the bliss that surrounded the bride and her groom. As the couple came together for the ceremonial kiss, many of the women guests yielded to an emotional tear, remembering their own wedding day or perhaps the wedding of a beloved son or daughter. Taking her new husband's arm, Sandra led the way to the wedding banquet, which turned out to be brilliant. The food and drink were superb. There were speeches, short and entertaining, that had people laughing; others were deeply touching, such as Joel Moreland's welcoming the bride into the family, an event he said couldn't have taken place had his grandson, Daniel, not have been restored to him.

Afterward there was a great deal of catching up to do as relatives who hadn't seen one another in ages came together and friends from either side of the bridal party were introduced to one another. Professional photographers were on hand to record the happy occasion. The press photographer, with a large video camera in hand, worked his way through the throng while guests took photographs destined for private albums. The bride found herself surrounded by old friends all wanting to embrace her; the groom found he had even more cousins than he had ever dreamt of. There were people everywhere: inside the flower-decked house, with all the French doors standing open to the garden; in the main reception rooms, the huge living room, dining room, library, garden room at the rear of the house. Young people sat all over the steps of the grand staircase, eager to make new friends and, who knows? meet the love of their life. Or dancing to the excellent band had already begun on the broad stone terrace that wrapped the rear of the mansion. Many more guests, champagne flutes in hand, were wandering about the beautiful grounds, admiring the flowers and the antique statuary. Some of the children had stripped off their wedding finery to dive near naked and shrieking into the lake, with inevitably a few adults who'd had too much to drink falling in to join them.

Cecile roamed freely with Stuart, the two stopping frequently to converse with family and guests. Invariably someone, most often a woman, told them archly, "You two will be next!" At such times Stuart always drew Cecile close, dropping a kiss on her temple beneath the lovely garland of silk flowers. "Can't come soon enough for me!" was his most favored response.

It was an answer that should have made Cecile glow. Instead something twisted inside her and on this day of days she found herself badly unsettled. Was it being witness to the love between Daniel and Sandra that had crystallized her long-growing uncertainties? Or was it having that man look at her as he did? She wasn't a temperamental woman—she rather prided herself on her composure—but that look had shaken her. To think that out of the wild blue yonder she had been plunged into what amounted to panic! Such things didn't happen to her. It didn't seem possible that a mere look could turn her world upside down. The answer presented itself. Because it was so primitive, so much man-woman, so irrevocably *physical*. She might as well have been standing on the balcony with her gown transparent. She had to force herself to stop quivering

For a fraught moment Cecile felt like slumping onto one of the stone garden benches, head in hands. There would be a terrible backlash from Stuart and his family if she ever thought to break her engagement. They, who were all so much *for* her, would overnight turn against her. Bitterness and anger would take hold, never to let go. She would be made to feel their public humiliation. In her heart she knew part of her appeal for Stuart and his family was her being Joel Moreland's granddaughter. She had grown up knowing that being the *only* granddaughter of one of the country's richest men affected her relationship with others. Some actively pursued friendship, others, motivated by envy became detractors behind her back. She was never one hundred percent sure who actually liked her for herself except for a trusted few, whose friendship *she* cherished. Even Stuart, by his own admission, was a man on a mission. He wanted to be a real player. He was already on his way. A very bright associate in a leading law firm, Stuart Carlson was looking at being made a full partner within a year or two. He had political aspirations, as well, perhaps borne of his longing to be in the spotlight. She had often teased him about his ambitions. Now she thought they were too overriding. Even in the past year Stuart had become increasingly bent on cultivating the *right* people and discarding those he judged as not really going anywhere. It seemed to her sadly false, though she realized Stuart wasn't alone in setting his goals on climbing the social ladder to the top rung. Marrying a Moreland greatly increased his chances.

And what of her mother? Cecile had spent her life trying to appease and placate her nerve-ridden mother, so she knew Justine would be devastated by any change of plan. For reasons she had never really been able to fathom, Stuart and her mother were huge allies. Of course, Stuart had always gone out of his way to charm her—very attentive, bringing wine and flowers, the special handmade chocolates her mother loved—but even that didn't explain it. She knew her mother saw Stuart as someone on side with *her*; a young man who would make a good son-in-law, who with her guidance could develop into a pillar of society; steady and reliable, a one-woman man who could be depended upon to honor his marriage vows. A judgment Justine knew in her heart of hearts didn't fit her husband.

ALL THE WHILE they were roaming, Cecile was very much aware of Stuart's arm clamped possessively around her waist. She couldn't bring herself to hurt him by breaking free, but it struck her that she wanted to walk alone, not linked to the man she had chosen to marry.

It will make it so much easier for you to find the stranger, said a harsh little voice inside her head. It was excruciating to have to acknowledge it, but it was true. She was actively searching for his tall striking figure among the milling crowd.

You idiot! the harsh little voice whispered on. *He's trouble. You know that. He's someone who can upset your whole life.*

She couldn't claim she had no portent of this. Every nerve in her body was shrieking a warning. Wasn't it extremely foolish then to ignore that warning when she should be listening? It was out of character for her to behave this way, but she found she couldn't stop.

Stuart told her repeatedly how beautiful she looked. "There's not a woman here to touch you!" Pride transformed his smooth, self-assured face, his *lawyer's face* as she thought of it. They were standing in the dappled shadows of a shade tree, he playing with her fingers. Slowly, almost reverently, he lifted the hand that bore his splendid diamond engagement ring to his mouth.

"Ceci?" He looked longingly into her eyes. "You have to marry me very soon. I'm *crazy* about you, don't you know?"

"I do, Stuart, I do!" Her heart felt as though it could break. How could she possibly betray him and his love? How could she even think about it? She had given her solemn promise to marry him. She'd had any number of admirers to choose from since the age of sixteen, but none she'd been able to take as seriously as Stuart. She wanted to marry. She wanted children. She loved children. She would be a good mother, shielding any child of hers from all the pressures that had attended her own childhood. There wasn't going to be any grand passion for her. No use waiting around for it. The knowledge was a factor in her decision to marry Stuart, who had many attractive qualities and, she believed, genuinely loved her. Everyone knew lightning strikes were dangerous, anyway.

There was absolutely no way out.

Stuart threw back his dark head and laughed triumphantly. "That's the very thing I'm desperate for you to say—'I do.' A June wedding would be perfect, wouldn't it, darling? We need to be together, man and wife. I know you love the idea of Morelands for the wedding, but surely you'd want to be married from your own home? You couldn't possibly disappoint Justine. Or my mother, for that matter, though she's neutral. She thinks the world of your grandfather. Morelands is an incredible venue, no denying that, but Justine and I have our hearts set on Melbourne. Tell me that's what you want, too, Ceci. I've known you for a dozen years and more, but sometimes I think I don't know you at all."

She had the eerie feeling that was true. She couldn't tell him that many changes were taking place inside her. In retrospect she realized she rarely confided in him. Stuart was a little like her mother in that he had a tendency to close his ears on what he didn't wish to hear. "Let's just enjoy today, Stuart," she begged gently. "I can't always do what you and my mother want. Oh, look—" she shifted her gaze gratefully "—there's Sasha Donnelly calling to us."

"I say, she's looking very glamorous." Stuart was distracted by the shortness of Sasha's skirt and the sassiness of the gala confection she had on her head.

"She is, and she's still carrying a torch for you," Cecile pointed out lightly.

JUST WHEN SHE THOUGHT the stranger must have left early, she saw him standing with a knot of older guests. Profound disappointment, even despondency, was transformed into soaring spirits. They rose alarmingly, threatening to make her airborne.

You fool! You're not even putting up a struggle.

She ignored the little voice. At the center of the group was her grandfather. Her mother and father flanked him, both of them looking extremely stylish; they were handsome people. With them were close friends of the family, Bruce and Fiona Gordon and the Ardens. Bruce Gordon and George Arden were among her grandfather's oldest friends and business partners. All of them were smiling warmly.

"Ceci, darling! Stuart!" Joel Moreland caught sight of them, gesturing them over. When they were close enough, he put out his arm to gather his much-loved granddaughter to his side. "I don't think either of you have yet met Señor Montalvan, who is visiting us from Argentina. When Fiona told me she and Bruce had a houseguest, I insisted he come along with them today." Joel turned his aristocratic silver head to smile at the well-to-do couple.

"Cecile, my darling—" he beamed down at her as he began the introductions "—may I present Señor Raul Montalvan from…"

She didn't hear another word for the roaring in her ears. Every dormant cell in her body fired into life.

Damn it, damn it! This isn't like you. Get a grip!

She might have been standing at a distance, looking at her double. The tide of feeling she was experiencing was not untainted with remorse, even shame. There was Stuart, her fiancé, proud and smiling by her side. She wore his ring. She should only be thinking of Stuart, while all the while she was racked by her attraction to another man.

He was even more stunning close up. Indeed he could have stepped out of a bravura painting. The bronze of his skin was in striking contrast to the dark caramel of his hair with its glinting golden strands. How dark his eyes were! Not black, but a brilliant dark brown with gold flecks. Their expression was very intense. She didn't think she had seen such intensity in a man's eyes before. They made her feel more conscious of herself as a *woman* than at any moment of Stuart's most passionate lovemaking. It was as though that dark seductive gaze pierced right through her breast to her heart.

"Miss Moreland, I've heard so much about you." He spoke with exquisite gentleness. "The whole of it glowing!"

This drew a smile from her grandfather, who Cecile guessed correctly had been singing her praises.

There was an intriguing hint of an accent. No more. It was a cosmopolitan voice, coming from deep in his chest, the timbre dark, beguiling, with a faint cutting edge.

Good manners demanded she extend her hand. "My grandfather has a very natural bias, señor. I'm very pleased to welcome you to our country." Her skin seemed to sizzle at his touch. She thought she flushed. He didn't shake her hand as she expected, but bowed over it in a way that showed his heritage. It was an entirely natural and elegant ritual courtesy that didn't demand his lips touch her skin. She didn't think she could have borne that given what the mere touch of his hand could do. His hands were as elegant as the rest of him, but she could feel calluses on the pads of his fingers and the palm. Was that the cause of that extraordinary surge of electricity?

Then it was Stuart's turn. He gave a hearty, "Happy to meet you, Mr. Montalvan." To Cecile's ears that didn't quite ring true. Stuart hadn't taken to the newcomer, she could tell, but he was shaking the other man's hand vigorously. "What brings you to the Territory?" he asked.

Montalvan gave a very European shrug. "Pleasure, business. I have always wanted to come to Australia." He spoke in a relaxed fashion, but the *gentleness*, it seemed, had been reserved for Cecile. "Your Top End is not so very different to my home in Argentina. Very beautiful, very isolated, hot and humid, plenty of rain when it comes, glorious vegetation, vast open spaces."

Joel Moreland nodded his agreement. "This is still largely frontier country, Señor Montalvan."

"Please, do call me Raul!" Montalvan turned to his host with a charming half smile.

"Raul it is," Joel Moreland responded, his expression revealing that unlike Stuart, he had taken a fancy to this young man. "Raul is in the ranching business," he informed Cecile and Stuart, "so we have a lot in common. His family have been in ranching for many generations. Ranching and mining, isn't that so? He's also a very fine polo player, I've been told."

"Not surprising, when he hails from a country that has won the World Cup every year since 1949," Cecile's father, Howard, contributed with an admiring laugh.

"True." Montalvan gave another elegant shrug of his shoulder. "But you have some wonderful players here," he added appreciatively. "I'm hoping I'll be invited to participate in a few matches during my stay. Australia is nearly as polo mad as Argentina, I believe."

"It's the great sport of the Outback," Moreland confirmed, "but we can't challenge your world supremacy. Don't worry, Raul, I'm sure we'll be able to arrange something. I used to be a pretty good player myself in the old days."

"I'm certain that's an understatement, sir." Montalvan gave a respectful inclination of his head.

"My father was absolutely splendid!" Justine, who adored her father, spoke proudly. "We have two polo fields on Malagari."

"That's my flagship cattle station toward the Red Centre," Moreland explained before turning to his daughter with a teasing smile. "The polo fields, my dear, are still there. You should come and visit sometime."

"I will, I will, I promise." Justine flushed slightly. "When I get time. Father breeds some of the finest polo ponies in the country," she added.

"So I believe." The Argentinian's expression lit up with interest. "My family breeds fine ponies, too, but nothing like Señor Moreland's operation, which we do know about in Argentina. I believe, sir, you sold ponies to our famous Da Silver brothers?"

"So I did," Joel Moreland said with great satisfaction. "A heroic pair! I've seen them play. Their team won the World Cup no less than four times, the last time—that was in the mid-90s—riding Lagunda ponies. That's my horse stud in the Gold Coast hinterland of Queensland where the climate, the terrain and environment are ideal."

"I'd love to visit it sometime," Montalvan replied. "It would be a great honor."

"And I'd be delighted to show you, Raul. Both Malagari, which is in the Territory and very dear to my heart, and Lagunda, way across the border. The flame for the game still burns very bright, but inevitably time has sidelined me. I still ride, of course. Now my son, Jared, was far more talented. He had effortless style, the physical strength and power to excel at the game. He had a physique like yours." Moreland had been speaking with spontaneous enthusiasm but he stopped abruptly.

"Very sadly, Uncle Jared died young," Cecile told their guest softly. She knew the comment had simply slipped out, borne of her grandfather's obvious liking for their visitor. Her grandfather rarely spoke his dead son's name. Nearly thirty years later, the pain was too great.

"I am so sorry," Montalvan answered quietly, briefly raising his hand to touch Joel Moreland's shoulder.

"Thank you." Moreland bowed his silver head.

"So where are you staying, Señor Montalvan?" Cecile asked with a return to her normal fluent poise.

"Why, with us, Ceci dear," Fiona Gordon, who had been Justine's chief bridesmaid and was in fact one of Cecile's godmothers, smiled fondly.

"Bruce and Fiona have been very kind to me." Montalvan flashed the couple a smile that was simply marvelous, Cecile thought. It had much to do with his fine white teeth against his deep tan, but it went further, lighting up his whole face.

Yet another powerful tool in his seductive armory, she thought, listening to him say he couldn't impose on Bruce and Fiona much longer.

"I'm thinking of leasing, perhaps buying an apartment overlooking the harbor," he told them. "As I've come this far, I intend to make my stay fairly lengthy."

"You have no one at home demanding your presence?" Stuart asked with the faintest lick of challenge. "Not married, I take it?"

No wife in her right mind would allow this man to roam at will, Cecile thought, acutely aware she was hanging on his answer.

"I'm still waiting for the *coup de foudre*, as the French say." Oddly, Montalvan echoed Cecile's earlier thoughts. "May I congratulate you on your engagement." He returned Stuart's gaze directly.

"You may," Stuart answered, blue eyes very bright. "Getting Cecile to say yes wasn't all that easy, but she's made me the happiest man in the world. Or at least as happy as Daniel on this day of days. It's been the perfect wedding."

"Indeed it has!" Justine gave a voluptuous sigh of satisfaction. "I can't wait until Cecile and Stuart tie the knot.

You've no idea, Mr. Montalvan, how long I've been planning it in my head."

Cecile, glancing across at her father, caught the rueful expression in his eyes. Planning was Justine's forte. What she planned had to come off.

THE CELEBRATIONS WENT ON long after the bride and groom had left for Darwin airport on the first leg of their honeymoon trip, which would take them to Hong Kong for a few days, then on to the great capitals of Europe. Sandra had thrown her beautiful bouquet from the upstairs balcony into a sea of smiling, upturned faces and waving, raised arms. There was a great deal of laughing and scuffling, especially on the part of the chief bridesmaid, Melinda, who had her eye on a certain someone in the bridal party, but despite the fact Cecile had just stood there smiling, the bouquet flew to her as though carried on guided wings. Because she made no move to catch it, it came to land on someone directly behind her who, with a swift movement of the hand, sent it back over Cecile's bare shoulder and into the arms she hastily raised. Sandra's bridal bouquet was much too precious to allow to fall to the ground.

"Oh, good for you, Ceci!" Melinda, disappointed, declared.

"Isn't that sweet? You'll be next, Ceci darling!" An elderly Moreland relative flashed her an arch smile.

There were shouts of delight, exaggerated groans of disappointment. Stuart, who had been cheering the loudest threw his arms around her and kissed her mouth. "That settles it, Ceci. We *are* next!"

Cecile kept her eyes fixed steadily on the beautiful waving bride on the balcony.

She knew *exactly* who was behind her, it wasn't her mind that told her. It was her body. She could *feel* him, feel his aura the warmth off his skin, the unique male scent of him that she inhaled into her nostrils. Jubilant at her side, Stuart got into a long, laughing exchange with another guest about where the bouquet had actually landed before being catapulted over Cecile's shoulder. "All's well that ends well!" he cried, and swooped to kiss Cecile again, reveling in the knowledge he was a much-envied man.

She ought to turn around. She *had* to turn around. She managed to do so, her eyes locking on his. The graceful little remark she made sounded quite natural and perfectly composed. It was important she did not let him see how much he affected her. Of course he *did* know.

She could weep for her own susceptibility. Especially now when she had given up thinking any man could evoke such a response. How could such things happen so fast? Nothing seemed real. Nothing was as it had been before. It was as simple and as momentous as that.

WITH THE BRIDE AND GROOM GONE, the party kicked up several more notches. Moet flowed like the water from a great fountain. Inside the house, the older guests settled into comfortable arm-chairs and sofas, relishing the opportunity for a good long chat away from the boisterous young ones. Youth was so wearing. Outside the music from the band was so compulsively toe tapping it had couples everywhere up and dancing: on the brightly lit terrace and in the grounds where the trees had been decked with thousands and thousands of fairy lights, around the huge pool area where they risked getting splashed. There was a lot of hilarity, a lot of flirting, abandoned kisses in the scented darkness, holding hands. Everyone clung to the magic of the day, the marvelous haze of pleasure. No one wanted it to end.

CHAPTER THREE

CECILE KNEW the moment he would come to her, though her head was turned away. She had, she realized, been waiting for him, as though she waited for him every night of her life. She had even deliberately engineered the moment she would be alone, by sending Stuart off for a cold drink she didn't want. She could see Stuart in the distance being detained by a group of their friends, which included a slightly tipsy Sasha who was holding on to his arm as if she didn't intend to let him get away. Her grandfather, who was enjoying himself enormously, was a good distance away from her, as well, his handsome silver head thrown back as he laughed at something one of his cronies said.

So *finally,* they were alone.

She hoped he couldn't see she was trembling. She moved back into the protective shadows, realizing every defense she had consciously or unconsciously raised over the years to protect herself lay demolished.

"A pretty spectacle?" He indicated the nighttime scene with a turn of his hand. It was a dazzling kaleidoscope of brightly colored dresses, many of them full-length and sweeping the grass. The illuminated gardens were extravagant in their beauty, their intoxicating fragrance unleashed by the warm air. The great shade trees stood like beacons of light, covered all over with tiny white bulbs that pulsed like stars.

"Yes, it's beautiful," she agreed quietly, thinking the man beside her added his own element of splendor. "Everything has gone so well. Granddad waved his magic wand and it all happened."

"The Man with the Midas Touch!"

Something in the way he said it, a barely perceptible nuance, wasn't quite right. She turned her head toward him. "So you've heard that already?"

He gave her a slight smile. "I couldn't tell you how many times."

"I'm very proud of my grandfather," she said, startled he had thrown her onto the defensive when, really, he had said nothing out of place.

"And he adores you." Was there the barest trace of mockery in that fascinating voice? She had the idea there was.

"That's fine by me. *I* adore him."

"I saw that very plainly. Would you care to dance?" he asked, not taking his eyes off her face. "I would have asked you earlier, but your fiancé has never left your side."

Until you sent him away!

She recognized that uncompromising little voice, resisted the accusation though her stomach gave a lurch. How could she say to him she was afraid to dance with him? It was a very strange sensation having a man's aura wrap her like a flowing cloak.

"I'm a little out of breath from the last dance," she said in a low voice, mortified there was a throb in it.

His eyes dropped for a mere moment to the rise and fall

of her breasts. "Come, Ms. Moreland. I regard that as an excuse."

"It *is* an excuse." What was the point of saying otherwise? The silent communication between them was as keen as a blade's edge.

"You ought not refuse me," he told her ever so gently. "I'm a visitor to your shores. I think I can say I have your grandfather's approval. But most especially because I was the one who caused the bridal bouquet to fall right into your arms."

"I realize that, Señor Montalvan." She couldn't laugh or smile.

"Please…Raul, I insist. Señor Montalvan is much too formal. I freely admit I maneuvered the bouquet because I was intrigued you weren't making the slightest effort to catch it. Why is that?" He held out his hand. "Come, you can't plead fatigue. You look like you could dance right through the night."

She was so acutely conscious of him she almost wished she were wearing gloves. Once again skin on skin proved so electric it was as though one or the other had thrown a switch. She had never experienced anything like it in her life. There had to be some scientific explanation. Did *he* feel it? She was certain he did. She felt once again the rough calluses. Why wouldn't he have them, a cattleman and an experienced polo player? They moved out of the shadows and he pulled her near, very quiet about it, yet she had the strangest sensation her body was unfurling like a flower. Where was Stuart now? Stuart, her safety net?

She had to say something, anything. This entire sizzling scenario couldn't be happening to her, but it was. "The party doesn't appear to be winding down." She was grateful her voice wasn't shaking like her hands. Dancing was a source of innocent pleasure and relaxation. It could also be a potent form of lovemaking with a certain person.

"Even the children are still running around." There was a note of amusement in his tone. "I wouldn't dare guide you anywhere near the pool. It's fun watching them splash, but I couldn't bear to see your lovely gown marked. Not many could wear a gown the color of crystal rain unless they were beautiful and had eyes like the diamonds you wear at your throat."

Her heart skipped many dangerous beats. "A charming compliment, but the color of my eyes is genetic. Both Daniel and I inherited our gray eyes from our grandfather."

"Gray doesn't say it," he said, studying her face so intently he might have been trying to discover her whole history.

She had half hoped closer contact might lessen some of his mystique, anything so she could regain her balance, but the excitement was fierce.

They were moving in a dream, their steps melding and matching as though their bodies were no surprise to the other. Indeed she fit so perfectly into his arms she wondered if those strong arms would leave an imprint on her. It was so wonderful, so exciting, so *scary,* she grasped as she had never done before how attraction could overpower. And with such violent attraction came the potential to destroy lives and ruin reputations.

The band segued into a haunting romantic ballad that struck a chord deep inside her. The blood coursing through her body was full of sparkles, hot sparkles from all the electricity that raced up and down her spine. She felt a dull heavy ache in the pit of her stomach as though she was about to start her period, which she wasn't. She knew what it was: powerful sexual desire that acted like an erotic charge. It brought on a physical change in her, like deep contractions in the womb. She, who had been brought up to be a fluent conversationalist as befitting a cultured young woman, could say nothing. Excitement was growing inside her at a tremendous rate. She couldn't shut it off. She was in thrall, so much less of herself, much, much, more of him.

Once his cheek touched her temple as he whirled her away from another couple, also intent on each other. She felt the faint rasp of his beard on her soft skin. He was a beautiful dancer. She might have known that from the way he moved. Did they have golden pumas in Argentina? she wondered. She was taken by the image. He was beautiful as a man can be beautiful, with an undeniably exotic air, but she couldn't see his *Spanish* heritage. His eyes were more a velvety brown than black. His hair so thick, and well-groomed, was a warm caramel softened by those sun-kissed streaks. If she hadn't known he was Argentinian and heard for herself that fascinating hint of accent, she wouldn't have known exactly *where* to place him. If Daniel had introduced an adventurous friend back from wandering the world, she would have accepted it readily. Suddenly there were many questions she wanted to ask him.

Not a good idea, Cecile! Her warning voice struggled to get through again. *He'll only be here for a short time. Then he goes back to where he belongs. Much wiser to keep your distance.*

Too late to tell her that now. She had moved into a new, potentially dangerous dimension.

Her grandfather had taken a strong liking to him—she knew her grandfather well—which meant lots of invitations would be issued to the visitor. Her own time in Darwin was short. When her vacation with her grandfather was over, she would have to return home to Melbourne to her work. For the past four years she had achieved her ambition, practicing as a child psychologist in a large private hospital that had excellent accreditation. It was work that was important to her, a career choice perhaps influenced by her own struggle in childhood. At any rate she had another life.

But how to shut him out?

Look on it as a brief encounter, the voice in her head instructed.

One could live a lifetime in an hour.

"So quiet?" he murmured. She had removed her lovely headdress, revealing a waterfall of raven hair that flowed straight and glossy down her back to her shoulder blades. From a central parting, the sides were secured behind her ears by two glittering leaf-shaped diamond clasps. It was a classic style that greatly appealed to him.

"I'm not usually." She allowed herself one roving glance across his face. His mouth was beautifully cut, firm but sensual. She wanted to reach out and touch it very gently with her finger, trace its outline. "You understand," she murmured, "weddings are very moving occasions."

"This one in particular," he agreed, drawing her, unprotesting, closer.

Thousands of twinkling lights from the trees poured over them. There was a cry from a night bird somewhere close by. Two perfectly pitched notes, in a descending cadence.

It was repeated.

God! She could hardly bear it! Her heart was thudding so hard it had to be moving the bodice of her gown.

The ache in her stomach wasn't fading—it was growing. It tormented her she could feel this hungry for sex. It was no romantic longing and so relatively harmless. She wished for sex with a perfect stranger. The very thought threatened her ordered life and disassociated her from her engagement. She could have been one of her own patients: an adolescent whose hormones raged out of control.

"One doesn't always see such a true love match," he remarked after a long pause. "It's commonplace in Argentina and many parts of the world for material considerations to be put first. Fiona explained to me how your cousin came to be restored to his family. It's an extraordinary story, though many families have dark secrets and tragic histories. Still…incredible to think it took all this time before his identity came to light. Your cousin deserves his great happiness."

"He does. Blood is very binding," she agreed in a low voice.

"No matter the separation." Again there was a certain nuance that caused her to look up at him.

"You sound as though you know all about the trials of separation."

"What gave you that idea?" He stared down into her eyes.

"You *do* know though, don't you?"

He was silent a moment. "You're obviously a woman of admirable perception. Separations happen all the time. Some perhaps in a way that others do not. Some separations bring misery and trauma, others make us, as they say, fonder. You and your cousin are very much alike. Anyone seeing the two of you together would assume you were sister and brother. You don't have a brother of your own?"

She shook her head with deep regret. "I'm an only child.

I would have liked a brother, preferably brothers and sisters, but my mother had difficulty having me, so no more family! It was wonderful when Daniel came into our lives, and now Sandra. We've become good friends. And you, señor, you have siblings?"

"Didn't I beg you to call me Raul?" His tone dropped low into his chest. It was almost a deep purr. "After all, I intend to call you Cecile."

He pronounced it in the French fashion. It sounded... lovely. Like being stroked. Featherlike strokes all over her face and up and down her body. He was using his voice like the finest of instruments. One could fall in love with such a voice, she thought shakily, even if the owner were plain.

That night bird called again. Was it serenading them? The scent of gardenias was heavy in the air, their waxy white flowers dazzling in the dark. "I don't think we'll be seeing much of each other, however."

"You say it like it cannot be," he challenged. "Your distinguished grandfather has already invited me to a dinner party he's giving Wednesday of this coming week. Perhaps you are wrong. I might be often on your doorstep. I understand you are staying with your grandfather for a month? There is much you could show me if you would only be so kind to a stranger to your country."

Kind? Kindness wasn't what he wanted from her, of that she was sure. Though he mesmerized her with his charm, the idea that he might have an agenda of his own wouldn't have shocked her. He could even be exploiting her. Such attempts had been made before, but she had easily staved them off. "I'm sure there are many others who would be delighted to play that role," she said with a slight air of irony.

He didn't appear to notice.

"But you'll have some time on your hands, Cecile. I could at least be some company, as your fiancé has to return to Melbourne."

She stopped dancing, aware of her burning cheeks. "My grandfather told you that?"

"He did when he issued his invitation."

A curious thing—he kept hold of her hand. "He also told me your fiancé is a lawyer with a prestigious Melbourne firm."

"He is," she said, defeated and unnerved by the thought that Stuart didn't mean as much to her as he should. How, if she loved Stuart, could she put herself into Raul Montalvan's hands? "He should make full partner in a year or so."

"You see yourself as the perfect wife to a man of law?"

"What's behind that question, Raul?" She withdrew her trembling hand and walked on.

"Ah. So I've made you a little angry." He caught her up easily, bending his head as if to search her expression.

"You would *know* if I were angry."

He only smiled. "Fire and ice. However, I don't think your eyes could sparkle any more dangerously than they do now. I apologize if I've somehow given offense. I never meant to. You asked if I had siblings. I have. A younger brother, Francisco, and a sister, Ramona, who is so beautiful she turns heads. But then you would know all about that." The resonance of his voice deepened. "So tell me, do you feel rewarded working with children who are in much mental pain? Your grandfather told me you were a child psychologist. I'd very much like to hear why you chose such a profession. It seems to me to reveal a deeply maternal streak, does it not?"

In her high heels she stumbled slightly over an exposed tree root and he swiftly steadied her. "Thank you," she murmured, fathoms deep in awareness.

"So?" he prompted with what sounded like real interest.

She made an effort. "I do love children. I want children of my own. My guiding star is to help ease the pain. It's greatly rewarding to be able to steer badly hurting young people through very real and sometimes just perceived crises in their lives."

He nodded agreement. "There are so many areas of conflict to contend with, especially during adolescence."

"Children are far less secure these days than ever before. Marriages break up, and the fallout can be very damaging. Some children tend to blame a particular parent for the breakup of the marriage. Usually the mothers. Daddy's gone and Mummy drove him away. This can lead to profound upset for the parent who has to bear the blame. Then again, I find a lot of the time that problems originate with the parents' behavior. They have one another and kept the children at arm's length. That can make change very difficult. Other parents persist in keeping up a front. They disguise, disown or actively lie about the part they play in these conflicts. Children are so helpless. They suffer loneliness, excessive stress and acute depression just as we do. I have a little ten-year-old patient at the moment, a girl called Ellie. I'm trying very hard to help. In fact, she's been constantly on my mind while I'm here on holiday. Ellie has a good many behavioral problems that are getting her deeper and deeper into trouble both at home and school. In some ways she's a contradiction. I'm prepared to back my initial impression she's highly intelligent, yet she's earned the reputation for not being very bright, even with her parents."

"Good people?" he questioned, frowning slightly.

"Good, *caring* people at their wits' end," Cecile confirmed. "So far I haven't been able to make a breakthrough, either, though it's early days."

"Then I wish you every success with young Ellie," he said, sounding earnest. "Perhaps she's grieving about something she can't or won't talk about? The innocent grieve. It is so very interesting, your choice of a profession. Surely you wouldn't have known suffering or conflict in your privileged life? A princess, Joel Moreland's granddaughter?"

She felt a moment of unease. "Is that your *exact* interest in me, Señor Montalvan? I'm Joel Moreland's granddaughter? I have to tell you I'm long used to it, consequently forewarned. I saw how you were secretly studying me while I was standing on the balcony."

"Perhaps I was only thinking how beautiful you were," he answered, smoothly turning her into his arms again. "As serene as the swans that glide across your lake."

She had little option but to continue dancing. "Somehow I don't think that was it. The look wasn't at all an admiring glance or even friendly."

"What was it, then?" he asked, his wide shoulders blocking the light.

She wished she could see his expression more clearly. "Extremely disconcerting."

"Perhaps that was only an illusion. I was simply admiring a woman exquisite in her beauty and outward appearance of serenity."

She couldn't fail to pick up on the *outward*. "You think something entirely different goes on inside me?"

"Would it be so strange if I did? I, too, am a student of psychology. No one could say it's a simple life any more than we are simple beings. The inner person and the outer person can be significantly different."

"Of course. It's no easy thing to become a well-integrated adult. We all continue to harbor the fears and anxieties we had as children, but we've had to learn how to master them or seek help. I see young patients in terrible self-destructive rages because they've had to live through years of conflict and un-happiness. I see a great deal worse, physical and sexual abuse sometimes where one least suspects."

"That must be extremely upsetting?"

"It is." She drew a deep breath. "I've seen children sent back to the care of the very people who've abused them and I've been helpless! Some of it I'll never get out of my mind. It's ghastly stuff. That's one of the reasons I needed this holiday with Granddad. It's not easy what I do and I can't always stand aloof. In childhood we all assemble the building blocks that go into making the adult."

"So when the building blocks are in extremely short supply and the conflicts never resolve themselves, one is left scarred and without an inner haven to shelter."

"Exactly." It was obvious he was following her words closely. "The violent pattern most frequently repeats itself."

He sighed, his breath warm and sweet. "It's difficult to dis-associate oneself from intense traumas in childhood. Didn't William Faulkner once say something about the past not being over or even past?"

"I'm not going to disagree with the great man."

"Me, neither. So you see we do have much to talk about, Cecile, if only our mutual interest in the development or the destruction of the human psyche. The great human values of love and honor coexist with hate and evil. Now, I must surrender you to your fiancé. He's heading very purpose-fully in this direction. I don't know that *I* would care to see my beautiful fiancée in another man's arms, either."

CHAPTER FOUR

STUART TOOK HIS LEAVE at noon the following day. Exactly one minute after Cecile drove her grandfather's Bentley through the front gates of Morelands, the argument broke out just as she knew it would, when there was no one around to overhear.

"Damn it all, I wish you were coming back with me!" Stuart exclaimed, his handsome face marred by an angry expression.

"You don't begrudge me my vacation, surely?" She winced. Even with her sunglasses on the sunlight was much too bright.

"I simply want you with me."

"I know." Stuart had been simmering ever since he'd joined her and Raul Montalvan the previous night, leaving her with the sensation she was caught in the eye of a storm. Even when they met up at breakfast, she'd sensed the continuation of his mood, but as a guest in her grandfather's house he could scarcely vent feelings of outrage or jealousy. She was very much aware he'd had to make a huge effort in the final hours of the party. The celebrations had continued unabated until after two in the morning. When they'd left the mansion, the grounds were thronged with the staff of the firm that supplied the huge marquees and the tables and chairs, among other things.

Cecile tried to remain calm. Inside she knew she was approaching her own crisis point in life. It was a real struggle to hide it; harder yet to fight back.

"I just hate the idea of your being away from me," Stuart said tersely, equally off balance.

"Goodness, it's only a month!" She tried a soothing, sideways glance. "We'll be speaking to each other every day."

"Count on it." He stared moodily out the window. "That bloody Raul made a hit with your grandfather."

"That's not very nice, is it, *bloody* Raul."

"I know it isn't, but I can't help it. He's too suave, too charming by half."

"That's his Latin blood," she offered by way of explanation. "You're not going to blame him for being charming?"

Stuart had the grace to look embarrassed. "I just wish he hadn't turned up. He's the sort of guy that stirs everything up."

God help her, hadn't Stuart put his finger right on it? "You are in an odd mood, Stuart. No sleep?"

"Not when you wouldn't join me," he said, sounding painfully rebuffed.

"Not with a house full of relatives, Stuart. I told you that wasn't likely to happen."

He gave an angry snort. "Sometimes I think you don't give a damn if you sleep with me or not."

Her heart was beating painfully fast. She hadn't asked for any of this. It had just happened. Anyone could become madly infatuated. It was what one did about it that counted. "That's not true, Stuart." Even to her own ears her response didn't sound terribly convincing, yet she enjoyed their love-making. Stuart was a considerate lover, able to give satisfaction and not lacking finesse. "Do we really have to ruin a beautiful day with all this? I promised to marry you, didn't I?"

"But, Ceci—" Stuart twisted in the passenger seat to stare at her "—you won't set the date. You've no idea how insecure that makes me feel. Hell, it's like Justine says. We should be married and expecting our first child by now. You told me you loved children. I'm no longer sure."

Normally slow to temper, she felt intensely irritated. "What an alliance you and my mother have formed! Both of you pushing me into marriage and motherhood like I was the wrong side of forty. I do love children, Stuart. I think my choice of a profession proves that. If you and my mother continue to hound me—" She broke off, breathing a sharp sigh of frustration.

"It's not like that." Stuart reached out to stroke her arm. "Darling, it's not like that," he said softly.

Nothing. She felt nothing. She was greatly shocked.

"We would never be guilty of that." Stuart faced front again as though he thought it crucial he, too, mind the road. "Justine just wants the best for you, Cecile. You can be very difficult sometimes."

That was grossly unfair. She shook her head weakly. "I thought I rarely gave trouble. In fact, I was the model child. Ask anyone. I always did *exactly* what was expected of me. I had to be top in everything, grades, sports, ballet, piano. I worked so hard to keep my mother proud of me. I was never under that kind of pressure from my father, thank God. I was always obedient and respectful. I've never played around. I've never touched drugs. My mother wants *her* idea of the best for me, Stuart. I'm not my mother. I love her, but I'm not like her. She means well, but she spends every day of her life making plans for me. She had to give up on Dad. I want her to stop. I'm twenty-six, but she continues to act as though one day I'll screw up. Maybe she's right. Now there's a thought! My mother has always been too focused on me as her only child. I wish to God I'd had brothers and sisters. Anyone to take the heat off me. It won't stop even after we're married. Not with you encouraging her. Or is *that* going to stop when you've finally won the prize?"

Stuart's whole face turned stony, an expression she rarely saw and decided she didn't like. "I don't deserve that, Ceci," he said coldly. "Of course you're a prize, but I'm genuinely fond of your mother. She's a marvelous woman."

"It's a pity you didn't meet someone like her," Cecile shot back. "You have so much in common."

Censure was in his voice. "You sound pretty darn resentful, do you know that? As a psychologist, you ought to know it. Justine and I do have a lot in common. We both love *you*. Look, I don't want to argue, Ceci. I'm like a bear with a sore head today. I had way too much to drink last night and I'm no drinker, as you know. It's just that I'm worried about leaving you here, especially with that bloody Argentinian hanging around. They fancy themselves as great lovers, you know."

Cecile took a deep breath, trying to rein in her anger. "Well, he certainly gives the impression he might be. You don't trust me, is that it? You were furious I was dancing with him. Your coldness to him made it pretty apparent. You didn't get the opportunity to take it out on me, not with a party going on. You're acting as though I can't conduct myself in an appropriate manner if you're not around, just like you're bloody well braking now with your foot while *I'm* driving the car. Do you think I'm going to fling myself at a complete stranger like in some fruity melodrama?"

"You want the straight answer? *Yes*," he said in a goaded voice. "There's so much about you, Ceci, that's beneath the surface. You act so cool and composed, but that could be your training. There was *something* between you, Ceci. You're trying hard to deny it, but I'm not a complete fool. I'm your fiancé, the man you're going to marry. Need I jog your memory? I have the *right* to question you."

"Really? I might have to start questioning if you're the right man for me. I hate people who go on about their rights, Stuart, unless it's the right to life, liberty and freedom. So to hell with your right to interfere with *my* freedom."

Stuart scowled. "You're being childish, Ceci. It's not like you to rebel. Maybe you *were* on too tight a leash as a child. My aim is to protect you. I've always trusted you in the past."

"How sad, then, I've committed a very serious breach."

"Ceci, you of all people appeared to be encouraging him." He turned to her, his expression deadly serious.

She groaned. "You just can't leave well enough alone, can you?"

"You think I *want* to speak like this?" His voice was a rasp. "I feel I have an obligation to point certain things out. I do respect your high moral standards, my darling. It's Montalvan I don't trust. You don't have much vanity, but you're a very beautiful woman. Who could blame him if he was attracted to you?"

"How the heck do you know he was?" she demanded, her anger fueled by feelings of guilt.

"Oh, he's attracted all right!" Stuart declared with great conviction. "You could have been alone on an island. Forget there were three hundred bloody guests all around you."

"You have to stop this, Stuart," she said. "My head is

starting to pound. Jealousy is a terrible thing. Lots of relationships can't survive jealousy. So we were enjoying the dance. No big deal. I reserve the right to choose the men I wish to speak to or dance with without consulting you, fiancé or not!"

Observing the hectic flush in her cheeks, Stuart backed down. "Of course you can, Ceci. It was the way the guy was holding you, looking at you, that put me in a rage. He knows bloody well you're *my* woman."

She felt like stopping the car and jumping out. It would be so much easier than trying to push him out. "Don't you love to get your tongue around the word *my*," she fumed. "You've got a whole list starting with *my* career, *my* ambitions, *my* political aspirations, *my* new house, *my* new Beemer, *my* fiancée. I'm right down the list." She realized in her agitation she was over the speed limit and quickly slowed. "Raul Montalvan is a beautiful, natural dancer. Why not? Argentina is the home of the tango after all."

"Ahhh, Ceci," he groaned, "You're making quite an effort to put me off the scent, but there was a little more to it than that. Even Sasha noticed."

"Sasha?" Cecile gave an incredulous laugh. "The two of you were spying on me?"

"Of course not." Stuart spoke in an aggrieved tone. "It was only by chance she spotted you."

"I bet!" She swung her head toward him. "Sasha always was a troublemaker."

"Actually she's very fond of you. She wouldn't want to see you put a foot wrong any more than I would. Women are very sharp. You catch on to things we men don't. But the way the two of you moved together it would have crossed anyone's

mind, even trusting ol' me. There was just some aura for
all to see."

"Could it have been an alcoholic haze?" she asked with
some sarcasm. She was rebelling against the accusations,
even as she knew she was in denial. "Sasha was sloshed. I
could equally well point out you had no objection to Sasha's
clinging on to your arm."

Stuart grimaced. "She doesn't mean a thing to me and you
know it. I bet you weren't a bit jealous of Sasha even though
she's a damned sexy girl. Doesn't that tell you something
about *our* relationship?"

"I've learned to trust you, perhaps?" Cecile maneuvered
the big car into the busy right lane so she could take the
freeway turnoff.

"You *can* trust me. I don't want anyone else but you, Ceci.
And I have some ethics, if that bloody Argentinian doesn't.
Who is he, anyway? He appears out of nowhere and makes
a beeline for you."

She felt like she wanted to sleep for hours. Shut it all out.
"One dance!" she said sharply. "You call that making a beeline?"

Stuart sat straighter, rubbing his trousered knees. "Steady
on."

Cecile gritted her teeth. "Do you want to miss your plane?
I've had a license since I was seventeen, Stuart. I've never had
an accident, which is more than I can say for you."

"Don't be so touchy!" He raised his brows. "I know you're
a good driver, very controlled and decisive about what you
do, but this is a big powerful car. Women shouldn't really
drive big powerful cars in my view, and you do have a
worrying tendency to be impetuous, especially if you're

running late. As for my *one* accident, how was I to know a bus was going to pull out in front of the car ahead of me?"

"By studying the road well ahead," she said tartly. "Look, let's stop this, shall we?"

"Certainly. I'm sorry, darling. I apologize. I was jealous. I freely admit it, but I can only say what I fear. To get to know this Montalvan would be to court danger. Knowing your grand-father, the guy's bound to be offered plenty of entertainment while he's here. He's not a suitable companion, that's all. I'm five years older than you. I work in an area where I see a lot more suspect characters than you."

"To hell with that!" she said hotly. "Do you see children and adolescents who've been sexually, physically and mentally abused? Do you see suffering on the grand scale? Little people who've been beaten, burned, tied up with rope or whatever is to hand, had their bones broken, their bodies violated and infected, been threatened with weapons? The most you see, Stu-art—you're so bloody pompous at times—is white-collar crime. The socially prominent scoundrels you help beat the charges."

"Well, really, that's a bit extreme, isn't it?" Stuart's voice was taut with shock. "And there's no need to swear. It scarcely suits you. I've never heard you call me pompous before."

"Clearly, sometimes you are!"

"This is too much, Ceci," he complained. "Personally I don't believe attack is the best form of defense. All I was saying is I don't think business-pleasure is all there is to it with this Montalvan guy."

"Why don't you have him investigated?" she suggested, suddenly very aware of Stuart's tendency to patronize her. "That should solve the problem."

Stuart, the lawyer, took the suggestion seriously. "It could be done," he said, nibbling hard on his lip. "All that charm, the expensive clothes, the handmade shoes, the solid gold watch, the meticulous grooming—it could all be window dressing. He could be an experienced con man, for all we know. There's nothing would suit a con man more than to latch on to a beautiful heiress. Seduce her if he could. He certainly latched on to you and your grandfather."

So he did, said that harsh little voice in her head. *He made a huge attempt to reach you and succeeded.* As a man, Raul Montalvan was very, very seductive. It was one way to cut across all borders.

"You can't deny it's a possibility." Stuart frowned as he searched her tense profile.

"Fascinating if you were writing a novel, Stuart, but I haven't the slightest doubt Señor Montalvan is who he says he is. I think you'll find he comes from a wealthy well-respected family. Bruce and Fiona must know all about him. I'm sure you could find the Montalvan estancia on the Internet, as they breed polo ponies."

"Maybe he's using someone else's identity," Stuart suggested, still frowning hard. "It's been done before today. Australia is a long way from Argentina."

She clicked her tongue angrily. "Nowhere is a long way from anywhere these days. Granddad would soon discover if Raul knew little about ranching, and polo isn't the sport for a man without means. Besides he has all the graces expected in the son of a cultured family. He's bilingual. I wouldn't be a bit surprised if he didn't speak other languages, as well. Italian, French, who knows?"

"I'm getting the strong impression you admire him," Stuart said angrily.

"I'd say a lot of people admire him," she said dryly. "Actually, Stuart, I'm on side with you. For all his charm, there's something mysterious about Raul Montalvan. Something steely, possibly dangerous? He's an enigma."

Stuart reeled back at some note—perhaps betrayal—in her voice. "Aw, bugger that!" he said with a burst of violent jealousy. "All I know is, such men are best left alone."

Such a pity, then, you've already burnt your fingers!

CHAPTER FIVE

CECILE GAZED DOWN the beautifully appointed dinner table, her eyes on her grandfather, who was swirling a deep ruby wine around his crystal goblet before drinking it and nodding to Robson, the major domo responsible for running the domestic affairs of the mansion smoothly. Her grandfather had always kept an excellent cellar, the best wines from home and around the world. The conversation at a table for fourteen guests eddied around her, her grandfather at one end, Great-aunt Bea at the other. The guest of honor for the evening was a well-known political figure, Senator Brendan Ryan. He sat to her grandfather's right, her mother to his left. She herself sat a few chairs away with Raul Montalvan sitting opposite her across the gleaming table, set with the finest bone china, sparkling crystal and solid silver flatware. A set of six beautiful caryatid candlesticks, her favorites, supporting tall white tapers were set at intervals down the table. Her late maternal grandmother, Frances, had acquired them in London when she and her grandfather were on their honeymoon. Grecian goddesses rose from domed circular bases to support the wax pans and sconces above their heads. Her grandmother had always promised them to her. Frances had doted on her, whereas Justine claimed she had spent a lifetime trying to gain her mother's love and attention. Sadly, from all accounts it was true. It was her uncle Jared, her mother's late brother, who had been the apple of Frances's eye. She had adored him to the exclusion of her daughter, a deprivation that had badly affected Justine and perhaps explained her unswerving, single-minded focus on her only child.

The scent of the wines mingled with the scent of the flowers in the low, very beautiful central arrangement of white lilies and orchids. Montalvan wasn't looking at her. He was talking to her friend Tara Sinclair, his tone too low for her to hear, but it was easy enough to read Tara's expression. She looked enthralled.

There, what did I tell you? It's not difficult for any woman to become infatuated with an exciting man. Possibly he doesn't even realize his hypnotic powers. Then again he most assuredly does.

Tara threw back her blond head and laughed. She was wearing a red silk dress cut low to show the upward swell of her breasts. She had lovely creamy skin, not a conventional beauty but attractive and vivacious. She and Raul appeared to be drawn together in an intimate joke. A peculiar feeling akin, not to jealousy, but to rejection rose in her. She had made a fool of herself the other night. She had quarreled with Stuart, sending him back home to Melbourne with no harmony between them. Of course he had since rung any number of times from his apartment and from work, but during these intervening days she had agonized over, not whether, but *when* to call off the engagement. She knew her mother's reproaches would go on forever, Stuart being her mother's idea of an excellent match.

I can't believe what you're thinking, girl!

She was beginning to tire of her inner voice. She hadn't really done anything stupid, thank God. She took a sip of her wine, no more, quickly turning to one of her old beaus, an architect, newly married, as he asked for her impressions of a recent showing of aboriginal art they had both attended. She was happy to tell him. It took her mind off Raul and Tara.

After dinner her grandfather asked her to play for them, as she'd known he would. She was a gifted pianist. Glad, in the end, her mother had forced many long hours of practice on her, so that she had collected a clutch of diplomas, all high distinctions, even before she left school. Ordinarily she was happy to perform for dinner guests, but tonight *his* presence made her incredibly nervous when nervousness had been bearing down on her all day.

Everyone took their seats in the living room, all in wonderfully mellow spirits, induced by good conversation and a truly memorable dinner. It had been definitely on the sensual side, with superb oysters topped by caviar, succulent garden-fresh asparagus to accompany the melt-in-your-mouth beef and small pots of velvety smooth, ever-so-seductive chocolate mousse to finish. Certainly Raul Montalvan appeared to have enjoyed it. She had the idea that in nineteenth-century France a bridegroom was encouraged to eat several helpings of asparagus before joining his bride in the connubial bed, just as Montezuma consumed copious amounts of hot chocolate before visiting his harem. Just looking across the table had been enough for her to be devoured by her senses.

Her grandfather went to the big Steinway grand, lifting the lid. It was a small task he loved. Her mother played, or rather, *had* played until her daughter's abilities had overtaken hers. After that, Justine never touched the piano again, which was an awful shame, because Justine desperately needed the relaxation. The magnificent Steinway her grandfather had bought Cecile some ten years back replaced the fine old Bechstein her mother had learned on.

Cecile settled herself on the ebony piano seat already adjusted to her height and particular requirements. Knowing she would be asked to play, she had spent an hour or so of the preceding days practicing. Her hands were slender, long-fingered, deceptively strong. Her technique had never let her down. Tonight, unfortunately, her emotions were all over the place. Should she not play well, her mother would be deeply disappointed in her and make a point of telling her so afterward.

Cecile bowed her head over the keys, her long graceful neck revealed by her hairstyle for the evening, an updated chignon. Normally she was very comfortable in this setting, surrounded by family and friends, none of them, outside of her mother, critical. For a moment her nervousness threatened to overwhelm her. She glanced up at the ceiling; the ceiling stared back. God, she was nothing without her confidence. No performer was. Someone was laughing, a soft little giggle. Sounded like Tara. Etiquette demanded an audience be quiet, but it was hard to quiet Tara, who wasn't a music lover, anyway.

What was happening to her? Stage fright? Panic attacks could happen right out of the blue. She had seen them with sad regularity in the course of her work, but she had never actually experienced one until she'd laid eyes on Raul Montalvan.

Play something easy. Start with a couple of Chopin waltzes. Everyone just wants to enjoy themselves.

She glanced down at her hands, wondering if she had simply lost it.

Then suddenly *he* was approaching the piano, asking her very charmingly if the Spanish composer Albeniz was included in her repertoire. He pronounced the composer's name in the Spanish fashion. She had never heard it sound so good. She had intended to start with a Brahms rhapsody, but Spanish music had always captivated her. She had kept up the repertoire. Why, given he was South American, had she not thought of it herself?

"As long as you don't expect me to measure up to the great Alicia De Larrocha," she said, finding she was able to breathe again.

"You're an artist, I'm sure." He looked deeply into her eyes. Then he moved back to his position on the sofa between Tara and Great Aunt Bea, who claimed to have been in her youth—she was now seventy-eight—a regular love goddess. Bea certainly liked good looking men, never depriving herself of their company.

The lights turned on again in her brain. Normally she would never have started with the very difficult "Malaga," one of the most passionate pieces of Albeniz's great work for piano, *Iberia*, but the fact he had come to her aid—his eyes told her that—fired her blood. She turned with a smile to announce to the room what she intended to play. She saw her grandfather clap with delight, turning his head to say a few words to his Argentinian guest. Bea gave her such an animated wave of her heavily bejewelled hands, Cecile thought for a moment she might get up and dance; her mother sat with a slight frown as though doubting whether, without practice, she could pull it off.

Thank you, Mother, for the vote of confidence.

She knew well how difficult it was to treat children whose parents, especially the mothers, were overly demanding. Her old professor at the Conservatorium had always refused to let her mother sit in on any lesson, even rehearsals for exams. *Helicopter mothers, Cecile, forever hovering over their children. I cannot abide them!*

She sat quietly for a moment before the keyboard, bringing all her concentration to bear. Then when she was ready she launched into the piece that in essence represented the wonderful dance rhythms of the *malaguena.*

NEVER FOR A MOMENT had he allowed his purpose for coming here to fade from his mind. What he wanted was revenge. It was a kind of mania, really. Sometimes more than others— when he was riding alone far out on the *pampas*—he saw himself as a grown man bound by the vows of his youth. A boy lost, his face hot and flushed with tears for all the misfortune coming his beloved grandfather's way. It was obvious even to him forces were at work to drive them off their land. Land that one day would be his. Land was everything. It spoke to him with a passion. There was an explanation for what was happening.

The Morelands.

"They're determined to ruin us!" He wasn't sure how he was going to achieve revenge—strip a powerful man of at least some of his prestige—but he was hoping ways and means would present themselves as he was drawn deeper and deeper into their world. He had achieved his prime objective of working his way in with little difficulty. It had turned out to be so easy he could scarcely believe it. He had the moti-

vation, now he needed the necessary guile. There would be opportunities. This family, like all families, had secrets. Dark, damning secrets that needed to be exposed to the light of day and public censure. Since he'd been a boy he had dreamed of striking a blow at the family responsible for his own family's long years of suffering and exile: the Morelands, with their powerful army of sympathizers and supporters.

His mother had found peace in her second marriage, giving birth to Francisco, his stepfather Ramon's heir, then two years later, little Ramona. His own father, who had been enticed to Argentina to play polo and was later employed by Ramon to help breed his polo ponies, was long dead, dying in hospital a few days after taking a bad fall at a home match. He would have survived the fall, only it was his blighted destiny to be trampled by his agitated pony. Polo, the way the *gauchos* played it, was dangerously fast in what was the fastest game in the world. What had happened to his father should have put him off playing polo for life, but he, too, thrived on the element of danger. Horsemanship was in his blood. He had inherited his father's speed and finesse and his near-complete range of strokes. Unlike his father when he played it was with *one* objective in mind: to win. He knew Joel Moreland had been a fine, enthusiastic player. He knew his son Jared rode as hard and fearlessly as the best. He knew a great deal about Jared Moreland, the predator, canonized in death.

What he hadn't anticipated was meeting this beautiful creature, Jared Moreland's niece. She couldn't be allowed to get in his way. Then again, he knew he had her at his mercy. If he could only bring himself to be so ruthless, she could play a big part in showing the all-powerful Morelands what it was like to suffer. He relived the moment he'd looked up to see her standing above him on the central balcony of the mansion. She had appeared in her wedding finery like some splendid apparition or a beautiful illustration out of one of Ramona's golden books of fairy tales. Her gown was a lustrous silver. She wore a crown of flowers on her head. That first sight of her might well haunt him the rest of his life, he thought bleakly. Just the sight of her had made him think for the first time he should be building his own life, not forever seeking revenge for a past that was gone. Were the vows he had made eternally binding? Why had she made him feel they no longer meant anything?

For long moments he'd been a stranger to himself. She hadn't been aware of him, so he continued to stare with this queer hunger, as a man might stare at the unattainable. She *shone* in her bridesmaid's gown. Her skin gave off a lovely, luminous glow. Her effect on him was unprecedented in his experience, when his family's adopted Argentina was full of beautiful women, his for the asking. He had not dreamed of *this*, when it was essential he remain true to himself.

She had turned her head; stared down at him, her beautiful face unsmiling. Impossible to smile at that moment. He remembered he'd saluted her in some way. She had acknowledged him, regal as a princess. He'd wanted to climb up to her, using the thick, flowering trumpet vine that wreathed the white pillars as purchase for his eager feet. He was a passionate slave to beauty in all its forms, but for no woman had he been aflame with a terrible desire. It was *unimaginable* she should be a Moreland.

He had known that at once. She was Cecile Moreland, very much her grandfather's princess and heiress. She was far more beautiful in the flesh than in her photos in newspapers and the social pages of magazines, arresting as they were. He'd made it his business to find out everything there was to be learned about the Morelands. He already knew much, since he had lived with that hated name since his childhood. He had started his updated research with the Man with the Midas Touch, Joel Moreland. He now knew where every member of the entire clan lived, what they did for a living, the circles they moved in, their particular friends, their habits. He might have been commissioned to write an unauthorized book on the family, entitled *A Study of the Morelands*. Joel Moreland, the patriarch, father of the dead Jared, was way up there with the richest men in the country. His interests were vast. He doted on the young woman who now sat at the piano, her raven head bent over the keys.

She could complicate things drastically if he allowed it. Or she could become the all-powerful pawn. He had no stomach for causing grief to a woman—certainly not one who had so easily ensnared him—but he couldn't forget how much the women of his family had suffered. His grandmother, his mother, his aunts. The entire family had been forced off the land as his grandfather went deeper and deeper into debt. Land that one day his grandfather had promised would be his. Land was everything. Only, his grandfather had gone bankrupt. His creditors had moved in and they had moved out. Exile was like an amputation. There was an explanation for it all, the never-ending problems and misfortune. The way the family was ostracized.

Moreland wrath.

"They're determined to ruin us, boy!" his grandfather had said, shaking an impotent fist at the clear blue sky. The

memory would always remain with him: the boy and the old man. The boy's face hot and flushed with tears, his heart as heavy as his grandfather's. What was to be his was no more. His inheritance, his future hopes had been swept away on a wind straight from hell.

Even in the middle of his tortured thoughts, Raul had sensed Cecile was under some strain, as intensely nervous as he was intensely on edge. He'd been observing her closely all through dinner even with her charming but frivolous friend's voice buzzing like a bee in his ear. He rose when Tara began to giggle softly, walked to the piano knowing intuitively he could restore her nervous energy. It was all part of their subterranean communication.

The instant Cecile's hands touched the keys, the magic of the wonderful opening bars put his somber thoughts to rest. He sat back simply to listen, to absorb the music and the spectacle of her beauty as she sat at the grand piano in her lovely chiffon dress. The color put him in mind of the jacarandas, native to the high deserts of adjoining Brazil. They grew everywhere in Argentina and in flower lit up the Montalvan estancia. He knew they flourished, too, in many parts of temperate and subtropical Australia.

She played beautifully, powerfully. More important, she had mastered to perfection the particular rhythms of Spanish music. His stepsister, Ramona, was an accomplished pianist, but nothing like this. He knew the piece she was playing. He knew practically every piano piece the composer had written, the *Iberia* suite well, although Ramona always said the "Malaga" was too hard for her. Ramona had played the "Suite Espanola" so often over the years he could have whistled every note. In fact, he did whistle the catchy melodies as he rode the *pampas*. Ramon had been the kindest and most generous of stepfathers, adopting him and lending him his name. But Ramon had his heir, Francisco, who would soon turn twenty-one. Stepbrothers, they had never grown close. There was the big difference in age. He was nearly eleven years older, and Francisco was burdened by an intensely jealous nature that came much between them. With him out of the way, perhaps Francisco could find himself and become a better man.

AS IT WAS A WEEKDAY, all the guests were ready to take their leave not long after midnight. The senator as he was leaving complimented Cecile on "a wonderful performance." The other guests, too, as they moved out the front door expressed their enjoyment. Tara, who had come with her parents, grasped Cecile's arm rather painfully, drawing her swiftly aside.

"He's not married, is he?" she asked excitedly, color in her creamy cheeks.

"You mean Raul?"

"What's wrong with you all of a sudden? Of course I mean Raul. He's *devastating!*" Tara rolled her eyes.

"Don't get your hopes up, girl. I understand he has six children. Argentinians marry early."

Tara elbowed her in the ribs. "You're joking! He's not married at all. *Is* he?"

"He says not. Do you think we can believe him?"

"Well, *I* intend to." Tara readjusted the bodice of her dress to better show off her cleavage. "Listen, Ceci, I need to see more of him. Can you arrange it? Don't tell me now," she whispered hurriedly. "Here he comes. I don't want him to know we're talking about him. Have coffee with me tomorrow, okay? I'll ring you."

"Fine. I look forward to it."

Tara directed a brilliant smile and a little flutter of her hand at Raul Montalvan, calling sweetly, "Hope to see you again, Raul!"

"Is someone giving you a lift?" Cecile inquired of him politely. Fiona and Bruce had had a previous engagement, so they weren't able to attend the dinner party.

"I don't need a lift." He looked down at her gravely. "Your grandfather has already asked. I intend to walk back to the house. It's a beautiful night, and only a couple of miles to the residence. I'm used to very long treks, so a couple of miles could scarcely bother me. That said," his handsome mouth twitched, "perhaps you can walk me to your front gate? I've been wanting to tell you for close on two hours how much excitement I heard in your playing. It gave me enormous pleasure."

"Thank you." She inclined her head. "And thank you for helping me through a nervous moment. Somehow I *froze* when I'm used to playing for company."

"Perhaps I inspired the nerves, so it was necessary for me to take them away."

"You're very sure of yourself, aren't you?" There was a spirited flash in her silver-sheened eyes.

"I could scarcely answer, sure of *you!*"

"Is that a challenge?"

"Only if you'll respond." He smiled. "Come…" He didn't wait for her to agree to accompany him, but gently took her arm.

"Where are you off to, Ceci?" her mother called brightly from the bottom of the grand staircase.

"Ah, the mother ever ready to watch over her chick," he sighed softly, bending his head to Cecile's ear.

"Only to the front gate, Mother," she replied just as blithely.

"Some mothers never really see their daughters as grown-up," he said.

"Please don't tell anyone, okay?" she said coolly when she felt a fever coming on.

THE LAST OF THE GUESTS' cars were in line to pull out of the open front gates, their rear lights glowing a hot red. In silence they walked down the short flight of stone steps that led away from the huge three-story, colonial-style mansion with its towering vine-wreathed white pillars and second-floor central balcony. Cecile's heart was racing ninety to the dozen, as adrenaline poured into her blood. Now she knew what being on a "high" was. She didn't need any drugs; she was sizzling with the fever of sexual attraction. She felt she was doing something tantalizingly illicit, yet at the same time she couldn't and wouldn't stop herself from going with him. There was simply no *chance* of stopping. It wasn't that she was so much afraid of *him*. She was afraid of herself. And why not? She didn't know herself anymore. The outwardly serene Cecile people were used to had been replaced by someone quite different. She was now a woman who was ready to take dangerous chances.

The night sky was glorious, crowded with stars that hung over the harbor. The sea breeze stirred the leaves of the trees and shook out the perfume of a million tropical flowers. They had moved beyond the wide semicircle of exterior lights from the house, but the huge lantern lights set into the massive stone pillars that supported the wrought-iron gates showed the path clearly.

"You grandfather has very kindly asked me to his flagship station, as he called it, Malagari."

"When will this be?" She lifted her head in surprise. She didn't know how to take it—things were moving so fast.

"Would you believe toward the end of next week?" he said smoothly. "He had to consult his diary. He told me he had promised you a trip also, that Malagari is one of your favorite places."

"*The* favorite," she said.

"I expect he will want you to come along as well." His voice dropped deep into his chest. "Perhaps we could enjoy some marvelous Outback adventure together?"

The very thought sent cascading ripples down her spine. "There's absolutely no way I can do that, Raul. You know I can't!"

"But you *can!*"

The way he said it thrilled her. This was the moment she should pull back, but he had the speed and grace of a big cat. With one arm around her he whirled her off the driveway into the dense shadow of the trees.

"Wait! *Wait*, Raul! What are you doing?" Her voice shook; her body trembled violently. She might have been stripped naked.

He ran a finger down her satin cheek. "Cecile, my behavior is wholly known to you."

It was a waste of time denying it. "That doesn't mean it's not wrong." She felt herself flush deeply.

"I know that, too—" his answer was clipped "—but I can't seem to help myself."

"Raul, I'm *engaged!*" She despised herself for using it as a shield.

"I remember," he said quietly.

"Then you must realize this shouldn't happen."

"Astonishingly it has!" He pulled her close. "And engaged isn't married. I don't much like your fiancé. I feel strongly he isn't the man for you."

Her agitation intensified. "I don't know what I'm expected to say to that. He's my fiancé. I love him. You don't know anything about Stuart. He's—"

He stopped her mouth with his own.

Delirium!

Moondust fell from the skies, settling like a golden net around them.

His kiss was so deep and so passionate all thought of withstanding it evaporated like the dawn mist. It was a total assault on the senses, too devastating in its power for a mere kiss. Sensation upon sensation rushed through her body, hot, sweet, incredibly fierce. If he had drawn her down to the thick grass where they stood, she wouldn't have resisted. Resistance was impossible, even though she knew she was flouting her own code of honorable behavior.

In moments it was over. She stood there panting, trying to regain some semblance of control. He was still holding her in his arms, but she couldn't get her balance back. It was moments more before she could pull away.

"Dear Lord!" She gave a soft moan, lamenting how much of herself she had delivered up.

"Look at me." His tone was quiet but commanding.

"No way!" She had to lean against a tree for support even though the rough bark caught at the fine fabric of her dress.

"*Please* look at me." He moved nearer. "You are the love-liest thing I've ever seen."

"Raul, go. Just go."

"You feel guilty?"

"Of course I feel guilty," she said angrily. "I'm engaged to be married. I'm kissing you. What sort of a person does that make me?"

His laugh was faintly discordant. "Maybe you're just setting yourself free? Maybe you've wanted to be free all along?"

"And maybe for your own reasons you would like to seduce me?" She threw out the challenge. Certainly it had happened to her before. "I actually knew someone who proposed to do that just to settle a bet. It isn't unusual for a certain kind of man to have that idea."

"Of course this certain man didn't succeed?"

She spoke in a contemptuous tone. "In the end he wished he'd never thought of it. He or his friend."

"So where are we now? Only a fool would mess with the Morelands. Is that it?"

"I wouldn't care to mess with you," she retorted. "Was that kiss a blatant example of what I might expect if I were fool enough to join you on Malagari?"

"I know you want to," he said with stunning self-confi-dence. "It should happen. It will happen, Cecile. You're the beautiful princess locked away in the ivory tower. It's time for you to break out." His hand rose to lift her chin, then slowly, voluptuously, he pressed another kiss onto her warm pulsing mouth. "Must you marry this fiancé of yours? He seems to me to be what they call a stuffed shirt. He isn't your soul mate."

"And you are?" Her voice betrayed high emotion, but she'd gone beyond caring.

"I can make you tremble," he pointed out gently. "I can make you open your mouth to me."

"The next step my thighs? I think not," she said sharply, a blue vein beating in her temple. "I must go back to the house," she said, albeit much too late. "If you're looking for a holiday affair—"

He caught her wrist, his sensuous voice abruptly harsh. "Don't talk such nonsense. I am as much compromised by whatever it is that exists between us as you are."

"Nothing exists between us," she declared with no truth whatsoever. "I'm to be married very soon to the man I love."

He gave a short laugh. "Forgive me, but isn't this a bad time to drag that up? It's humiliating, I know, to lose control, especially for someone who represses emotion. Both of us appear to have been blindsided. Fate works in strange ways, Cecile."

She shook her head, feeling like she wanted to cry. What had happened to her self-control? It was sliding away from her. "I must go back." She started to move toward the path and the beam of light. Her high heels were sinking into the grass, and again he took her arm.

"Ah yes, Mamma will be waiting," he said in a sardonic voice. "I picture her now, on the central balcony, a pair of binoculars in hand. She's an impressive woman, your mother, but very controlling. You must try to get past that, Cecile."

She surprised herself by a confession. "Sometimes I think I never will. I'm caught, you see, by love and…compassion."

"Useful tools when one needs to apply emotional blackmail," he said. "How did your engagement happen?"

She gave an angry little laugh. "Maybe I was bored. Maybe I felt pressured into it. Maybe I felt my youth ticking by. I want children." She shrugged a little. "Surely you have no right to question me. Let's say, I fell in love. Stuart loves me."

"*That* part I believe," he said, sounding grim.

"Do you always talk this way to strangers?" She was angry that she felt incompetent to deal with him. "I have to tell you, student of psychology that you are, you know nothing about my mother, my family, my fiancé, nothing about me, except I play the piano rather well—"

"And you forget everything and everyone in my arms." He turned her toward him.

"You don't need to remind me." She drew away as if he were the devil himself. "I think I should make a vow right now *never* to go back into your arms again."

"Will the moon never come out again at night?" He gave a brief, sardonic laugh.

She had trouble even thinking of an answer. Instead, panic rose in her like a flock of startled birds. "Raul, you must stay away from me."

He touched her cheek "That, too, seems to be out of our control. Your grandfather appears bent on throwing us together."

"He's simply being kind." Even as she said it she was tormented by the notion he was right.

"Perhaps he doesn't think your fiancé worthy of you, either?" Raul suggested. "You deserve better. Already I know a side of you he will *never* see. I'm sure he tells you your playing is very *nice?*"

"Well, he would, as he's tone deaf. You should never have kissed me, Raul," she told him bleakly.

"You should never have kissed me back." His answer was calm.

"I'm ashamed."

"I'm quite certain I'm not," he clipped off. "He wants to *own* you, Cecile."

There was too much truth in what he said, however unpalatable, for her to deny it.

"It can't be a fate your grandfather would want for you. You are your own woman."

"Yes I am, though I won't be if we continue like this." She turned her face sharply toward the house. "I can deal with my problems by myself, you know."

He shrugged. "Forgive me if I thought you could use some help. It seems to me from what your grandfather has told me, much has been expected of you."

"Hasn't much been expected of you?" she countered. "Who *are* you, anyway?" She couldn't conceal her unease.

"Perhaps someone you need?" While she sounded angry, he sounded calm, almost fatalistic.

Her eyes, more accustomed to the low level of lighting, registered the expression on his face. "You don't appear to me as a *friend!* I confess a concern you might have some private agenda."

"But of course I have!" He made a little foreign gesture with his hands. "I can promise you that."

"I don't care for the sound of that."

"But you don't want to *stop* seeing me."

She had no idea how to cope with him. *None!* Not when he had come at her like some blazing meteor from out of space. How could a mere mortal reach her in unreachable places? It didn't seem possible otherwise. She turned on her heel, throwing her words over her shoulder. "Don't draw me into your plans, Raul Montalvan, whatever they are. I'll say good-night."

He raised a mocking hand. "*Buenas noches*, Cecile. Until we meet again!"

CHAPTER SIX

SHE WAS UNDRESSED, ready to climb into bed, when her mother tapped on her door.

"May I come in for a moment, Cecile?" Justine, in one of her collection of luxurious satin nightgowns and matching robes, swept in before Cecile got a chance to say yea or nay.

"It must be important if it can't wait." Cecile, long used to these late-night encounters with her mother, slumped onto the bed, her head already pounding and in a whirl. "It's well after one."

Justine spun around, a handsome, dominant woman whose frequent aggressive actions masked deep insecurities. "Be that as it may, I have something very serious to say to you, Cecile. I don't believe it *can* wait. I'll be off in the morning, as you know. Your father and I have a big function to attend Friday evening."

"Fire away then," Cecile answered, unable to keep the weariness out of her voice.

Justine pursed her mouth at her daughter's response. "*Don't*—I beg of you—don't when you've finally got your life together, allow anything to threaten it."

Realistically speaking, wasn't it a possibility? "Words to

live by, Mother," Cecile said. "Anything in particular bring this on?"

Justine moved to one side and took a seat in a brocade-covered armchair. "Don't take that tone with me, Cecile. Your manners have slipped. You used to be very respectful. I'd like you to remain that way. It's the least you can do when I've devoted my life to you. You've been reared in the lap of luxury with every advantage. You've had much love, not to say adulation. I certainly never had that. My mother scarcely acknowledged my existence. We, however, have been very close. I'm very proud of that. You've always heeded my advice and acted on it. Maybe I didn't want you to pursue your career, which must be very ugly and distressing, but I didn't put up any real objection."

Cecile stifled a snort. "How can you say that, Mother, given your numerous objections? It was Dad and Granddad who supported my desire to become a child psychologist. You might challenge Dad and you did, but you've never challenged Granddad."

Justine's outraged expression showed she didn't like that fact pointed out. "I *adore* Daddy. You know I do." At fifty Justine didn't find it at all incongruous she should continue to call her father "Daddy."

"But you've never forgiven him, either," Cecile pointed out quietly. What made her say that, however true? How many times in one day could she shock herself, Cecile thought.

"Cecile, what are you saying?" Justine sat straight, holding her shoulders rigidly.

"Something I've known for a very long time. I'm not trying to upset you, Mother, but I think I should tell you, *you* upset me a lot of the time. You're too ready to interfere in my life, always advising, exhorting. There's always something, if not wrong, not quite right with what I'm doing, no matter what it is. Sometimes I think I'm not the daughter you wanted at all, though God knows I've tried to be. I saw your face tonight when I announced I was going to play the 'Malaga.' Anyone would have thought I was about to disgrace you."

"Nonsense!" Justine rejected that firmly. "I merely thought you wouldn't do yourself justice. I'm sure you haven't practiced that piece in ages and it's technically very demanding."

"But I did play it well?"

For the first time Justine's taut expression relaxed. "You were wonderful, Cecile. I've always been very proud of you. Haven't I told you often enough?"

"Forgive me, Mother, you have. What are we talking about here, anyway?"

Justine pursed her lips again. "I understood you to say I've never forgiven Daddy. Whatever prompted that?"

"The truth, Mother," Cecile sighed. "You grew up believing Granddad didn't do enough for you." She held up her hand as her mother went to interrupt. "I scarcely mean in the material sense. You didn't think Granddad supported you enough against Nan. He gave you love, support, comfort, solace when you didn't get those things from your mother, but—"

"Believe me, I *didn't!*" Justine said harshly, stony-faced.

"Grandma cared more about Granddad and Uncle Jared than she cared about you?" Cecile asked gently.

"Some women are like that," Justine said bitterly. "Husbands and sons are the only ones who matter. Daddy was away so much of the time. It was always business, business,

business. I had no one but servants to look out for me. In many ways I was a lost child. I know my mother loved *you*, extraordinarily enough, but she skipped a generation. She never bonded with me. Ask anyone. Ask wicked old Bea. There's another one who loves you and not me."

"You won't let yourself be loved, Mother," Cecile said. "I think it must have taken Granddad—a very busy man as you say—a long time before he realized what was going on with you and Nan, the lack of warmth and affection. But it wasn't Granddad's fault any more than what happened to Daniel and his poor little mother. It was necessary for Granddad to be away on his many business trips. We've all benefited from his great success. His family and any number of friends and charities. It seems incredible to me now that Nan was so cruel to Daniel's mother."

"Ah, Johanna! She was just the maid, a no one!" Justine sighed. "Let me tell you your grandmother did have a cruel streak. No way was Johanna, however pretty, going to be allowed to get her hooks into Mother's beloved Jared. My mother solved the problem by driving Daniel's mother away. Now Daniel's back."

"You don't want him back, though, do you, Mother?" Cecile brought it out into the open.

Justine's fine, regular features sharpened. "How dare you say such a thing!"

"Aw, Mother, admit it. You think you know me. I know *you*. I already love Daniel. You've tried very hard to do the right thing. You've acted perfectly, but it is *acting*. You're Daniel's aunt, his own flesh and blood, but you have no feeling for him. Is it because you fear Granddad's love for Daniel will lessen his love for you? It won't. You should feel secure in Granddad's love."

Justine sighed deeply. "Well, I never have. I know Daddy loves me, but he would have gotten over *my* death a whole lot sooner than he's survived Jared's. You can't know what it's like, Cecile, to forever walk in someone else's shadow. When Jared died I wanted to be dead myself. I know my mother would have sacrificed me in an instant to save Jared. She *knew,* I'm convinced of it, that Daniel's mother was pregnant when she sent her away. That meant she sent away her own grandchild, but she didn't care. She had Jared. Thank God Daniel is more like Daddy than Jared ever was. Otherwise I couldn't abide the sight of him. You're right, I can't take to poor Daniel, I'm sorry."

"You will in time, Mother. Give yourself a chance. You know the source of your bitterness and resentment. Daniel had no part to play in that. Daniel was an innocent victim. He's *good,* like Granddad is good. You'll come to see that."

Justine looked unconvinced. "Cecile, I'm hoping I'll have little to do with him, though I do like Alexandra. She's a lovely girl. It's *you* I'm worried about. I want to prevent something bad happening here. You're attracted to this Raul Montalvan, aren't you?"

"Definitely." Cecile saw no point in not admitting it. She had given herself away. "Tara found him extremely attractive, too."

"Then leave him to Tara," Justine said in a clipped voice. "Let Tara entertain him. She'll *love* that. I can see his very obvious attractions, but I don't trust him. Daddy is so generous with his time and money I'm sure he'll be wanting to entertain this young man while he's here. My advice to you, and it's good advice, stay clear of him. He's most definitely trouble. I know Stuart was very concerned."

Cecile flared up. "You don't mean to tell me Stuart discussed the subject with you."

"He didn't have to," Justine answered irritably. "Stuart and I are on the same wavelength. Besides it was *appallingly* obvious our visitor was attracted to you. I don't have to remind you being a Moreland gives you added brilliance. He could be on the lookout for a rich wife for all we know."

"So you think he's a fortune hunter?" Cecile's hackles were well and truly up.

Justine smiled bitterly. "I was an heiress myself, Cecile."

"What's that supposed to mean?"

"It means that made a difference to your *father*," Justine said dryly, shocking her daughter. "I know you think I blind myself to the truth. Most of the time I do, but I have my moments when the shutters come down. Your father and I have a good stable marriage. Each of us got what we wanted. He will never leave me. I'm absolutely certain of that. If he ever tried it, I'd ruin him."

"Oh, Mother!" Cecile sighed deeply, thinking Justine had more of her own mother, Frances, in her than she ever imagined.

Justine stood up, putting a hand to her thick, deeply waving hair, one of her best assets. "Promise me you won't see any more of this Raul Montalvan, Cecile. I can't trust Daddy not to throw you both together. I don't think he truly appreciates what a good husband Stuart will be for you. You have a lot going on inside you, Cecile, that needs curbing. Don't think I'm not aware of it. You seem to be searching for some new way of defining yourself when you're on the threshold of marriage, your life settled. Your job is to be a good wife to Stuart and raise beautiful children."

"You don't think *my* future development is important, Mother?"

"Of course it is," Justine said irritably. "You have the rest of your life for self-development. Look at me. I've been a great asset to your father as you will be to Stuart with some help from me. I love you, Cecile. You've always made me proud. Don't let me down now, I beg of you. Raul Montalvan, no matter how fascinating, is nothing but trouble. Such men always are."

CECILE SAW HER MOTHER OFF at the airport, her mother reluctant to let go of her dire warnings until the very last minute, then drove back into the city to have coffee with Tara.

"Tell me first—" Tara put a hand across their al fresco table to grab Cecile's "—did he say anything about me?"

Cecile made a play of looking back at her friend blankly. "Who?"

"For God's sake, tell me." Tara shook Cecile's hand.

"Can we order first?" Cecile asked mildly. "Terrible to say it, but with my mother gone I feel like a kid let off school. When was this anyway?"

Tara looked at her friend with dismay. "When you were walking with him down the bloody drive," she responded tartly. "I *saw* you, but I promise I won't tell the pain in the ass."

The pain in the ass was Tara's private name for Stuart. "Shouldn't you avoid those precise words when you're talking about my fiancé?" Cecile suggested, withdrawing her hand from Tara's surprisingly strong grip. A petite five foot two, Tara was a featherweight due to a strict dieting regime, which veered by the week from one method to another, none of them particularly healthy.

"Why? He's just so bloody pompous," Tara responded, thinking she couldn't bear the idea of her beautiful Cecile marrying Stuart Carlson. "Okay he's good-looking, he's clever, he's the man destined to marry the beautiful Cecile Moreland and go right to the top of the tree, but he's too much the go-getter and he's got bugger-all sex appeal."

"You're not sleeping with him, are you?" Cecile asked.

"If I thought it would stop you marrying him, I would do it in a split second," Tara said with some force.

"Ah, Tara!" Cecile shook her head. In the space of a few hours, her oldest, closest friend was saying one thing, her mother the very opposite. She picked up the menu, ashamed of the fact she had to make a real effort to dredge up a few words in Stuart's defense. "It's as well I'm used to your straight shooting, sweetie. In fact, I love you for it—most of the time—but let me assure you, Stuart's libido is in good working order. I can see why Mother has always considered you an unsuitable companion for me."

"Ah, yes, Mother," Tara replied gleefully. "Gee, you know, if she were only twenty years younger *she* could marry Stuart. They always seem to have such a lot in common."

"They do." Cecile's tone was dry.

"He's not the man for you, Ceci," Tara mourned, shaking her lovely blond helmet of hair. "You're angelic on top, but you're hot and spicy underneath. You can't fool me. We've been friends since we fell into Joel's pond."

"You pushed me in, you mean," Cecile said, recalling the hot afternoon when the two of them had first met at one of her grandmother's garden parties. Six going on seven, complete opposites.

"I was jealous of your party dress," Tara admitted, a nostalgic smile on her pert face. "And *you*. You looked like a little princess and you spoke oh so prim and proper, but you turned out to be a lot of fun. You never told on me, either. But to get back to the delicious Señor Montalvan. I bet he'd be a *wonderful* lover! Did he say anything about me?"

Cecile took her time to answer, not knowing what to say or in what direction she should steer her friend. "Actually he didn't," she said after a while, "which doesn't mean he didn't find you a very attractive dinner companion."

"Oh I hope, I hope!" Tara clasped her hands together in an attitude of prayer. "He's *gorgeous!*" she raved, "and the bloody *voice!* Mel Gibson with a bit of Antonio Banderas thrown in. He doesn't actually look South American, though, does he? Not like South Americans look South American, if you know what I mean. You know, the raven hair and the flashing dark eyes. He could be a very sophisticated Englishman, Australian, American, only for the fascinating trace of accent and I suppose, the manner. Now *that's* South American. What's he here for, anyway? I tried to question him very discreetly."

"You, discreet?" Cecile cocked an eyebrow.

"You don't think I can be discreet?"

"Frankly, no!" Cecile shook her head.

Tara didn't take offense. Her mother told her that all the time, and her young brother, Harry, called her *motormouth.* "Anyway, he was charming but very astute at not answering my questions. Joel's taken quite a fancy to him."

"Yes, he has," Cecile agreed, lifting a hand to a waiter. Tara was one of the few people, certainly of her age group, who called her grandfather Joel. But then, Tara was a great flirt and it amused her grandfather, who had always found Tara as engaging as her mother found her "vulgar." Not true and rather cruel. Impetuous, impulsive maybe, but very loyal.

"I overheard Joel inviting him to Malagari," Tara went on excitedly.

"Puh-leeze, you were *listening*," Cecile chided her.

"So I was!" Tara gave her infectious gurgle of laughter. "I might as well confess it, you know me so well. Are *you* going? I got the feeling it was quite soon."

"I don't know." She would need serious counseling herself if she did.

"Come off it!" Tara scoffed. "No woman in her right mind would turn down the opportunity of spending a little time with Señor Montalvan."

"There is the fact I'm an engaged woman," Cecile suggested. "The accent is on the second-last syllable, by the way. Mon-*tal*-van. I think there are a few Spanish marks thrown in the spelling, like the French acutes and graves and cedillas and what not."

"What's a cedilla?" Tara asked with interest.

"Didn't you take French?"

Tara put a finger to her cheek, turning her large blue eyes upward. "Let me think. *Henri Quatre est sur la Pont Neuf.* I know, it's the little comma thing."

"Right. It's under *c* to show it's sibilant."

"Okay, do you have to keep reminding me you've more brains than I have? So it's Mon*tal*van? I *see*. I call him Raul. What does Raul mean, smarty-pants?"

Cecile laughed. "I imagine it's the Spanish form of Ralph." She broke off as the waiter came to take their order.

"So like Raul, you haven't answered my question. Will you go, too?" Tara asked.

Cecile sighed. "Tara, I can't go running off with devilishly handsome Argentinians."

"Force yourself. Or look on it as a kind of escape from

Stuart. You've got nothing in common with him. It's all that pressure your mother puts on you! God, does she ever stop? I know mothers nag, but your mother takes the cake. I've worried about it for years. Why does she think Stuart is so great, anyway?"

Cecile rested her chin on the upturned palm of her hand. "God knows."

"There you go!" Tara crowed. "That wasn't the response of a woman in love. Wake up to yourself, girl. There must be at least two or three billion men left in the world for you to choose from. Me, I'd just like to take a shot at Señor Montalvan. I've never ever seen anything quite like him. He's got wonderful shoulders, don't you think? A wide back too. He looks great in his clothes. I'm just stopping myself from contemplating him without them. The thing is, if *you* go, Ceci, you can ask me. Well? Why are you staring at me like that?"

"Don't you have a job to go to?" Cecile asked, giving herself time to mull over Tara's proposal.

"Sure, only I work for my dad," Tara gloated, "which means I can easily persuade him to give me some time off. Especially if I'm going with you. Unlike your mother with me, *my* mother holds you in very high regard. You're my friend. I would never wish to steal your fiancé, but I sure would like to steal Señor Mon*tal*van away."

"Be my guest," Cecile offered in a wry voice.

Tara took her literally. "Bloody hell, you *mean* it?" Zesty as always, Tara jumped up from her chair to give Cecile a big hug. "I can come?"

"Don't get too excited," Cecile said gently. "I can *ask*, Tara, but it's up to Granddad."

Tara resumed her chair, waving a nonchalant hand. "Then

we don't have a worry in the world. Whatever you ask, Joel gives. Anyway, Joel's got a soft spot for me."

"Because you give him heaps of blarney." Cecile smiled.

"Would you *mind!* I love him. Joel is a beautiful man, everyone's image of a distinguished gentleman. Anyway, I've been asked to Malagari plenty of times before. Raul is going to love it!" Tara's blue eyes grew dreamy. "I can see myself sitting across the campfire from him. Dingoes are howling in the hills. I shiver. Immediately he gets up to comfort me. The night is full of stars!" She exhaled blissfully. "Romance with a capital *R,* wouldn't you say?"

"Now that you mention it, yes."

"Next day we go exploring our great desert monuments, Uluru and Kata Tjuta. We pick wildflowers in the canyons. We go horse riding—not far, I'm not much good on horses as you know. Swim in a billabong—who needs suits? Make love on the warm sand. It turns into an orgy. Hey, all I need is a chance!"

CHAPTER SEVEN

THE LANDSCAPE BELOW them put Raul in mind of the pictures coming back to Earth from Mars. It was also the fantastic fiery-red landscape he inhabited in his dreams. Now he was regarding it afresh. His mother had escaped the country of her birth, in truth still too heartsick to ever wish to return. He had never escaped, no matter how far away they had settled. From the moment his mother had arrived in Argentina all those years ago, she had made herself fit in by sheer force of will. She had escaped them all: the people who had thrown the maiming sticks and stones, blaming her simply because of who she was. He and his dad, who had never given a tuppenny damn for what anyone said, had never made a successful transition, not that his dad was given much time to fit in anywhere.

Later on, after that terrible grief had been sprung on his mother and him, Ramon with his money and his beautiful estancia had made himself their deliverer. The fact that his mother was meltingly lovely and courageous had a lot to do with it. Still, Ramon had been good to him even when he'd been a hurting, hotheaded, wildly rebellious boy—practically a savage without the controlling hand of his father—but he had never learned to think of Argentina as his home or his future. He had always been determined that one day he would go back. One day he would make the Morelands pay. He would chase down all the people who had hurt his family. He would solve the puzzle and fulfill his ambition to once more walk his desert home.

Now Moreland's granddaughter and heiress with her silver-rain eyes and her beautiful face had literally fallen into his arms. That rocked him to the core even as an ungentle voice inside his head, cried out triumphantly, *Yes! Yes!* He didn't have to work on any other plan beyond her. He could, however, with his inside influence and knowledge, throw a considerable spoke in Joel Moreland's plans for doing business with Argentinian polo pony breeders and front-line players. A word here, a word there, and it was done. He was as trusted within the Argentinian industry as was his stepfather, Ramon.

Raul continued to look earthward, averting his head to conceal his expression from watching eyes. Had he known it, it was darkly brooding with a turbulent edginess. Yet he had to be careful not to alarm anyone. No one was to see he was plotting anything, but the urge for revenge had become almost meat and drink. Now it was laced with a perverse sense of misgiving. A woman, almost a stranger to him, was at the center of his changing heart. Old scores had to be settled surely? He had to keep remembering that. The slur on *his* family's name had to be lifted.

Beneath them the great inland desert captivated him. It was an endless world of fiery colors: bloodred, bright rust, strong yellow, burnt umber, dusty pink and glaring white. Land always had filled him with a fierce exhilaration. He worshiped the land like some early pagan, the roar of the winds, the fantastic electric storms that rolled back and forth without delivering life-giving rain; canyons that in severe drought opened up unexpectedly right at one's feet. Floods that concealed these undulating red dunes and the isolated mesas, set down as they were in the great emptiness. It was unlike any other part of the world. He realized he had never experienced quite this level of nature worship riding the gorse-covered *pampas* that stretched out to the majestic snow-capped Andes, though their isolated splendor and the wonderful horses had consoled him greatly. He would be forever grateful to Ramon and Ramon's beloved Argentina, but his heart, his *wild* heart, belonged to only one place.

It was the Timeless Land that truly called to his heart.

To the south the endless plains, parched by the blazing sun, met up with eroded ranges that in the distance glowed an extraordinary purplish-blue like the heart of a black opal. Infinite stretches of the living desert lay to either side. It took monsoonal rain from the tropical north or winter rains from the south to carry here to transform the barren Inland into a world of flowers of immense numbers and incomparable perfume. He still remembered as a small boy waking up to a wonderland, jumping out of bed and without bothering to dress, racing out into the horse paddocks to be one of the first to witness the desert flora burst into ecstatic life.

The exhilaration he felt was not unmixed with a deep melancholia that had begun the moment they flew out of the tropical Top End with its crocodiles and magnificent lily-covered lagoons and into the arid Red Heart with its all-pervading atmosphere of deep time. The Northern Territory was bigger than France, Italy and Spain put together, but within its borders lay two vastly different climatic zones: rain forest and desert.

On no account could he allow his melancholia to grow to the point it would swamp him. There would be plenty of ghosts down there on Malagari. Ghosts on the other side of the purple ranges where lay hidden the small operation his family had worked for five generations. Through thick and thin, through drought and a terrible bush fire that had claimed the life of his great-uncle Harry, they had held on to it. He wondered what had happened to it after his grandfather had been forced off. His granddad, a man of tremendous strength and energy, had died of a massive heart attack exactly six months later. That terrible event had drained all the life out of his grandmother. She had survived, eventually falling back on the loving kindness of her married sister who lived far away in the South Island of New Zealand.

So much that had gone catastrophically wrong, and all in a lamentably short time. What had his grandmother called the family suffering? *All the afflictions of Job*. His uncle Benjie had been only fifteen going on sixteen when his life had changed within the space of a few minutes. Benjie was more a big brother than an uncle. He had been killed in a bar fight at the age of twenty-two. What had been his assailant's intention? Murder? Of course the man had denied it strenuously, but he had been charged with manslaughter and given a ten-year jail sentence with parole after six. He'd be long out by now. Probably had his old job back on Malagari. Joel Moreland wasn't just a very rich man. He was an Outback icon. So many people, through his vast interests, relied on him for their livelihood. He had then, as he had now, a veritable army of henchmen to do his bidding.

Yet how could a man who looked and acted as straight as a die in deed and word be so cruel? How could a seemingly delightful man like Joel Moreland, so kind and distinguished, go to such remorseless lengths to punish a boy who had been unfortunate enough to be in the wrong place at the wrong time? Not only the boy, his entire family, as though they had all connived to cause Jared Moreland's death. It hadn't been Benjie who had triggered Jared Moreland's violent end. Jared Moreland, who had been the instrument of Johanna Muir's catastrophic fall from grace, had by his callous behavior contributed to his own death. Innocent high-spirited Benjie had been used as a pawn in a murderous game.

Beware those of you who are left. The exile is back!

MORELAND'S PILOT BANKED into a right turn lining up the private jet for Malagari's runway. At the far end he could see the roof of a massive hangar far bigger than the one on the Montalvan estancia. The silver roof glittered in the hot sun, the surface giving off shimmering waves of heat. On the roof was emblazoned the name of the station, Malagari, in royal blue, the edges picked out in red. On the ground to the right of the hangar was a towering flagpole from which the red, white and blue of the Australian flag fluttered. Beneath it flew a pennant carrying the colors of the station with the addition of a white circle of stars. He knew that was a Moreland logo.

The tires thumped and bounced hard on contact with the first-grade all-weather strip, sending a cloud of red dust over the wings. He could have managed the landing better, though it was okay. He could see from the flags there was a brisk cross wind. The brakes made their usual high-pitched squeal, then the pilot cut the engines back to idle, taxiing toward the hangar.

They had arrived.

He looked across at Cecile, who was looking out the porthole. Her friend, Tara, was chattering ninety to the dozen in her ear. Cecile's wondrous femininity that put him in mind of a white lily was strangely enhanced by the almost masculine severity of today's outfit, tailored black linen slacks, a silk camisole showing beneath a deeper cream linen safari-style jacket. A wide embossed leather belt with an ornate silver buckle was slung around her narrow waist. Her friend, on the other hand, wore a short, bright blue dress that exactly matched her pretty eyes. While Cecile had greeted him at Moreland's private airstrip with deliberate formality, her friend had stood on tiptoe to kiss him on the cheek. No chance of a kiss or embrace from the woman who barely a week before had swooned in his arms.

There were intense moments in life, Raul mused. Some were more intense than others, but he had never for all his traumas experienced anything approaching the power and complexity of the feelings he was trying to master now. A few feet away from him she sat, a gold clasp gathering back her long hair, totally unaware of what was in his heart. She had that inviolable self-assurance that came with being a beautiful woman of class and money. It would be so easy to hurt her. He would hate to hurt her for a thousand and one reasons. He wasn't a cruel man by nature. But he had been shown a way, perhaps the most symbolic way, to avenge Benjie and his family. Benjie might have turned out the great loser, but Raul reminded himself Benjie was a better man than the scoundrel who had been Moreland's only son.

Pain twisted in his stomach. The bitter irony was he'd had

no way of knowing the powerful effect a woman of a hated family would have on him. This was a woman who inspired love, not hate.

ON THE GROUND the heat was like a dry oven. He reveled in it; felt it soak into his skin, already darkly tanned. Off in the distance the mirage was playing its remembered tricks, creating inviting vistas of phantom lakes. Chains of them shimmered in the distance, their shores surrounded by tall waving desert palms.

"My man will be here shortly to drive us to the homestead, Raul," Moreland told him, gripped by his own pleasure at being back on Malagari. "Ah, here he is now."

Raul turned slightly. A dusty Land Rover was roaring cross-country, eventually driving up onto the huge concrete platform that surrounded the hangar on all sides and met up with the runway. The engine cut and a big bearded man in his early fifties stood out of the vehicle waving a hand.

"Afternoon, all! Good flight I hope, sir?"

"Couldn't have been smoother, Jack," Moreland said cheerfully, turning to his guest, while Cecile and Tara stood smilingly to one side. "Raul, I'd like you to meet Jack Doyle, my chief steward on Malagari. Jack has worked for me in one capacity or the other for close on thirty years. His wife, Alison, is our resident chef and housekeeper. Ally's in charge of the domestic staff all of them our own aboriginal girls, born on the station. It's a large house. Needs a lot of maintenance. I'm lucky to have such loyal employees."

"Glad to meet you, Mr. Doyle," Raul responded, shaking the other man's hand. *Jack Doyle*. He knew the name. Doyle had moved up in the world. One did when one delivered big on *loyalty*.

"Likewise," Doyle said with a friendly grin. "And it's Jack. No one calls me Mr. Doyle. Welcome to Malagari, Raul. Ah…Miss Cecile—" Doyle turned to smile at her with open affection "—it's great to have you back. We've been missing you. You too, Miss Tara. What practical jokes have you lined up for us this time?"

"Got to be a surprise, Jack," Tara told him breezily.

"Best get us up to the house, Jack," Moreland intervened. "It's pretty darn hot on the runway."

"Right, sir. I'll just load on the luggage."

"I'll give you a hand." Raul was already moving to do so.

"Gee, thanks, mate!" Jack gave their visitor a quick smile. Miss Cecile's fiancé had never on any occasion made such a suggestion. There were servants to do things like that. Delusions of grandeur, Jack always thought.

Ahead of them, set in a desert garden of greens and ochres and flourishing orange-and-scarlet bouganvillea blossom, was the Malagari homestead, an oasis in the wilderness. He had seen pictures of it in pastoral magazines and large coffee table books of historic homesteads, but nothing had prepared him for the heroic scale of the place nor the raw majesty of its setting. In a way, it was rather like the first glimpse of Uluru's great dome, rising out of the infinite plains. Malagari appealed to his heart, his senses and his mind when he had wanted most deeply to loathe the place. The surrounding gardens, huge by any standard, would depend on bore water from the Great Artesian Basin for survival. He knew that. The homestead, he thought, depended on its great overhanging hipped roof to anchor it to the bloodred earth and take care of those who sheltered beneath it. The main single-story structure had wings that formed a squared-off U. Only a man of Moreland's immense wealth, cattle king and business magnate as he was, could afford it.

Raul knew the station, all 10,000 square kilometers of it, carried a Santa Gertrudis herd of over a quarter of a million. It formed one of the largest operations in the country and certainly the world. Malagari was the Moreland flagship of the arid zone. The Moreland flagship of the Top End, the tropical zone, was Kumbal Downs. Kumbal, he had discovered, ran around 100,000 Brahman. There were other stations in the chain, vast Opal Creek in Queensland's Channel Country for one, Lagunda in Queensland another, but Malagari remained the backbone of the operation just as it had in Raul's grandfather's day.

"This is it!" Joel Moreland announced proudly, waving an arm toward the historic homestead.

"It's splendid!" Raul was able to respond without difficulty, which was as well since Moreland's keen regard was leveled on him. "A desert paradise." Raul turned to admire the courtyard's central marble fountain. It was playing in the blazing fire of noon, creating an aura of coolness. The great bowl, one in a tier of three, was supported by four magnificently carved rearing horses. It would have to be horses for a man who had lived his life in the saddle.

"Italian," Moreland said, following Raul's gaze. "Cost a fortune, plus another fortune to get it here. I bought it in Rome, one of my favorite places in all the world, not long after my beautiful Ceci was born. Right, girls, we'll go inside. Must protect those beautiful complexions." He put an arm around his granddaughter and Tara, turning them toward the house. "Come, Raul. We'll get settled, then we'll have lunch.

Jack can attend to everything. I can't wait to hear what you think of the interior. Ceci has been my most recent decorator. She knows exactly what I like. I have to say my late wife and I didn't always see eye-to-eye in that department. Frances had more of a city eye, if you know what I mean. I'm an Outback man through and through. It was Frances who chose to live in Darwin, which I enjoy—it has its own fascination—but in latter years she rarely visited Malagari. In that sense Justine is like her mother. She's a city girl at heart. My Ceci isn't." He dropped a quick kiss on his granddaughter's gleaming head.

So why then did you choose a man who means to keep you pregnant in the suburbs? Raul thought.

Cecile sensed it as if he had spoken his thought aloud. His expressive glance subtly mocked her, catching her up in the now familiar black magic. For a moment she had the strong impression he was going to address her directly. To make it worse, although her grandfather had never interfered in her choice of Stuart or openly criticized any aspect of his behavior, she knew he had never taken to Stuart the way he had so obviously taken to Raul Montalvan.

Damn him!

Raul saw the light flush color her high cheekbones, felt her little wave of hostility. She tilted her chin. It only served to enhance the lovely line of her throat. He was becoming very aware of the fact that she wasn't slow to pick up on his wavelength, read his thoughts. He would have to be careful there. Her friend, Tara, turned her head over her shoulder to smile at him. He couldn't help knowing Tara was attracted to him, but like a madness, he had his heart and his mind set on Cecile.

Raul followed them through the deeply recessed double

doors, which appeared to have been carved from Indian teak, and into the world of the very rich. The floor of the grand entrance hall was covered in a wonderful mosaic tile that brought him up short. It had all the glowing colors of a Persian carpet.

"Again an Italian artisan." Joel Moreland smiled at his guest's look of appreciation. "It's beautiful, isn't it?"

"Indeed it is." Raul glanced around him. It was a very handsome house, but as they continued on their way he saw the decoration had been handled in a manner that welcomed.

Inside all was serene, cool and quiet. The main rooms he was able to glimpse through tall pedimented archways of dark gleaming timbers. The furnishings, the pictures, all the valuable objects around the place—one such resting on a console in the entrance hall looked like a Tang Dynasty horse and probably was—created an aura of richness, but the overall effect was one of a comfortable, inviting, large country house. There was a graceful *balance,* Raul thought, like Cecile Moreland herself. The spaces between the beautiful paintings were exactly right. Some of the large canvases depicted the very best of aboriginal art which he knew was attracting a world following. He found himself seduced. Cecile, he noticed with some irony, walked with easy familiarity past all these treasures. Outback royalty, he thought, staring after her.

The color scheme was pale: ivories and creams and dusky golds. It made a cool contrast to the dark timbers, as did the light and airy drapes that billowed gently at the series of broad French doors. The floors weren't carpeted in the desert heat. They were polished to the color of golden honey, the hardwood scattered here and there with magnificent rugs. There were intimate womanly touches to counteract the sheer richness, books, flowers, a very pleasing juxtaposition of objects. He caught a glimpse of an ebony concert grand in the living room. She had a most indulgent grandfather, this Cecile. Life would have been idyllic for her as she was growing up, loved and indulged at every turn. Unlike his, her life had not been vandalized.

Alison Doyle, the housekeeper, came rushing out to greet them, a little flustered, excusing her late appearance as having to get something out of the oven. Introductions began again. Doyle's wife was a slim attractive woman in her late forties, auburn hair, lightly freckled skin with bright blue eyes and a sunny smile.

"I've got everything ready for you, Mr. Moreland," she said. "Lunch in a half hour if that suits?"

"Fine, Ally, fine!" Moreland said, in his easy charming voice. "I know I can always rely on you. I've brought a couple of CDs for you to add to your collection. Ella Fitzgerald and Peggy Lee."

The housekeeper's face lit up. "That's great. Really great!"

"Ally has discovered the great female jazz singers," Joel Moreland turned to Raul with a word of explanation. "I don't think anyone has topped Ella."

"I know I'm going to love them," Ally said. "Now if you'll excuse me I'll get on with preparing lunch." She gave another smile that encompassed them all, then moved off.

"If you'd like to come with me now, Raul, I'll show you to your room," Cecile said.

"Thank you." Raul turned his eyes away from her to smile at his host. "You have a very beautiful home, sir." He was able to say it with perfect sincerity.

"Look here, you've got to make it Joel." Moreland

didn't hold back on extending the friendship. "You can't keep calling me sir."

Raul flashed his illuminating smile. "I'd be delighted to call you Joel if that's your wish." He gave a slight inclination of his head. "I'm looking forward to hearing from Cecile which parts of the homestead have benefited from her elegant hand."

"Why, nearly the lot!" Tara told him blithely. She was relishing the fact that she was here with him. "Ceci is multitalented. You know, good at everything!"

Cecile laughed. "Easy to see Tara are I are old friends. She likes to praise me. My attentions most notably, Raul, have been directed to the living room, the formal dining room and the library. It's a big house. I'm working my way through it gradually." She turned her head to her friend. "You're in the Blue Room, Tara. I know how much you like it."

"I love it!" Tara responded, the excitement she was feeling evident to all.

IN THE ELEGANT GUEST SUITE that had been allotted him, the French doors stood open to the garden and the warm desert breeze. Cecile walked briskly toward them, wondering how on earth she was going to handle this inflammatory situation, though she felt fortified by having Tara's company. Raul followed more slowly, moving out onto the broad veranda that ran the length of the entire building at the rear.

"The casuarinas are what I call monumental," he remarked after a while, his tanned, long-fingered hands spread out on the balustrade as he gazed at the magnificent desert specimens, four in all, that graced that section of the garden. Around their base to a considerable depth were planted the extremely hardy sunbursts of the blue flowering agapanthus.

Cecile glanced at him in surprise. She had now joined him at the balustrade, but keeping a distance away. "You have casuarinas in Argentina?"

That was a slip. "Well, I know what they are." He shrugged.

"You're very knowledgeable about our native desert plants. Yet you can't have been here very long."

"I'm sure there's one in Fiona's garden."

"No, there isn't," she said. "They don't grow in the torrid zone."

"All right, I've seen a picture." He moved his hand along the railing so it covered hers where it lay.

"*Don't,* Raul," she said, low voiced. "Nothing can come of this." Yet he had only to touch her hand for *something* to happen.

"I can't stop this thing between us any more than you can," he answered, the golden sparkles in his eyes catching the light. He didn't remove his hand.

She had to do something. Anything. Only, she was overtaken by the incredible languor he was able to induce in her body while her mind remained on high alert.

"Come here to me."

Four simple words to make up a sentence, yet the effect on her was electrifying. She should have been shocked at his audacity but wasn't. Instead she tried to imagine herself physically putting up barriers…

He straightened and pulled her toward him, fluidity in his every movement. He kept one arm around her waist. "I understand you're perturbed at having me here."

"Why wouldn't I be?" She arched back slightly, looking up into his face. "You're increasing my fears, Raul. You're not doing anything to dispel them."

His velvet brown eyes smoldered. He was trying hard to crush his own feelings of vulnerability without much success. She was not what he had been expecting at all. "I want to kiss you," he said, abruptly abandoning control. "I want to bury my face in your neck, between your breasts. I want to pull your beautiful hair out of that clasp. I want to stroke it with my hands. Feel how soft and silky it is. Do you mind?"

Before she could answer, if she could even find her voice, he lifted his free hand and removed the gold clasp that held back her long hair. Immediately it slid forward, rippling around her shoulders.

"Does your fiancé ever sit with you and brush it?" he asked, smoothing a sensuous hand down a long glossy coil. He had seen Ramon brush his mother's long, thick blond hair many many times. Probably a prelude to their lovemaking.

"No," Cecile answered shakily, fighting an overpowering urge to move right into his arms. Finish this thing they had started.

"You sleep with him?" His hand slowed as he studied her face closely.

"Is that so strange?" she countered self-consciously. "He's my fiancé. I'm going to marry him."

"You're wrong," he said, his voice curt. "You're not going to marry him. I think you already know that. My sister now, Ramona, will go to her bridegroom a virgin. I find I hate the idea of that man touching you."

She could see it in his face. Hear it in his voice. "You have no right to hate," she said. "No right at all."

"Haven't I?" he answered, still in that oddly curt voice. *Careful,* Raul thought. *Careful.* He lifted a hand to encircle her nape. Her beautiful hair cascaded over his hand and wrist.

He allowed his callused thumb to massage her skin. How cool her skin was! Smooth as satin.

Cecile could have moaned aloud from the pleasure he was giving her. Perhaps she did. "Things must be different in Argentina," she breathed, realizing how wonderfully well he knew how to touch. Stuart had never stirred her like this even in the wildest throes of their lovemaking. All those sharp little contractions she associated with being touched by this man were starting up again, stabbing deep into her vagina. She touched the tip of her tongue to suddenly parched lips.

"You are *so* beautiful," he said, lowering his head. His mouth was very close. "Lift your face to me, Cecile." He spoke very quietly, but the effect was infinitely powerful.

"Where are we going with this, Raul? The consequences could be disastrous." She was terrified, too, someone would come and catch them in this compromising tableau.

"Need you ask?" He bent his head then, kissing her so softly but so passionately, his mouth savoring the texture of hers, the kiss might have lasted through eternity. "What bright spirit impelled toward delight was ever known to finger out the cost?" His arm remained locked around her as though he knew without being told that the sexual languor that had overtaken her could cause her to sway.

Her heart was beating so high up it was almost in her throat. Her mouth was open to his. His to hers. Their tongues mated. There could be no one else like him in the world.

So this was how a woman fell from grace? If he had picked her up and carried her back inside to the bed? Impossible to do anything now, but if the opportunity arose? God, she hadn't just gone out on a limb, she had already made her decision. The only honorable thing left to her was to break her engagement. That thought, the sudden flare of resolution, gave her the strength to pull free.

There was no look of triumph on his face at overcoming her every scruple. Rather, his expression was deeply brooding. "I wonder which one of us will surrender first?" he said in a perfectly hard, considering, way.

His words burned into her. "I ought to have you thrown out," she muttered, realizing she was wound up as tight as a spring. If there had ever been a moment to reject him, it had long passed.

"I daresay you would have in the old days." There was a flash of sexual antagonism in his own eyes. "You look like a princess. You even act like one. So ready to turn imperious."

"Because you frighten me, Raul. You really do." Frantic in case they were interrupted, she tried to draw back her long hair, but skeins of it escaped. "Please, my clasp, give it back to me."

"When I thought to souvenir it." He loosened a long silky strand of hair that had twined itself around her throat, then removed the clasp from his pocket and put it into her trembling hand.

"Thank you," she said raggedly.

Somewhere along the corridor a door shut firmly.

"That's Tara," she said with a touch of panic. She looked at him with a plea in her eyes. "How do I look?"

"Exquisite," he said, openly mocking. "You have the most astonishing eyes. Silver. You know the name Argentina come from the Latin word *argentums*, which means silver?"

"Yes," she said, breathlessly. "Do you prefer dark eyes or light? You must have had many affairs. Women and girls with hair as dark as my own but flashing black eyes?"

That smile touched his handsome mouth, lighting up the tiny space between them. "I forget that part now I've met you."

"You're trying to seduce me, aren't you?"

"Aren't you doing the same with me?"

All the magnetism in the world was in his eyes.

WHEN TARA FINALLY CAME to the open doorway, Cecile was pointing out three splendid Chinese bronzes that sat atop a yellow rosewood cabinet. "Tang Dynasty," she said, amazed her voice sounded quite normal. This particular guest room had been furnished with a male guest in mind. The color scheme was neutral, the furnishings Oriental.

"So what do you think of your room, Raul? Pretty classy, eh?" Tara all but danced into the room, her hair a light nimbus around her pert, glowing face. She was feeling so happy it was all she could do not to pinch herself to prove it was really happening. Her attention, so deeply focused on Raul, allowed the highly nervous Cecile to beat a swift retreat to the door, speaking over her shoulder as she went. "Bring Raul to the garden room when you're ready, Tara," she said, worried there might be some lingering touch of agitation in her voice. "That's where we'll be having lunch."

"Will do!" Tara called, so busy smiling at Raul she wouldn't even have noticed if there were. Tara was longing to question this fascinating guy about what he would like to do that afternoon. He would probably want to go horseback riding. She wasn't much of a rider unfortunately. Mounted so far from the ground always made her nervous, that and the long neck that stretched away in front of her. She'd had to work hard in the early days to overcome her fear of horses, but Cecile had coached her to the stage she could tell which end of the horse was which and if given a quiet work horse she could not only stay on but manage to look quite fetching in the saddle. She'd brought a brand-new outfit with her, bum-hugging sexy moleskins, glossy new riding boots. Raul seemed the sort of guy that noticed those things. Tara shook out her blond hair and began to ask him if Buenos Aires was as exciting a capital city as everyone said. This was one Argentinian who knew how to take a woman's breath away!

CHAPTER EIGHT

As WAS HER ROUTINE when she visited Malagari, Cecile rose at dawn to take an early-morning gallop before the heat of the sun became too fierce. She had always loved these early-morning rides, moving about the stables complex, talking to the stable boys, who were always up and about, fluttering and fussing around their charges, feeding, cleaning, grooming, exercising. No point in trying to wake Tara to accompany her. Tara wasn't an early riser; neither did she take much pleasure in riding. Let her sleep.

By the time she reached the cobbled yard, the sun was rising in its fiery glory, dispelling the layers of pinks, indigos and pale yellow on the horizon. Blue light was starting to pour from the sky, the legions of birds were shrieking and whistling as they called to each other, and the desert wind was busy lifting the tantalizing mauve river of mist that hovered over the garden, blowing it away.

As chance would have it, there was no one around, though it was clear work had already begun. The place was lit, and fresh, sweet-smelling hay covered the floors. She walked about, speaking affectionately to the horses, Arabs and Thoroughbreds, all groomed to a silken shine. The horses nodded and whinnied back before she turned her attention to her favorite mount, the beautiful palomino, Zuleika, a separate breed from the others. Horses were just like people, Cecile thought. They had different, sometimes highly individual, personalities. Zuleika was the perfect match for her—or that part of her personality that was mostly hidden. The palomino with her golden coat and light blond mane and tail was sweet-tempered but high-spirited, with a sense of adventure and a certain unpredictability that often kept Cecile on her mettle.

Humming beneath her breath, Cecile pulled the girth tight and adjusted the buckles automatically while Zulelka tried a playful nip or two with her teeth and stamped her lively feet in a show of pent-up energy. The palomino was as eager for a gallop as she was. In fact, Cecile had to hold her back until they were well clear of the home compound. Then she let loose.

The blood sang in Cecile's veins. It was glorious! Such a thrill to have a spirited horse beneath her, a horse that was galloping strongly, pulling at the bit, its hooves thudding into the ground. Moments like this she lived for. They were just what she needed to clear the mad jumble of thoughts out of her head.

A mile from the Pink Lady Lagoon she relaxed the pace. Way across the flats she could see a large mob of cattle being moved toward a water course, which at this time of year would be full of shallow, yellowish water from the clay bed. The omnipresent flights of budgies, a symbol of the Outback, swirled above her in long ribbons of emerald and gold before finally flying off toward the lagoon where she herself was heading. She wondered what her grandfather would have lined up for today to entertain their guest. He had been talking about flying to Lagunda, deep across the border, sometime soon. Lagunda was a working station and one of the country's premier polo farms, producing outstanding polo ponies shipped anywhere in the world where playing polo was a passion. She'd overheard Raul telling her grandfather he'd played in his first tournament when he was fourteen. His team had won. He was now on seven goals, so he had to be pretty darn good. No surprise!

Yesterday her grandfather had set a cracking pace. She was particularly proud of his stamina and fitness. He had always taken pleasure in having young people around him. In the afternoon, after a leisurely lunch, they had traveled in the Land Rover around the station, so Raul could get a good idea of the operation. The two men, despite the huge age difference, had quickly developed an excellent rapport. Indeed one might have thought Joel Moreland had long been Raul's mentor. Her grandfather drove; Raul joined him up front, both of them keeping up a near nonstop conversation with the emphasis on station operations. She and Tara sat in the back throwing in a comment from time to time. Hers, informed, as it should be, Tara's so frivolous it had made them all laugh.

As the afternoon wore on, it struck Cecile, that the Argentinian was perfectly at home on a big Australian cattle station. He was deeply familiar with a station's workings, was able to communicate easily with the station staff, in particular Brad Caldwell, the station manager who had risen through the ranks. Raul loved and knew horses right down to the yarded brumbies awaiting "schooling" from Brad. Most significantly Raul gave every impression of being at one with their desert environment, which, after all, in character was unique in the world. She'd had an idea she intended to check out: that the vast plains of the Argentinian *pampa* were black soil and wonderfully fertile like Queensland's Darling Downs. That would make a stunning contrast to the aridity of the Red Heart, with its fiery, shifting sands, yet Raul Montalvan seemed as much at home in Australia's Red Centre as was her grandfather and for that matter, herself. It struck her as somewhat unusual. Of course he had been reared in vast open spaces, but a lot of visitors to Malagari found the isolation and the sheer starkness of the wild landscape with its infinite horizons quite intimidating. Not so Raul. Cecile had caught many of his passing comments as they had traveled around the station. The man was fathoms deep.

Approaching the Pink Lady Lagoon, so called because of its thick mantle of exquisite water lilies, Cecile noticed off to her left, parallel to the line of river gums, a swirl of red dust that resolved into a horse and rider traveling at speed. She knew the horse, the magnificent, black-as-coal stallion, Sulaiman. He was being given his head. Out in the open she recognized the rider, Raul Montalvan. Instantly she felt a mad rush of blood to her head. She should have noticed the stallion wasn't in his stall. Their powerful rhythm over the ground flooded her with a breath-catching emotion.

He rode splendidly. She had been prepared for that. He was Argentinian raised on an estancia, but he had obviously adapted in the blink of an eye to the Australian saddle. She was stunned. So, he had set off before her! No time to make her escape either—horse and rider were coming right for her. No way she and Zuleika could outrun them. Zuleika, in fact, was becoming jumpy and excited so by the time Raul had slowed to join her she'd just got the palomino under control.

"Buenos dias!" He swept off his wide-brimmed hat with an engaging little flourish that showed his background. "Pretty horse." He studied the palomino with a smile. "You must learn how to handle her."

"I beg your pardon?" Cecile's chin came up before she saw the teasing look in his eyes. "You're joking of course."

"Do you mind I joke?" he asked, his eyes moving over her face and lovely supple body with an admiration he didn't bother to hide. "I thought I might see you out on an early-morning ride."

She breathed in deeply. It was exciting just to look at him. In fact, he was so damned handsome it nearly brought tears to her eyes. "No doubt Granddad told you?" she said, sounding a little vexed.

"Saved my having to ask," he mocked. "Do you wish to ride down to the lagoon? The horses would appreciate a breather. This Sulaiman is magnificent." He leaned over the stallion's neck, stroking it with his hand.

"He is. How did you get used to our type of saddle so quickly?"

A smile flickered across his dynamic features. "Cecile, I've learned more about riding than you can ever imagine. Do we go down to the lagoon or not?"

"If you give me your promise to—" She broke off, not quite knowing how to continue.

"Not to play games?" he asked with a wicked glint in his dark eyes.

"Exactly."

"But it's no game I'm playing," he assured her. "I should tell you I can't help admiring *your* riding style."

"But you haven't had time to judge it."

"On the contrary, I took time out to watch you put the palomino to the gallop. A remarkable display. I was tempted to run out and applaud." He inclined his head in the direction of a copse of trees. "I hid back there, sorry I didn't have a camera with me. I've seen a lot of women riders where I come from, but you're as good as the best."

"Praise indeed." She sounded cool, but her nerves were running riot.

"The simple truth," he said.

Sunlight filtered a greenish-gold through the avenue of feathery acacias and bauhinias that lined the banks of the lagoon on one side. On the other was a stand of coolabahs, and at their arrival, a flock of gorgeous parrots exploded out of it and rose high above the canopy. She saw Raul lift his head, an expression of pleasure passing across his face. He truly did understand the bush.

Cecile dismounted quickly, tying the reins to a low branch before making her way across the expanse of golden sand to the water. The beautiful pink water lilies were profuse, holding their heads above the silver-sheened dark green water. She had removed her akubra, and now she bent to the crystal-clear stream to splash her face with water, throwing back her head afterward to let her skin dry in the warm breeze.

Cooled and refreshed, she began to take deep, calming breaths. One thing she was really afraid of was this new lack of control in herself. She had never believed in love at first sight. She still didn't. But she had since been converted to *desire* at first sight. Its suddenness, its power, though it was far more than sexual attraction that was between her and Raul Montalvan. Whatever it was, it had real meaning to it. She was *dying* for him to touch her. When had she ever been dying for Stuart to touch her? It was like she was a different woman. This sensuality, this awareness of her body, had come over her all at once. If ever a man had power over her, it was Raul Montalvan.

He came behind her as though he easily read her thoughts, pulling her hair free of its thick plait so it uncoiled across her back. Then he turned her to him, speaking in his dark, faintly accented voice. "You were with me last night," he said, staring deep into her eyes. "Was it a sin to dream it, Cecile? You were with me when I awoke at dawn. I think you are beginning to possess me. What more could you wish to know?"

"If it's *real?*" she answered very seriously.

His nod was solemn. "You think we need more time?"

She turned her face away. "I don't know what to *think,* Raul. Since I first laid eyes on you I haven't been doing much thinking."

"It upsets you to *feel?*"

"No problem if one can handle it," she said wryly.

"Isn't being able to *feel* a miracle?" he asked. "Some people can go through life not even knowing what the word means." His finger stroked her flawless white skin. She wore a touch of lipstick, nothing more. "You look ravishing first thing in the morning," he said. She was a truly beautiful woman, his for the asking; but the enormous *want* he felt for her could so easily turn to love and thus wipe out any thought of reprisals. It was turning into a big dilemma with the joke on him.

Little currents of electricity activated the muscles of his hands. He cupped the perfect oval of her face, conscious his fingertips were rough against that magnolia skin, then he lowered his head and pressed his lips to hers as if her mouth was luscious fruit and he was ravenous.

"Raul!" It was a noble exercise in restraint for Cecile to voice a protest. Only, he ignored her, continuing to nibble on her lips and then the tip of her seeking tongue.

"Don't worry," he whispered into her open mouth. "I'm only kissing you. I promise I will only kiss you until you break your engagement."

"And what happens then?" She was shocked by the heart-broken sound of her voice. "We run away together? We create a scandal? What is this, anyway, Raul? A want, a need, a simple desire?"

"*Simple?*" He drew back, contemptuous of the word. "Simple desire is not an agony. There's such affinity between our bodies." He set his hand to doing what he desperately wanted. He palmed her breast, his long fingers shaping it, taking the tender weight. It was delicate, yet full. He wanted to tease the nipple with his tongue. Instead, he thumbed the bud, feeling it come erect.

Instantly passion seized her. Cecile arched her neck while a soft moan gushed from her throat. Her shirt clung damply from all the splashing at the stream. Beads of water glistened on her skin at the V neckline of her shirt. Her nipples were now ripe little berries that strained against the thin fabric. She had this violent need to be against him, her breasts crushed to his chest. Why had Stuart never had this effect on her? She had wanted Stuart, but never with such intensity. She should feel guilt, but the strength of her feelings brushed the guilt off.

"Look at the contrast of my brown hand against your white skin," Raul said in an hypnotic voice. He had slipped open a button on her shirt so he could splay his fingers against the upward swell of her breast. "I've never felt such desire for a woman in my life!"

It was so strange the way he said it that she opened her eyes, fixing them on his face. His expression seemed to say his desire for her made him both defensive and angry. "You sound as though you don't want it at all."

He breathed in deeply. "There's this thing called losing control, Cecile. Losing oneself in a woman could mean losing one's own identity."

"Has it never happened to you?" She tilted her head to one side.

He laughed. Not a happy sound. "A couple of weeks ago I wouldn't have thought it possible. You are something utterly new to me, Cecile."

"And it upsets you, though you're trying to cover it."

"As you are trying to cover your beautiful breasts." He shifted her hand away. "Why don't you take the shirt off altogether? It would make it so much easier for me to caress you."

Like him, she exhaled hard. Arousal and anger were naked on her face. "I daresay it would, but I think we should call a stop."

"*This* time," he said, narrow-eyed.

"You're assuming there will be a next time?" Her voice had sharpened.

"Tell me you don't want it."

She bit down on her bottom lip. "Tell *me*, Raul. Am I part of some plan? Watching you makes me think so. What goes on inside your head?"

Her beautiful eyes begged him to tell her. For a moment he even *wanted* to but it was all so complicated and she wouldn't want to ever see him again. "Maybe someday I'll share it with you." His shrug lifted his shoulder. "For now I can tell you it was no plan of mine for the two of us to become enmeshed. It just…happened."

"Maybe the novelty will wear off as quickly as it started," she said, a certain bleakness in her words. She wanted him to keep on doing what he was doing to her; she also wanted him to stop.

His smile turned cynical. "Perhaps we shouldn't miss the opportunity to find out."

Cecile drew away. She was a woman who had once had self-control. "I think not. I'd better obey my inner voice. Do you have one?"

"Yes," he acknowledged. "But no matter what it tells me, fate holds the cards."

She had no answer to that. "I know so little about you, Raul. Even our being here together is completely crazy. Forget Fate. We're ignoring all the *rules!*"

"Which astonishes you?"

She looked away. "I don't want to be astonished at myself."

"I wouldn't have thought you a coward." He watched the shadows play across her face.

"Pretty close," she said, thinking what would be in store for her once she broke off her engagement.

He read her mind. "You can't be frightened of this fiancé, surely?"

"I'd be a darn sight more frightened if I tried to break off any engagement to *you!*"

"It wouldn't happen."

She shrugged and raked her long hair from her face. "The few things I do know about you, Raul, I don't understand."

"No matter!" He couldn't stop himself from kissing her

again. It was brief, but so much harder than before. The need just got worse and worse. He slipped the button of her fine cotton shirt back into its hole. "Anyway," he said smoothly, "we have a whole week and more to fill in the gaps."

"While you content yourself with your dreams."

"Of course! Remember what I told you?" He caught her left hand, lifted it to the sunlight so the diamonds blazed. "We don't sleep together until you get rid of this ring. Why are you wearing it? I don't remember your wearing it last night at dinner."

She hadn't, but she had put it on this morning in a rush of guilt. Was she really willing to break Stuart's heart, or she stopped short thinking, badly damage his pride? "This has nothing to do with Stuart, has it?" she asked very quietly. "I've sensed that all along."

His smile was crooked. "Which clearly shows you have very sensitive antennae. It has absolutely *nothing* to do with your fiancé," he confirmed.

CECILE KNEW she should say something to Stuart. God knows he rang every evening…but she should say it to his face. In the whirlwind days that followed she couldn't seem to summon up her courage to even give a hint. Night after night in bed she composed opening sentences in her head:

Stuart, the last thing in the world I want to do is hurt you…. Stuart, I'm so sorry. I never meant it to happen this way…. Come right out with it, girl! *Stuart, I don't love you. I don't think I ever loved you….* No, too cruel. *Stuart, I've been thinking a great deal about this and I've come to the sad conclusion we're not really meant for each other.*

And then there was the house under construction. *God, oh God, please come to my aid.*

God, no more than her mother would understand what she was doing now. Guilt racked her. Why had she taken so long to discover she didn't love Stuart? She was twenty-six not sixteen. She was a professional woman, earning the respect of people she admired. She thought she knew her own mind. In all probability if she hadn't met Raul, she would have gone ahead and married Stuart. Made her mother very happy. Or would she? Maybe a wedding wouldn't have gone ahead at all. She wasn't lying to herself. Her doubts had set in well before she laid eyes on Raul Montalvan. But now having done so, the question of whether she would marry Stuart was settled.

She went over and over the burning issue so much sometimes she wanted to scream, and once she started to cry in the shower from sheer frustration, unable to figure out what was happening in her life. Yet for the most part she was being carried so high on a wave of euphoria she wouldn't have swapped places with anyone on the planet. So the days passed in a blaze of excitement. Raul was a sorcerer, placing a spell on her.

Her grandfather couldn't bear to sit still, either. It was almost as though he had decided to fill up every moment of the rest of the life that was left to him. It would have worried her greatly, only he was looking wonderfully well. Eating well. Full of energy.

"What do you think?" he announced one morning at breakfast. "I've finally been able to line up a couple of matches for Saturday afternoon. I've been waiting on Chad Bourne, but he's back and rarin' to go. The Farrington brothers are available. I thought Raul could team up well with them. They're all fine horsemen, Chad much more experienced—he plays the sort of game I imagine Raul does—but you have to even the teams up. As for the other team, Vince Siganto will captain it with Chris Arnold and the Dashwood twins, Mart and Matt. I thought we could have a party to follow. People will travel for miles to attend. We have to give them a good show, turn on our stuff. What do you say?"

"Sounds like a great weekend coming up." Raul smiled at the other man's enthusiasm. "What do I do for a polo pony? We've only got four days. I have to get to know the animal. One's horse has a direct effect on the play, as you know. I generally play to win."

"I'm sure you do." Joel Moreland beamed his pleasure. "Don't worry, I'm having one of my very best polo ponies trucked in. It will be here by midday, a Thoroughbred gelding. Called it Churchill, plenty of guts and needless to say he's well trained. I don't think you'll have any problems." He turned his silver head to smile at Cecile. "You girls can take care of the party, can't you? Whatever you want, have it flown in."

"Who's to come to the party, Granddad?" Cecile asked.

"Everyone who turns up." He laughed. "Best make it a big barbecue out of doors."

And to heck with the numbers! Cecile thought. She should have some idea how many would make the trip to the station most likely from Alice Springs by Thursday if she started to ring around now. In the Outback, where horses were a passion, people loved the game. Once word got around a game was on with high-calibre players, they could count on having quite an influx of spectators. Then there were the two teams with their womenfolk and personal entourages. Just as well she'd had plenty of experience handling her Granddad's impromptu parties. Tara would be a big help; her family did a lot of entertaining. She was pleased Tara was having such a good time even if she knew her friend was disappointed she wasn't getting enough of Raul's attention.

"He probably would like to spend some time alone with me," she lamented to Cecile in a quiet moment, "only that never seems to happen. Joel is a dynamo. He's over seventy, but he's getting around like a teenager. Do you think Raul likes me?"

"Come on, everyone likes you," Cecile said. "Don't feel bad. There's nothing wrong with you. He's probably got a girlfriend back home in Argentina. A dazzling *señorita* called Brunhilde."

"You're joking. Even I know Brunhilde is German."

"All right, Carmelita, then."

"I think maybe he has." Tara gave it her consideration. "He's a pretty dark horse. I'm starting to think there's *some one*."

"I'd be amazed if there weren't," Cecile said dryly.

"I guess." Tara drew a deep sigh. "It's not every guy who can make your knees buckle."

"Anyway, you really want to live in Argentina?" Cecile smiled. "It's a long way away and you're a real Daddy's girl. I always thought you were interested in Chris Arnold. He'll be here at the weekend."

"So he will!" Tara said, brightening somewhat.

CECILE LOWERED HERSELF into a planter's chair on the veranda, feeling a little tired. Getting this party organized had taken time and effort, but at last she had everything under control. Tara, usually a bundle of energy, was pretty looped. She had gone off for a lie-down. It was now Thursday;

Saturday morning everyone would start arriving: players, their entourages, friends and spectators. They were flying in, coming by charter bus, driving overland in convoys of dusty 4WDs. Generally speaking, everyone had a wonderful time at polo matches, and when the matches were on Malagari where the hospitality was legendary, they could expect the crowd she had catered for. Any food left over could easily be distributed among the station staff and the nomadic aboriginals who traversed the station on walkabout.

One such was Loora, a pure-blood aboriginal woman who had to be, on her grandfather's reckoning, a good twenty years older than he was, which put her well into her nineties. Nineties or not, Loora looked and acted like a sprightly seventy-year-old, an eater and collector of a great variety of native seeds, nuts, bean-sprouting plants and edible fruits that grew wild across the desert plains. No one knew more about the botany of the desert than Loora. For tens of thousands of years the aboriginal people had been like scientists, probing the secrets of the wild bush around them. The early settlers, including her own family, had relied on the aboriginal people to reveal many of the secrets they had unlocked. Which plants were poisonous, which fruits were edible, which contained medicinal compounds, which had therapeutic qualities, which were hallucinogenic. Aboriginals in remote communities of Western Australian were already harvesting and selling their fragrant sandalwood to leading French perfumeries, the sawn sandalwood sent to a distilling plant from whence the aromatic oil was airfreighted to France's top perfume houses.

For decades Loora had been harvesting various barks off the desert trees for her paintings, a collection of which was hung on one wall of her grandfather's study. Loora also collected a bonanza of wild fruits that included wild plums, wild rosella, desert limes, wild pears and many types of berries, which were probably packed with antioxidants. These she presented in an attractive basket she had woven herself at Malagari's kitchen door whenever she was on walkabout. Her grandfather had gone to the trouble of having the plums tested, seizing on the idea they might be a wonderful source of Vitamin C. Loora had known they were, decades before a Darwin laboratory came back with a glowing report.

Yesterday when Cecile and Raul were returning from a practice session at the polo field, they had encountered Loora on her way to the homestead, basket in arm. Raul had stopped the vehicle, astonished to hear from Cecile the old lady was considered to be well into her nineties. Loora, who had spent her entire life traversing the desert, had been moving along in a quite vigorous fashion, her full head of snow-white hair unprotected from the rays of the sun, which were still very strong even though it was coming on to sunset. Cecile's mind went back to the strange encounter, which had been very much on her mind…

"IF YOU ARE what you eat we'd better find out what it is she's eating," Raul said, half joking, half serious as he stopped the Jeep.

"One hundred percent organic bush tucker," Cecile replied. "The aboriginal traditional diet, plus the fact Loora's always on the move. God knows how many miles she walks every day. She lives her life in the open air without all the stress that goes into *our* lives. I suppose the utter simplicity of life helps and she's doing what she loves to do."

"So let's say hello." Raul was already climbing out. "I don't like her carrying that basket. It looks heavy."

Cecile called a greeting. Loora answered with a big smile that displayed fine teeth, a startling white against her black skin. Even her skin was in the sort of condition a woman half her age might envy.

It was when Cecile turned to introduce Raul that Cecile was caught entirely by surprise.

Loora laid her basket down, then went right up to Raul as though she recognized him. "I know yah, don't I?" Very softly she touched his arm as though eager for him to answer. "Yeah, I know yah," she repeated.

Cecile looked on, puzzled. Raul, however, stood perfectly still, seemingly unperplexed by Loora's behavior. "How can you tell?" He spoke slowly, his accent to Cecile's ears far more pronounced than usual.

Loora lifted a bony arm to tap several times on her right temple. "I got the gift!" she murmured. "I got it when I was just a little one."

"I can see you're clever, Loora," Raul said, "but I come from far away. A country called Argentina. It's in South America."

"I know South America." Loora tapped her temple again with a clawlike hand. "Longa go part of Gondwanna Land, but it break away. You not one of dose people, are yah." It was a statement not a question. Loora flexed her tight facial muscles into a smile. "You come from different direction. Beyond the ranges." She pointed off in the distance to where the sun was slipping down in a splendor of crimson, gold and purple behind the glowing ridges. Ridges that in prehistory were once sand on the shores of the inland sea. "I walk over dere many, many times collectin' stuff in me dilly bag. You belong *dere*. Nasty times. I see it!"

Raul continued to stare at her. "You know all that just from looking at me?"

"Was given to me," Loora explained. "The gift—the double power—it goes right back to the Dreamtime. Besides, I've seen your face before." She lifted her head and stared at him keenly.

"No," Raul replied, shaking his head. "*No,* Loora."

Loora stepped closer, saying the word *no* over as though testing its meaning, then giving it some deep thinking. "So Loora got it wrong," she said eventually. "I don't know yah."

"Not possible," Raul said quietly, "but it's a pleasure to meet *you,* Loora. Let me take that basket for you. It must be heavy."

"Used to havin' me hands full," Loora said, but let him pick it up, something she didn't always allow.

"You'll come up to the house, Loora?" Cecile invited. "Say hello? Everyone will be pleased to see you. My grandfather is at home."

"You always kind to me, missy," Loora said. "I say thank you. You ready to learn plenty about woman-business. You fall in love with this fella?" She cocked her head to one side, chuckling as embarrassment whipped color into Cecile's cheeks. "Got no man now. He die longa longa time ago. Up there in the sky with the old people now. This one got a restless spirit!" She gazed up at Raul for a moment. "Bold fella! Spirit wrestling goin' on inside, though."

"I've sensed that, Loora," Cecile said, her eyes seeking Raul's. What did she really know of him except that he had become very important to her?

"Never mind." Loora leaned in to Cecile, her voice dropping to a mere whisper. "He got powerful magic, as well. Magic important. I know." She brought up a hand, spoke from behind it. "He brings a child."

Cecile gasped. The whites of the old woman's eyes grew large. "I'm sorry, Loora," Cecile said, shaking her head to indicate she didn't understand.

Loora spoke again, even more quietly, though her words seemed to *roar* in Cecile's ears. "He bring a child," she repeated, her gaze more intense than ever.

LATER ON FROM the veranda outside her bedroom, Cecile caught sight of Raul walking away with Loora across the home gardens into the mauve mist of twilight. Raul had his sun-streaked head—it was so much blonder now—bent to the old aboriginal woman's. They were obviously deep in conversation.

What about? With no contact with the aboriginal people, how had he so easily made a connection? She couldn't pretend to know. So much about Raul Montalvan was a mystery. In some ways she could lock in to his thoughts; in others she had no key.

Then there was the thing that had most shocked her, which even now made her swallow. *He brings a child.* Did that pronouncement carry a warning? Or could Loora have possibly meant the tranquil little desert wind that aboriginal artists sometimes depicted as a child? There were human figures to represent east winds, west winds, soft winds, harsh winds, winds that brought great dust storms, others that brought thunder and lightning flashing across the desert skies. How could she remain calm when a tribal woman of acknowledged powers had made such a profound pronouncement?

RAUL AND THE STATION MANAGER, Brad Caldwell, had been meeting up late afternoons to acquaint each other with their playing styles and to trial maneuvers. It was when they were taking a break that Brad brought up Jared Moreland. It could never be said then that he had initiated the conversation, Raul thought, settling in to listen while endeavoring to keep the intensity out of his expression.

"He was a damned fine player," Brad said, wiping sweat from his eyes as he sprawled his long limbs on the grass. "Played his shots like you. Sorta graceful, if you know what I mean. Some players are as rough as guts. That's what brought Jared to mind. We were pretty much of an age. He was a few years older and Joel's son and heir of course. In other words, one hell of a broad canyon between us, but he was a good guy. No side to him like his old man."

"He died in a freak accident, I understand." Raul contrived to sound sympathetic. "The family don't speak about it and naturally I don't ask."

"Well, you know there was a bit of controversy about that." Brad chewed thoughtfully on a blade of grass. "Not at first. In fact, not for a few years. It was supposed to have been just a kid who was involved, but the rumors got started the kid hadn't acted alone."

"What?" Raul heard his voice snap, but he was unable to prevent himself.

Brad gave him an odd look. "Actually I get nervous just talking about it."

"That bad?" Raul swiftly modified his tone. "Sorry if I overreacted. You really shocked me."

Brad shrugged his big shoulders. "Kinda shocked us all. Talk was there was some bad blood between Jared and one of the stockmen. A guy called Frank Grover. He was pretty friendly with Jack—Jack Doyle up at the house."

"Ah, yes, Jack." Raul leaned back, trying to take in a vital piece of information totally new to him. "Did you have any idea what it was about?" How had it happened Frank Grover's name had never been mentioned within his family? "Surely Joel knew everything there was to know concerning his son's death?"

Brad offered up a deep sigh. "I tell you, mate, Joel in those days wasn't in the frame. Losing his son almost destroyed him, though he managed to soldier on. Too many people depending on him in one form or another. It was the missus, Mrs. Moreland, Joel's wife—a powerful lady—that stirred up a hornet's nest of trouble for the kid's family. Ben Lockhart, that was his name. Nice-lookin' kid. Looked like butter wouldn't melt in his mouth. Good people, the Lockharts, so they said. It was a crime they met with such bitter enmity from the missus. Lockhart went broke—starved out I reckon, so much bad feeling whipped up by you know who—and the creditors moved in. The whole lot of 'em moved away. I remember the sister, Lori, Lorianne or something. Boy, was she a looker! Had this glorious head of thick wavy hair. A bit like yours, only lighter, a dark blond. A real shame!" Brad shook his head from side to side.

For a moment Raul felt he really was a stranger in a strange land. There was a terrible tension right through his body. How did Moreland's wife get into this? "So what caused the bad blood between Jared and Grover? Do you know?"

Brad's lean face wore the laconic expression of a man for whom life held no surprises. "No big mystery! A woman, what else? Frank was real sweet on Johanna Muir, a maid at the homestead. Very pretty she was, too, but not a patch on that Lori. Turns out Jared was pretty keen on her, too. Can you beat that! With all the girls he coulda had, he falls for the housemaid. Got her pregnant, anyway. Turns out that baby was Daniel, you know, Daniel…?"

Raul nodded. Daniel Moreland wasn't one of his faceless figures. In fact, he had liked him. "I was at the wedding. Daniel is Jared and Johanna's son."

Another wry smile from Brad. "Nothin' would have come of it if Jared hadn't been killed. People reckon he would have married her. I say *no,* not with *that* mother! Not to speak ill of the dead, but she was a regular monster mum. Odd because Mr. Moreland is one of nature's gentlemen. The missus drove that girl away. One day she was there, the next she wasn't, and she would have needed help. You don't just walk off into the desert. Somehow she was spirited out. Then on top of it, Jared was killed. I'd have believed it if someone told me the missus had had Johanna killed off. I tell you, Mrs. Moreland was ruthless when it came to her family. She thought the sun rose and set in her son's eyes. Me, I'd have run a million miles from her. Maybe Jared would have, only he was destined for disaster."

A kind of numbness was spreading through Raul's body. Why hadn't his family ever pointed a finger at Mrs. Moreland? Joel Moreland had been the sole aggressor, according to his mother. Now Brad Caldwell, who would be in a position to know, said it was the *woman* who had been filled with visceral hatreds. He needed time to think about this. This wasn't the story he'd always been told. The past was unraveling and it wasn't in sync with his mother's version of the sad tale. "So Frank Grover hated Jared Moreland. Is that what you're saying?"

"Sure! Frank started to hate him when he found out about the affair. I reckon Johanna might have told Frank she was pregnant. Got him all fired up. He was one for the booze when he hit town. I know he got tanked up the minute we hit the Alice. Not that he couldn't hold it. He was one of those guys who liked to hang tough."

"And that's how Jared Moreland got himself killed?" Raul realized he was giving off too much intensity, but thankfully Brad wasn't looking at him.

"You know what they say, crimes of passion!" Brad gave a heavy-hearted sigh.

"So how did the boy come into it?" Raul asked, aware all the certainties he'd carried in his head had fled him. "What did he have to gain but a long prison term?"

A strange smile distorted Brad's mouth. "Maybe the kid had nothin' to do with it, after all," he said in his lazy drawl. "Maybe he was *pushed* off that fence. Coulda happened, a quick shove. All the crowd was interested in was the bulls and the broncos. No one woulda noticed. But one way or the other both Jared and the boy finished up in the path of one mad, stampeding bullock. Jared was kinda known for his reckless courage. He had a real cavalier way about him. I remember he moved without hesitation to protect the boy. In doing so, o'course, he got himself killed. There were minutes of utter silence, like we'd all turned deaf and dumb, then all hell broke loose. It was like there'd been an assassination. The crowd came together in swift judgment. Including me, I'm sorry to say. Always regretted it. But at the time, it was a big thumbs-down for the boy who had done something monumentally stupid. In the crowd's eyes Ben Lockhart was guilty of murder, not just criminal recklessness. He had to pay for it somehow. A man was dead. Joel Moreland is revered in the Outback. Everyone knew how much he adored his only son. Hell, Jared was hardly more than a boy himself. Just twenty-three years old. I'm gettin' a clear image of him now. That bullock did a job on him, I can tell you that." Brad shuddered, fighting off the vision. "Somethin' terrible!"

Raul, who had seen plenty of blood spilled on sand, couldn't talk about it, either. "Where's this Frank Grover now?" He had to find him, speak to him.

Brad snorted. "God knows! You'll have to ask Jack. He might know. Last I heard of him he was workin' on a croc farm in North Queensland. That was years ago. He wasn't wanted here after Jared's death. I figured the missus told him to pack up and go. She would have known he was sweet on Johanna. She probably told Frank where Johanna was. That's if she knew. The woman knew *everything!*" Brad shook his head gravely. "Suppose we'd better try another few shots? You're a great player. It's a privilege to be on the same team."

Raul came to his feet, feeling so profoundly disturbed he barely heard the compliment. He had hated the name Moreland for so long. In particular, Joel Moreland, the Man with the Midas Touch. Now it seemed, if Caldwell could be believed, his family had found the wrong Moreland guilty. A deep sense of frustration was building inside of him. What he desperately needed was hard evidence to prove it was so. Either way, the Morelands had acted like feudal barons.

CHAPTER NINE

THE BREEZE WAS UP. All around the playing field plastic multicolored pennants flapped, sounding for all the world like ocean waves breaking on the shore. The crowd of spectators had been building all day. Now they sat on three sides of the field in high good spirits waiting for the match of the day to begin. Chris Arnold, an exuberant pilot and captain of one team, had actually landed his Bell helicopter on the middle of the field and taken off again before Jack Doyle, who was in charge of proceedings, rode over to tell him to get the hell off. The crowd had loudly applauded Chris, who was well-known on the circuit, except for those who got the worst of the flying red dust.

Marquees had been set up to serve tea and coffee, soft drinks and light refreshments, sandwiches, pasties, sausage rolls and so on. There was a bar for a cold beer or two, but that was it. No one wanted any drunken behavior or a fight to break out, though Cecile was sure a few of the spectators— not the regulars of whom some had been coming for years— had managed to sneak in a couple of cartons. Everyone mixed well at these occasions, entering into the spirit of things, the rich station owners, stockmen, station workers, town folk from the Alice, a smattering of tourists, all dressed pretty much the same in cool casual gear, their heads covered by the ubiquitous wide-brimmed akubras, both sides rolled up, which somewhat defeated the purpose.

For Cecile, however, the excitement of the day was marred by the fact that Stuart and her mother had thrown a few things into an overnight bag, chartered a flight and turned up on Malagari at ten-thirty that morning. Great-aunt Bea had hitched a ride, as well, which was fine with Cecile. She was very fond of Bea—they'd always been close—but when her autocratic mother teamed up with Stuart, the nerves of Cecile's stomach all twisted in knots. Neither her mother nor Stuart had ever shown the slightest interest in the game of polo, but it became obvious both of them were truly concerned about Raul Montalvan's continuing presence on Malagari.

Then there was the matter of setting the wedding date! One couldn't go on and on with an engagement. One had to tie the knot. Her mother, Cecile realized, wouldn't stop her campaign until Stuart was her lawful wedded husband.

"How much do you love Stuart?" Justine asked the moment they were inside her bedroom door. She didn't wait for an answer. "You've done enough sleeping on the matter, Cecile. My advice is set the date and do it *now*. This very weekend. I don't think I need tell you people are talking about this Argentinian."

"Talking? *What* people?" Cecile looked as amazed as she felt. "We're here in the middle of nowhere, Mother, not back in Melbourne with all the gossips looking on."

"Word gets around nevertheless," Justine said, her voice taut with concern. "Doesn't he have somewhere else to go? And why is Daddy making such a fuss of him?"

Cecile laughed without amusement. "I should think that's obvious, Mother. He really likes him. Raul is very much at home on Malagari, and he's mad about polo, just like Grand-dad."

"Well, I'm sorry to say I don't like him." Justine passed judgment, tight-lipped.

"But then, who *do* you like?" Cecile asked. "Apart from Stuart, that is. Look, Mother, we can't go into this now. I'm busy and I'm a little tired. We had to fast-track this event. You know what Granddad's like when he's caught up by an enthusiasm."

"The whole thing is a waste of money," Justine said, dismissing the event as a triviality. "All those people! Freeloaders, I call them."

"They're *Granddad's* guests," Cecile pointed out. "It's costing *you* a big fat nothing."

Justine's eyes flashed. "No need to speak to me like that, Cecile. You say you're tired. You don't look it. In fact, I've never seen you look better." Justine sounded quite irked. Cecile was wearing a lacy white halter-necked top that plunged a little too much for Justine's liking, with an eye-catching skirt printed with huge cobalt, yellow and white flowers. She wore yellow wedge-heeled sandals on her feet. Her long hair was pulled back from her face, but flowed freely down her back. Even mothers could feel stabs of jealousy from time to time, Justine thought. It was hell to grow old.

"Malagari has always agreed with me, Mother—I love it," Cecile was saying, aware her control freak of a mother was as mad as a wet hen.

"Which has always struck me as really weird. I was never happy here." Justine turned away, removing an emerald kaftan richly embroidered around the neckline and sleeves from her suitcase and putting it on a padded hanger. "I'm highly tempted to say you've got a crush on this foreigner. He's certainly got an interest in you."

"You really should refrain from using the word *foreigner,* Mother," Cecile chided her mother mildly.

"How else can I put it?" Justine demanded to know. "This whole thing has gone far enough."

"So you've come to save me from myself, is that it?"

"Of course I have, you poor girl!" Justine drooped onto the bed, holding her hand to her head. "If only you'd listen to me. The very last thing I want is an argument, but there's a little *situation* going on here. You can't deny it. Well, not to a woman like me. I know men. Raul Montalvan will go back to Argentina where I'm sure he has a string of women panting on his return. This little flutter or whatever it is will be over. That's life. I just don't want you left crying. I don't want you to jeopardize your future, all our plans. And I beg of you not to humiliate Stuart with this. You may not believe me, but tongues are already wagging."

That was the last straw for Cecile. "Don't you mean *your* tongue, Mother? I bet Stuart rings you every night for a powwow right after he's spoken to me."

Justine's finely cut nostrils flared. "Don't speak to me that way, Cecile," she said, looking mega-offended. "I'm not stupid. I'm your mother. I know you backward. As soon as I laid eyes on Raul Montalvan, I sensed trouble. There's something about that young man. He's dangerous. Too hard to handle, let alone tame. Stuart on the other hand is perfect for you."

Cecile started walking toward the door. "He's perfect for *you*, Mother," she corrected, "but unfortunately you're taken. Now, I really must fly."

"Very well, Cecile," Justine said in a wounded voice. "Run away. Ignore my advice. What a thankless job it is being a mother."

CECILE WAS MOVING head down along the corridor when she almost collided with Bea coming in the opposite direction.

"What's up with you?" Bea put two hands to her head to straighten her zebra-patterned turban, which sat high above spectacular dangly earrings and platinum kiss curls. "You were coming like an express train."

"Oh, I'm sorry, Bea!" Cecile said, looking at Bea with a feeling of gratitude and affection. Why was Bea always so cheerful when her mother never was? Why was Bea's voice always filled with such friendliness and warmth when her mother invariably sounded so bloody hoity-toity, as befitting her position of prestige and privilege? Bea loved a laugh. Her mother acted as though a laugh was frivolous. Oh hell!

"Having a few words with Mother, were we?" Bea rolled sympathetic eyes. "When is she going to stop trying to boss you around?"

"It's way too late for that, Bea." Cecile shook her head. "She *can't* stop. She doesn't know how."

"There must be a medical term for it," Bea pondered. "Something that ends with *itis*. Of course there *is* the menopause thing. It knocks some women about, but I took a good dose of hormones. You're not out of love with Stuart, are you, dear girl?"

Bea, who had grown considerably shorter over the past few years, tilted her turbaned head to look at the much taller Cecile, sounding hopeful. "Could be," Cecile lamented. "Why do you think Stuart and Mother are here?"

"Checking up on you, my darling. Need you ask? So, you're out of love with Stuart and in love with another man? Have I got that right?"

Cecile bit her lower lip. "Oh, Bea, I'm acting so unlike myself."

Bea, whose outfit for the day was a kind of haute-couture tribal, patted Cecile's arm, setting her dozen or so bracelets a-jangle. "Well, I have to say he's pretty damned *hot!* I won't mention any names of course."

"You'd better not." Cecile sighed. "I have to do the honorable thing, Bea. I have to tell Stuart I can't marry him."

"Well, he was only on probation, wasn't he?" Bea asked, very reasonably.

It was a very Bea-like answer. "It's all very well for you, Bea. You've always been a bad, bad girl."

"So I have!" said Bea, with complete satisfaction. "You on the other hand had the misfortune to be saddled with Justine for a mother. You're worried how she's going to take it?"

"Of course! But shouldn't I be more worried about hurting Stuart?"

"Look, he'll survive, lovey. He really will. You can't get yourself arrested just for breaking an engagement. It happens all the time. Look on the positive side. It would be far worse if you went ahead and got married. The thing that really amazes me is how you got engaged to him in the first place. You don't even speak the same language and he's so bloody *smug!*"

"I thought I loved him, Bea," Cecile said with some sorrow.

"Who could fall in love with a lawyer?" Bea argued. "The way they talk to you! You'd swear you were in a courtroom.

My advice to you, my darling, is get it over with. Your mother has to stop trying to run your life. You'll meet someone else *if you haven't met him already?"*

Cecile shook her head as Bea underscored her words. "Not *Raul,* Bea. If that's what you're thinking."

"Can *I* have him, then?" Bea joked. "Charmed the pants off you, has he?"

"Not as yet, Bea." Cecile frowned severely. "And you are a bad, bad girl." Tears glittered for a moment in her eyes. "It's frightening what I feel, Bea," she confessed. "I don't understand what's happening to me."

Bea swooped on her and kissed her. "Well, they do say falling in love is a madness," she pointed out very gently. "But nothing can beat it, believe me."

"It seems not!" Cecile's voice shook with emotion. "I used to be so...so..."

"You don't have to explain it to me, love," Bea said. "I wasn't always this goddamned old and dyeing my hair." She pulled at a platinum kiss curl.

"You? You'll never be old! Look at you today! Not many people could carry off an outfit like that! You're enormously chic!"

"Thank you, darling." Bea's smile was complacent. "When I was your age I was a household name for glamour. Nowadays I'm just a wealthy pampered old bat. You don't think it's a wee bit over the top?" Bea lifted her arms in an exaggerated model's pose.

"Well, it *has* to be because you're so *amazing,*" Cecile said, putting her arms around her frail great-aunt and hugging her. "Why wasn't I one of a dozen kids, Bea? Then Mother would have had a lot of us to get around, not just me. Why did it have to happen she could only have *one* child?"

Bea stared at the floor directly in front of her, apparently mulling that over, then she lifted her head, earrings swinging. "I think it's high time I told you all that 'only one child stuff' is a disgusting case of guff. I'm not saying Justine didn't have a tough time having you, but you were her first. Lots of women have a tough time with the first baby. The thing is, Justine had no intention of ever trying again. She had better things to do with her time."

For a moment it wasn't easy to take that in. Cecile opened her mouth to speak, but no sound emerged. "What are you saying, Bea?" she asked finally. Her voice held no anger but a lot of sadness.

"What I should have said long ago, dearest girl. Justine hated childbirth so much she was never going to try it again. There was no physical reason why she couldn't have more children. I know your father wanted more, but he couldn't have *everything* now, could he? Justine was the wife he wanted and she's been a good wife in many ways. I believe they look on it as a successful business partnership. There's something else, too. Justine was able to avenge herself for his other women by not giving him more kids. There was just poor little you for Mother to take care of and run your life. Hell, for all I know you could have been Justine's one-night stand."

"Bea!" Cecile protested even though she was about ready to believe anything.

"Sorry, love! That was in bad taste. I apologize. I'm sure they have a sex life. But next time your mother gives you the baloney about how she suffered so much having you she was advised not to have any more, tell her that ain't so. You can tell her wicked old Bea clued you in. I don't mind. I should have done it long ago. Of course it's not all Justine's fault." Bea shook her head slowly. "My dear sister-in-law Frances was a woeful mama. She ignored Justine for most of the time and got down on a prayer mat to worship her son. There's lots of stuff you don't know about this family, Cecile. Most of your mother's problems stem from the past. You can't afford to worry about what she thinks. If you don't love Stuart, you must tell him so. Let it go on any longer and things will only get worse." Bea pulled her great-niece to her and kissed her.

"I know that, Bea," Cecile murmured. "I'm glad you're here with me. I'll tell him this weekend before he leaves. I can't confront him now. Not with this match on and the party. I think he already suspects bad times are coming."

"And this is one of those times," said Bea prophetically.

THE CROWDS THAT HAD gathered around the marquees were back in their seats or sitting on rugs on the grass to watch the main match. A lead-up game had been played earlier with teams of modest handicaps from various stations, but now a great chorus of cheers broke out as the players for the big event of the afternoon took the field. There were four players to a team, two to ride offensively, the third and fourth to play back in the defensive position. In the Outback, polo, a difficult game to learn, let alone the most dangerous, wasn't just a game. It was much much more, like the jousts of old. Chris Arnold's team wore sapphire-blue-and-yellow jerseys; Vince Siganto's team, which included Raul and Brad Caldwell, wore red-and-white with their numbers on a wide white band on the short red sleeve. Brad, at forty-six, was the oldest player, but he was wonderfully fit and played regularly. Even so, he knew his playing days were coming to an end. Earlier Cecile had overheard Raul talking to Vince in the area where the polo ponies were being held. Both of them looked magnificent in their gear, white breeches, colorful jerseys, high polished boots, which emphasized their lean, long-legged muscular bodies. They weren't at the time wearing their helmets. Second-generation Italian, Vince, who was distinguishing himself internationally as a polo player, had thick raven hair that glistened in the blazing sunlight. In strong contrast, Raul's hair, bleached by the desert sun to coppery blond, burned like fire. Their body language spoke of easy camaraderie, but where she had been expecting them to be speaking English as a matter of course, she found their conversation was being conducted in mellifluous Italian.

Why be surprised?

For all of the play Stuart sat beside her in a collapsible chair battling manfully to look and sound enthusiastic. Her mother and Bea, along with the usual socialite friends, were part of the group sitting behind them under the shade of the trees. Tara, always popular, sat on Cecile's other side looking very fresh and pretty in her favorite blue. A short distance away under striped umbrellas a young group from the Alice had congregated. They were fervent followers of the game and well-known to Cecile; one of them kept up a running commentary that Cecile found both well-informed and funny.

It was evident right from the start that both teams were pretty evenly matched, which was the charm of the game. The best players—and it immediately became obvious who they were, going by their individual handicaps—were Vince, Chris and Raul, so the rest of the players were allotted to one team or the other to ensure neither team was hopelessly outclassed.

Raul, charging at full tilt, scored the first goal.

"Oh, well played!" Tara called excitedly, clapping her hands.

"That was a bit reckless, wasn't it?" Stuart whispered into Cecile's ear. "Frankly this game is so dangerous I think it should be condemned."

"Lighten up, Stuart!" she said. "Far from being reckless that shot was played with great finesse. Just look at Granddad down there." She turned her head to where her grandfather was sitting amid a group of pastoral men, all friends, all former polo players with a vast affection for the game. "He's loving it. So are the rest of them. Try to appreciate the horsemanship and the courage and skill of the ponies."

"I'm just worried some reckless fool is going to gallop right into us." Stuart shuddered, his eyes on Montalvan as the man made another full free swing. Montalvan's teammate Brad Caldwell was very wisely giving him plenty of room. Stuart could just see that mallet connecting with Brad's head, helmet or not. *Show-off,* Stuart thought, upset by the burst of cheering at Montalvan's dashing display of skill. A few minutes later the crowd leapt to their feet as Vince took a forward pass from Raul, shooting for goal. The larrikin in the crowd beside them let out an ear-piercing whistle that Stuart thought should have startled the horses. But then again, could you startle a horse that was used to having a club swung near its head?

"What the heck is this all about?" Stuart was driven into asking. He couldn't follow the game at all, mainly because he didn't want to. Though he had never dared tell anyone he didn't actually enjoy the Melbourne Cup—the nation's and the horse racing world's big event—all that much, either, except for the socializing and having his beautiful heiress fiancée on his arm.

"It's a battle of wits, Stuart," Cecile explained patiently, knowing Stuart was bored by the game. "See what Raul is doing? He's endeavoring to eliminate his opposite number. Some do it by blocking, hooking, barging, all sorts of tactics designed to slow the other man down. The crowd's getting so excited because he's doing it with speed and intelligence. No roughhousing. They appreciate that. Try to think of it as a very fast game of hockey on horseback. The rules are much the same."

"I prefer hockey," Stuart muttered.

"God, you're a spoilsport, Stuart!" Tara groaned. "They ought to put it on your epitaph."

"Not behind the door when it comes to airing your opinion, are we, Tara?" Stuart merely lifted supercilious brows. "Lord knows how Ceci has continued so long with your friendship."

"Ditto!" said Tara.

EIGHT CHUKKAS WERE PLAYED with four-minute breaks for the players to change ponies. At halftime the score was 6-4 for the Red team. Three of the Red team's goals had been scored by Raul, the other three by Vince. Chris had scored three of the four goals for his own team. The rest of the match promised to be the cliff-hanger the crowd wanted.

And to everyone's pleasure and excitement it was. The Red team finally won by the narrowest of margins and Cecile presented the impressive trophy to Vince Siganto amid much cheering. It had been a great match and everyone was in the best of spirits. It was now sunset. The barbecue was due to start at 6:30 p.m. In the meantime the crowd was free to roam the station and use the facilities at the staff quarters. The evening's entertainment would include line dancing, which usually proved to be a lot of fun for all age groups. The only exceptions to the universal good behavior were a couple of youths dressed in flashy cowboy outfits who had obviously been consuming alcohol from their own source.

Cecile saw Jack Doyle lead one away, probably to give him a good talking-to, the other, less boisterous and sedate enough until Jack was out of sight, then took it into his head to dart in and out of the milling crowd like an exuberant ten-year-old. Had he continued what he was doing he would have eventually been stopped and by someone, only soon he changed tack and made off quietly toward the enclosure where the polo ponies were being held. Once there, he slipped under the rope, whooping softly. The ponies began to bunch up, tails swishing, not happy to have him there.

"Hey, fellas! Take it easy!" The youth tried to cajole the restless animals. It would really cap a great day if he could get on one's back. "Only havin' a bit of fun!" he explained, looking around him in case a horse minder turned up. Horses thrilled him, not that he could afford one of his own. Maybe he could catch himself a brumby and train him. That Argentinian guy was the quickest and most daring rider he'd ever seen. He'd give anything to be able to ride like that.

Cecile walked down the path to check on the animals.

God, what the hell is that kid doing here? She wondered. *The silly fool is going to spook the horses.*

Cecile picked up her pace, her level of alarm rocketing as she saw the youth raise his arms to shoulder height before spreading them out like wings. Who was he supposed to be, Batman? Next he lifted himself up onto the toes of his boots, and before she knew what he was about, kicked out vigorously as though at an imaginary ball.

"Get out of there!" she yelled, breaking into a run.

He didn't even appear to hear her. Instead, to her acute anxiety, he gave vent to a great raucous squawk like a bird. Perhaps he was supposed to be an eagle? The string of ponies reacted just as she knew they would—with fright. Didn't he know horses could inflict a lot of damage on a person? The horse closest to him reared in a display of raw animal power. Too small to be trained as a racehorse, it was nonetheless a threat.

Too late the cowboy saw how very precarious his position was. He gave one long drawn-out wail, which only served to further spook the horses. The most troubled horse reared again, its front legs beating the air, before it broke free of its restraint and plunged past the youth, who miraculously was able to throw himself out of the way.

"Yikes!" he screamed, tears gushing spontaneously into his eyes with the agony of a struck elbow.

Oh my God!

Cecile stopped running and stood her ground as the horse bolted out onto the rough path. Those that had wandered into the vicinity frantically fell back, looking for cover. No one was prepared to intervene or stop the horse's mad flight for the very real fear they would get kicked or trampled.

Cecile, herself, felt an instant of paralysis, but she stalwartly spread out her arms, calling "Whoa!" in a voice not all that much above normal level but with enough command in it for the horse to get the message and skid to attention. It was all about communication. She rarely encountered the horse that wouldn't do what she wanted. She hoped to deflect the runaway to the side opposite the packed crowd.

The horse read her signals and faltered in its tracks. This was a horse well used to commands. But Cecile's hopes were short-lived. There was a loud whooping yell from behind the trees and the animal was spooked again, breaking into a gallop...

FARTHER OFF, Raul had been waylaid by an elderly polo aficionado who was bent on congratulating him for his fine play, but even so he noticed the crowd had changed shape. Always alert, especially when crowds and horses were in close proximity, he held up a staying hand to his companion, concentrating all his attention on what was happening around him.

"Something's wrong," he said to his admirer, then without looking back, took off down the path toward the pony enclosure.

"What's happened?" he called to a middle-aged couple who were beating a hasty retreat through the trees.

"Bloody horse loose, mate!" the man answered, still running. "Some stupid bugger spooked it."

He *knew*, and afterward he marveled that he did know, *she* was in danger.

Raul had never run so fast in his life. It was as though he had been given a shot of a powerful speed-enhancing drug. He saw station men coming from all directions. He was by far the closest. Cecile was standing perfectly still in the horse's path. He heard her call "Whoa!" in much the same sort of voice he himself would have used in the same circumstances. The animal obeyed, nearly skidding to a stop. All might have been well, only from near a stand of trees someone let out a great whoop. The horse was off again.

He could wait no longer. Any thought of revenge on the Morelands evaporated like smoke. This was *Cecile*. Raul arced like an arrow out of the crowd and shot toward his target then gathered her to him. Strangely it wasn't fear he felt but a crazy kind of exultation born of his iron determination to free them of danger. "Here he comes!" he told her, locking his arms around her like a vise.

Cecile's heart seemed to cease beating. She thought he would crack her ribs such was the steel of his grip. They would go down together. Another dreadful accident for the Morelands. Perhaps fatal.

Time crystallized. So this is how it happened, she thought. Her uncle Jared's face sprang to mind. Did he know terror with a rampaging bullock coming right at him? Or like her did he feel the numbed acceptance of someone facing a firing squad?

TO THE CROWD who witnessed what happened—and would talk about it for many a long day—it was an extraordinary act of bravery. It didn't seem like mortal man could react so swiftly. It was more a blur of movement that brought to mind the spring and pounce of a lion. Transfixed with horror, people looked on in sick fascination as two entwined bodies blasted as if out of a cannon across the rough track before crashing to the ground on the other side. It was mere seconds before the horse exploded past the very spot where Cecile had been standing and continued on its mad flight. The man had turned his body at the last minute so the woman was almost completely cushioned from the worst of the fall.

"God almighty!" A brother of one of the players gasped in high relief and admiration. "That's the gutsiest thing I've ever seen."

There was a ragged chorus of agreement.

A DISTANCE OFF, Chris Arnold and Brad Caldwell, working together, had managed to get the trembling polo pony under control. The pseudo cowboy, formerly full of mischief and now condemned as a "brainless young fool," was moaning and groaning, his arms pinned behind his back by a big burly spectator. "Arrest me. Go on, arrest me. I didn't mean no harm. How did I know the bloody horse was going to bolt?"

Ashen-faced and panting, Justine Moreland ran awkwardly, to her daughter who could so easily have been run down and pummeled into the dirt. "Cecile!" she cried, her mouth working with emotion. "You bloody idiot!" She turned her head to vent her rage on the youth with a passion she rarely showed. Her brother Jared's death inevitably came to mind. "I'm going to press charges! You wait and see!"

Joel Moreland, who had moved off some time before, now arrived back on the scene, his tall frame crumpling at the sight of Cecile and Raul lying prone on the ground. For a moment he had to be supported by his friends. "Tell me they're all right?" he begged as Jack Doyle ran to him. "Go to them, Jack."

Cecile was the first to sit up, though it was obviously a struggle for her.

"Thank God! Oh, thank God!" Justine's face was ghastly with shock.

Cecile couldn't speak. She was winded and hurting, but she reached out a hand to her mother, looking dazedly into Justine's tortured face. For all the difficulties between them it couldn't have been plainer her mother loved her. Behind her mother were Bea and Tara, their faces similarly pale and stricken. There was no sign of Stuart, but Cecile wasn't looking for him. He had probably run for his life.

Cecile twisted her aching torso to look down at Raul. He

was lying with his eyes shut, apparently unconscious, but her fevered inspection revealed no external signs of injury, apart from a rapidly swelling lump on his head. Blood trickled from where the skin had been broken. There was blood on her white halter top. *His* blood.

"Oh, Raul!" She found her voice, bending over him with breathless concern. Her tone of voice and the expression in her eyes reflected her powerful feelings for all to see, but she was oblivious to everyone but him.

"He's coming round," Justine said with relief, putting aside for the moment the fact that starkly revealing expression on her daughter's face was deeply perturbing. "Look— he's opening his eyes."

"Let me take a look there, lovey." Jack Doyle was with them, dropping to his haunches beside Cecile. Swiftly he took in the disposition of Raul's limbs. Everything looked normal. "Praise the Lord, that's all I can say!" Jack breathed. "I reckon he's okay." Jack looked into Raul's dark eyes. "How yah goin' there, fella?" he asked gently, taking note of the bump on Raul's head where his hair was matted with blood. "How many fingers, mate?" He held up three fingers of his right hand.

"Three," Raul answered instantly, putting a hand to his bleeding head. "What did I hit?"

"The tree." Jack chuckled. "You must have a pretty hard head there, mate. Like to squeeze my hand? Right. Let it go."

"Let's get them both up to the house, Jack," Justine said, some color returning to her face. "That head wound needs a sterile dressing. Ahh, here's Daddy. He looks terrible. Oh, poor Daddy! This shouldn't have happened. Sometimes I hate bloody horses," she raged. "They're so unpredictable, the

brutes! Daddy's got George Nelson with him." George
Nelson was Joel's friend and personal physician.

"There's the Jeep coming," Jack said. "Let's have Dr.
Nelson take a look at you both before we do anything else."

"I'm all right," Raul protested, pushing himself up into a
sitting position, though he was very pale beneath his dark tan.
"I've had plenty of spills before today. How are *you,* Cecile?
Did I hurt you? I'm so sorry."

"Hold on, mate!" Jack gave Raul several comforting pats
on the shoulder. "You're a bloody hero!"

"No! No way!" Raul shook his head, then winced.

Cecile, whose eyes were blazing out of her face, reached out
to lay a tender hand along his cheek. "We're both safe, Raul."

Dear Heaven! thought Justine, all her worst fears confirmed.
When had she ever seen such a frank expression of love on a
woman's face? When had she ever seen her daughter look at
Stuart that way? The answer was *never.* Where the hell was he,
anyway? Wherever he was, it was too late.

"Chris and Brad have the horse under control," Jack Doyle
was saying. "That kid and his mate will never be allowed on
Malagari again."

"Don't be too hard on him," Raul said, Benjie's fate never
far from his mind.

"Don't you go worrying about a thing, Raul dear," Bea
exhorted him. "You saved our darling Ceci's life. I'm going
to include you in my nightly prayers for the rest of my life,"
she declared fervently.

"*You,* Bea?" Justine whipped her head around to challenge her aunt. "When did you start praying?"

"About five minutes ago, Justine," said Bea. "Aren't you
glad they were answered?"

An Important Message from the Editors

Dear Reader,

*Because you've chosen to read one of our fine romance novels, we'd like to say "thank you!" And, as a **special** way to thank you, we've selected <u>two more</u> of the books you love so well **plus** two exciting Mystery Gifts to send you — absolutely <u>FREE</u>!*

Please enjoy them with our compliments...

Pam Powers

Lift here

How to validate your Editor's "Thank You" FREE GIFTS

1. Peel off gift seal from front cover. Place it in space provided at right. This automatically entitles you to receive 2 FREE BOOKS and 2 FREE mystery gifts.

2. Send back this card and you'll get 2 new Harlequin *Superromance®* novels. These books have a cover price of $5.50 or more each in the U.S. and $6.50 or more each in Canada, but they are yours to keep absolutely free.

3. There's no catch. You're under no obligation to buy anything. We charge nothing—ZERO—for your first shipment. And you don't have to make any minimum number of purchases— not even one!

4. The fact is, thousands of readers enjoy receiving their books by mail from The Harlequin Reader Service®. They enjoy the convenience of home delivery...they like getting the best new novels at discount prices BEFORE they're available in stores... and they love their Reader to Reader subscriber newsletter featuring author news, special book offers, book reviews and much more!

5. We hope that after receiving your free books you'll want to remain a subscriber. But the choice is yours— to continue or cancel, any time at all! So why not take us up on our invitation, with no risk of any kind. You'll be glad you did!

GET TWO *Free* MYSTERY GIFTS...

SURPRISE MYSTERY GIFTS COULD BE YOURS **FREE** AS A SPECIAL "THANK YOU" FROM THE EDITORS

The Editor's "Thank You" Free Gifts Include:

- Two NEW Romance novels!
- Two exciting mystery gifts!

Yes! I have placed my
Editor's "Thank You" seal in the
space provided at right. Please
send me 2 free books and
2 free mystery gifts. I
understand I am under no
obligation to purchase any
books, as explained on the
back and on the opposite page.

PLACE
FREE GIFTS
SEAL
HERE

336 HDL EFU4   135 HDL EFY4

FIRST NAME
LAST NAME
ADDRESS
APT.#
CITY
STATE/PROV.
ZIP/POSTAL CODE

(H-SR-08/06)

Thank You!

The Harlequin Reader Service® — Here's How It Works:

Accepting your 2 free books and 2 free mystery gifts places you under no obligation to buy anything. You may keep the books and gifts and return the shipping statement marked "cancel." If you do not cancel, about a month later we'll send you 6 additional books and bill you just $4.69 each in the U.S., or $5.24 each in Canada, plus 25¢ shipping & handling per book and applicable taxes if any.* That's the complete price and — compared to cover prices starting from $5.50 each in the U.S. and $6.50 each in Canada — it's quite a bargain! You may cancel at any time, but if you choose to continue, every month we'll send you 6 more books, which you may either purchase at the discount price or return to us and cancel your subscription.

*Terms and prices subject to change without notice. Sales tax applicable in N.Y. Canadian residents will be charged applicable provincial taxes and GST. All orders subject to approval. Credit or debit balances in a customer's account(s) may be offset by any other outstanding balance owed by or to the customer. Please allow 4 to 6 weeks for delivery.

CHAPTER TEN

THE BARBECUE WENT AHEAD. Everything was in readiness, the crowd had to be fed, so as they said in the theater the show must go on. Cecile couldn't claim she remembered much of it afterward. Shaken and bruised—the discolorations were already coming out—she was fussed over all night. Good-hearted efficient women cheerfully banded together to take the running of the party off her hands. They were all very experienced at these outdoor events and had no difficulty feeding the large crowd and keeping them happy.

For once her grandfather had retired early, reassuring them he was feeling fine, only a little shaken by the events of the afternoon. George Nelson had checked four patients over: Cecile and Raul, and also Joel and Bea, the latter of whom had had a sudden attack of tachycardia. All four had been given the all-clear, though Dr. Nelson had recommended they have an early night. Even so he had checked on Raul, Joel and Bea at frequent intervals during the evening. In Raul's case, though he was a splendidly fit young man, any injury to the head was potentially serious. Raul admitted under questioning to "a bit of a headache," but he showed no other worrying symptoms.

Both men, however, took the doctor's advice and made a reasonably early night of it.

"I'll never forget what you did today, Raul," Joel Moreland told him as they said good-night. He squeezed Raul's hand in gratitude. "If there's any way I can help you—with anything—you have only to say."

"You've already been kindness itself to me." Raul could speak with sincerity. "There are a few questions I might ask you one day."

"Ask them now!" Joel Moreland stared into the young man's eyes, frowning a little in perplexity.

"I don't think so," Raul said. "A bad shock can't be underestimated. You need your rest."

"I am a bit shaky," Joel admitted. "It was so eerie this afternoon. Time stood still. I've never got over the death of my son. I never will. Had anything happened to Cecile, indeed *you*, I seriously doubt I could have gone on."

"I understand that," Raul said quietly. "One day perhaps you can talk to me about Jared's death." *Starting with the truth,* Raul looked into Joel Moreland's remarkable eyes. "It might help."

Joel gave a sad, twisted smile and placed his hand on the young man's shoulder. "My gut feeling is you'll understand. Good night now, Raul. You sure you're feeling okay?"

"I'd do it again without hesitation," Raul answered.

For a long moment Joel Moreland's eyes remained on the dynamic young man who stood before him. "Anything to protect Cecile, eh?"

Raul's strained-looking face broke into a smile. "Whatever it takes."

AN HOUR OR SO LATER, having said her thank-yous and good-nights, Cecile made her way into the house, her head aching and her nerves frayed. Dr. Nelson had given her something to take before bed, but the reality was she and Raul could have been very badly injured or killed today. For that matter, her beloved grandfather could have suffered a heart attack, his color had been so bad. Not that there was anything wrong with his heart to date, but one never knew. The incident had cast a pall on the evening. And then there was Stuart. And her mother. So many times over the past few hours she had seen them with their heads together. Would it ever stop? Stuart had belatedly arrived on the scene, claiming he had been making his way back to the house for something. He then proceeded to make a big display of loving relief and gratitude to Raul. He had been very solicitous ever since. He had even given her her own space for most of the evening, even though he'd stayed close.

She hadn't, however, reckoned on his following her back to the house.

"Ceci!"

She came to a halt in the entrance hall, waiting for him to reach her. She didn't feel up to talking about anything now.

"Could I talk to you for a minute?"

"Can it wait until morning, Stuart?" she asked quietly.

Her plea and the paleness of her face did no good. "I promise it won't take long."

"All right. Let's go into the library," she said, leading the way. There, she switched on the light, taking comfort from the familiar surroundings. It was a world of columns and dark gleaming timbers; bookcases filled with hundreds and hundreds of leather-bound books, a mahogany ladder to reach the top shelves; rich upholstery and rugs, several large canvases of hunting scenes, two Georgian library tables, piled with books, a desk and chair in one corner, two large globes, terrestrial and celestial on stands. She loved this room. It calmed her. It might calm Stuart.

"Sit down, Stuart," she invited, herself sinking into a wing-backed chair. "What is it that can't keep?"

Stuart pulled up his burgundy leather armchair so their knees were almost touching. "Us, Ceci," he said. "I wasn't really sure what was going on before I arrived, but I do now. You're besotted with Montalvan."

Cecile dropped her head in her hands. "Oh, Stuart!" she breathed, thinking it was finally time to get this thing over with no matter how she felt.

"Be honest with me now," he said. "And don't hang your head. Look at me, Ceci, if you don't mind. What are you afraid of?"

She pulled herself together at his faintly hectoring tone. "There *are* things in life to be afraid of, Stuart. However, I'm not afraid of you. I deeply regret that I must hurt you, but you have to know the truth. I have fallen in love with Raul Montalvan, Stuart. I never meant it to happen."

"You mean you *let* it happen," he shot back accusingly. "Your mother's been right all along. You're not really what you appear to be."

Should she scream in frustration or burst into tears? She did neither. "Perhaps I'm not," she agreed. "I suppose we don't really know ourselves until someone who has the power to do so holds a mirror up to our real selves. I thought I loved you. But what I called love then and what I call love now are two very different things. I'm sorry, Stuart."

"You mean love's ugly twin, don't you?" Stuart's voice had a contemptuous edge. "It's all *sex* with this guy, isn't it?" Stuart's eyes brimmed with hatred.

"I haven't had sex with him, Stuart."

"Liar!" he said bitterly. "Your mother told me you had."

That shook her, but only momentarily. "Now that *is* a lie, Stuart. I'm certain my mother said no such thing."

"Indeed she didn't," Justine thundered from the open doorway. She sailed into the room in her glamorous kaftan and closed the door firmly behind her. "What I did say in the past was I didn't *trust* Raul Montalvan. But after what he did today, putting his own life on the line for Cecile, has left me and our family indebted to him forever. So she's in love with him, Stuart. Who could blame her? He's certainly an extraordinary young man. Maybe it will work out, maybe it won't. Either way—I'm very sorry, Stuart, I realize you're hurt—my daughter is no longer in love with you." Justine smiled tightly. "There it is! We had plans, but that young man knocked them all down with one look from those dark eyes."

A strangled groan from Stuart. "So you're turning against me too, Justine?" he cried. "You've been right behind me up until now."

"I know. I know." Justine put a heavily be-ringed hand to her head. "Stuart, you can't make me feel worse than I do already. I think you're a fine young man. I can't help it if Cecile has fallen out of love with you."

"How do you know she truly has?" Stuart demanded quite savagely.

"Because I *said* so, Stuart," Cecile answered. "The way you and Mother rattle on together as though I'm not in the room is quite extraordinary. I'll say it again, Stuart. I'm very sorry it has come to this, but I can't marry you. I'll return your ring in the morning. I've told you how I feel about Raul. I should point out, I'm not at all sure what Raul feels about me. Certainly he's as attracted to me as I am to him, but right at this moment I don't know where any of it is going. There's so much we don't know about one another."

"You can say that again." Stuart's handsome face darkened. "So he's a glamorous sort of character and he can play polo. He's here on a *visit!*"

"It's not about Raul," Cecile said. "It's about *us,* Stuart. There *is* no us. You're quite right. I'm not the woman you thought I was. Almost certainly I wouldn't make you happy. Our engagement was shaky for some time before Raul came into my life."

"Don't you think you're just trying to justify what you've done?" Stuart asked, his characteristic composure shattering like glass. "We were very happy. Everyone said so. Justine told me pretty well on a daily basis how happy she was about us."

"I had no right to do that, Stuart," Justine suddenly confessed, her supreme confidence in herself shaken. "Call me a very interfering woman. I am. Cecile is far better able to choose the right man than I am."

Stuart totally lost it. He sprang to his feet. "This is an appalling situation. You've made a fool of me, Cecile. I'll never forget that. Neither will my family. Do you know or even care I was going over *our* house with the architect only a few days ago? What about that?"

"My husband and I will take care of the house, Stuart," Justine said in an effort to placate him. "You won't suffer any financial pain."

"I should bloody well think not!" Stuart swore, his breathing fast and shallow.

"I think that's enough now, Stuart." Justine held up her

hand. "You and my daughter aren't the first young couple to call off an engagement and you won't be the last. There's no stigma attached to it, nor should there be. The hurt is regrettable."

"The hurt and the *humiliation*," Stuart answered, the muscles in his lean jaw working. "I'm telling you both now, I'm not taking this lying down. I'm going to dredge up every bit of information I can on Raul Montalvan. Okay, he is who he says he is, I've already checked that out, but you can bet your life a guy like that with his eye for women, and their eye for him—" he gave a hard cackling laugh "—will have a few secrets tucked away he doesn't want anyone to know about."

Cecile looked up at him, smiling sadly. "Stuart, if Raul has love children all over Argentina, it wouldn't help *you*. Our engagement is done. Please try to forgive me for the hurt I've caused you. I should have done this a long time ago. We really aren't suited, are we?"

Stuart gave that odd cackling laugh again. "Skip the self-delusion, Cecile. Raul Montalvan wrecked our engagement. I swear I'll get the dirt on that guy, and when I do you'll be the first to know."

NEXT MORNING when Raul walked onto the veranda outside his room, he saw Jack Doyle at the side of the house, giving instructions to a couple of groundsmen. He took in a lungful of pure desert air, trying to rid himself of the lingering miasma of his dreams, nightmares really, intensely vivid, that were connected to the deaths of both Jared Moreland and his uncle Benjamin. Not used to any kind of medication, he put a lot of the feverish brain activity down to the sedative, or whatever, Dr. Nelson had given him for the painful lump on his head. It was still aching and not all that much diminished in size.

He wondered how Cecile was this blue cloudless morning, heavy with the aromatic scents of the bush. The birds were darting through the trees showing flashes of incredibly brilliant color as they called to one another. Beautiful butterflies were drawn in large numbers to the profusely flowering lantana. He watched them fluttering, wondering how he had kept himself from going down to Cecile in the still of last night. Even the thought made his blood stir. The need to reassure himself she was all right had been overwhelming, but so was the need to be with her, to hold her lovely supple body in his arms. More than anything, to make love to her. Once he had seen them on opposing sides, but that feeling had passed. She was in his blood. It was as simple and as hopelessly complicated as that!

Since speaking to Brad Caldwell, the station manager, he had awaited his moment to strike up a conversation with Doyle. With any luck at all, it might lead to his finding out where Frank Grover, Jared Moreland's alleged rival, might be. Whether the man was in or out of the country, Raul silently vowed he would find him. There were a whole lot of questions that needed answers. No way would the Benjie he so lovingly remembered have been involved in any plan to hurt a living soul, let alone Joel Moreland's only son. The most likely scenario could prove Brad right. Someone with a pressing motive had pushed Benjie into the arena, certain that Moreland would be the first to go to his aid.

Chiseled features taut, Raul walked down into the garden and rounded the east wing of the house.

"Well, now, how's it goin'?" Jack Doyle called out a

friendly greeting the moment he spotted him. "Bet you've got a sore head."

"It's not too bad, thanks, Jack." Raul smiled at the older man, digging his fingers into his thick hair.

"That's a relief. No ride this morning?"

"I think I'll leave it until this afternoon," Raul said wryly. "It was a great pity Mr. Moreland had to be there yesterday. He was badly shaken."

"Sure was!" Jack agreed. "He's never got over what happened to Jared, even if he never lost the Midas Touch in other ways. I suppose it was trying to block out the grief that drove him to concentrate so fiercely on his business affairs."

There was irony in that, Raul thought. Even cut down, Joel Moreland had remained a workaholic and an increasingly formidable business mogul. In his seventies he was still very much in charge. Raul stared off across the garden to where a large flock of sulfur-crested cockatoos were making a commotion. "So what were the circumstances of Jared's death? Do you mind my asking, Jack? I only hear snatches here and there. I've never had the full story. Brad told me a little about that terrible day. About the young fellow that was held responsible for the tragedy."

"Just a kid—I remember him well," Jack said. "What he did—or what he was thought to have done at the time—was incredibly stupid and wild, but according to those who knew him, which I didn't, he wasn't wild at all. He did, however, have a passion for rodeo, which we all know is a pretty foolhardy recreation. What's the pleasure in courtin' broken bones, countless bruises and mashed insides? I've seen guys who've had their thumbs ripped off calf ropin'. Jared had a passion for the arena as well. It was real dangerous and his mother was very much against it. Even Joel, who used to have a lot of fun with the ride-'em-cowboy routine when he was young, begged him to wrap it up. Got 'im all the same. That was one mean, murderous beast that killed him."

"He must have been very brave, as well as tough." Raul found he was having to revise just about everything he had been told about the Morelands as a boy growing up.

"Brave like *you,*" Jack said simply. "Nuthin' fake about it. Real guts."

"He would have known he was taking a terrible risk."

"Nearly pulled it off," Jack lamented, "only he tripped on something and went sprawling flat on his back in the dust. It was bloody horrible, I can tell you. I had nightmares about it for years."

"You said something Brad implied, Jack." Raul was anxious to keep the conversation going without alerting the other man to his deep-seated fixation. "There was some speculation the boy could have been pushed, wasn't there? Brad spoke about bad blood between Jared and a friend of yours, Frank Grover—I think I've got the name right."

"Name's right, but Brad gave you a bum steer about the *friend.*" Jack slapped at a biting insect on his arm. "Grover was no friend of mine. How the hell did Brad figure that? We worked together. Rode together. We weren't mates. Hell, I didn't even like the guy. He had real pale, pale blue eyes, kinda empty. He was mad about Johanna, the little housemaid up at the homestead. I guess you know that story?"

Raul nodded and changed the subject. "What I saw of Daniel I liked. He and Cecile could be twins."

"Ain't no one as beautiful as Miss Cecile," Jack said, eyes twinkling.

"You won't get any argument from me," Raul said dryly. "So where is this Grover now? I gather he no longer works on the station?"

"Crikey, you wouldn't wanna know," Jack leaned toward him, near whispering. "He was taken by a croc up in North Queensland about four years ago."

No! That Grover, the bastard, was dead was the one thing Raul hadn't counted on. He was so busy trying to rein in his crushing frustration he barely heard the rest of Jack's story.

"It was in the papers," Jack was saying in a matter of fact voice. "Silly bugger was sitting on a jetty fishing, legs dangling apparently, and a bloody croc reared up out of the water and bit him near in two. They shot the croc when it was just doing what crocs do. Grover was the fool. Any mug would have known better. To make it worse he'd worked on a croc farm for a few years. Got a mite too complacent."

Raul could have smashed his fist into the trunk of the tree they were standing under. "Is it possible Grover pushed the boy, or is that theory just plain crazy?"

Jack took a deep breath and slowly let it out. "Actually not," he said. "No one considered it at the time, but I think Grover let a few things slip one time when he was drunk. He hated Jared for stealing his girl."

"And was she his girl?" Raul tried to moderate the intensity of his tone.

Jack shrugged a broad shoulder. "Lordy, I wasn't close enough to any of them to know. Grover was a good-looking bloke even if he was a bit strange. Johanna couldn't have thought to look as high as Jared. Hell, he was the boss's son. His mother had big plans for him, which didn't include no little housemaid. Maybe Frank *was* her boyfriend, at least for a while. I don't know. All I do know is Johanna was pregnant by Jared."

"Could it have been a deliberate ploy to get Jared to marry her?" Raul was compelled to ask.

"God knows, mate," Jack shook his head. "Who knows what goes on in anyone's head when sex is involved? Fact is, Daniel is the result and Daniel is Joel Moreland's heir. It wouldn't pay to start talkin' about Frank Grover, or the boy. Some things it's better not to discuss. Especially around here. Jared's memory is stained with blood. Lockhart was the boy's name. He was killed, too, believe it or not. It was like a bloody jinx was on all of them. All of them gone."

Raul fought down the racking cry that tore at his chest. "It's a very strange and disturbing story," he said. "You must have some opinion, Jack. You were there that day."

Jack's blue eyes went hazy with memory. "I thought the same as everyone else. It was an act of sheer bloody criminal stupidity had caused Jared's death. Everyone was so shocked and angry they wanted to tear the kid to pieces, poor little bugger…though he wasn't little at all. He was a big strappin' fella. Neither Joel nor Mrs. Moreland were there on the day, but Mrs. Moreland—now there was one terrifyin' lady— she was determined the boy and his family would be punished. She had the power to make it happen. The More- lands were even then huge Territory benefactors. It only took a word in someone's ear to make it pretty difficult for the boy's grandfather to run his property and get help when he needed it. Hired hands, mechanics, truckers, fencers, contract choppers, suppliers of all kinds, even vets had pressing reasons to be somewhere else. The word had gone out, you see. Most stuck with the strength, for fear of reprisals. I reckon Mrs. Moreland would have turned on them. The old boy couldn't get any additional credit from the bank to tide them over the bad patch everyone was experiencing. They came down mighty hard on him when they were lenient with others. It finally finished up with the bank foreclosin' on their station. No one in their right mind would have crossed Mrs. Moreland or, God forbid, been the cause of the death of her son. It wasn't until some years later that the rumors starting goin' the rounds. All of us quick to condemn had to sit down and reexamine the whole event and the people who could have been involved in some way. To this day nobody actually *knows*. Nor will we ever know if it was a horrific accident or bloody murder. I feel real bad about the whole thing. So do most of us, I reckon. Ben Lockhart might have been an entirely innocent young man."

Nevertheless he was condemned and is now dead.

THE STRAIN BETWEEN HERSELF and Stuart was of such magnitude Cecile judged it would be easier for everyone if she didn't accompany her mother, Bea and Stuart to the airstrip where the charter plane waited. She would bid her farewells at the homestead.

Now she stood on the veranda with Justine and Bea. "God knows what your father is going to say, Ceci," Justine said with that familiar note of censure in her voice.

"No, no, *no!*" Bea protested, waving her arms in the air. "Don't start that again, Justine."

Jaw set grimly, Justine ignored her. "There's going to be a scandal," she said. "Judy Carlson is a truly dreadful woman."

"Ho, ho, we all thought you liked her!" Bea winked laconically at Cecile.

"Keep out of this, Bea, would you?" Justine's nostrils flared, then deflated.

"Lighten up, can't you, Justine?" Bea groaned. "It'll be a nine-day wonder and Howard won't lose any sleep over it. He wants his daughter to be happy. Stuart was a terrible choice for Ceci, anyway. Where the hell is he, by the way?" Bea looked behind her into the interior of the house. "Uh-oh, take cover. Here he comes."

Stuart strode out onto the veranda with a very aloof expression. "Sorry to keep you waiting," he said icily. "I just wanted to have a word with Montalvan."

"Did you find him?" Bea asked with the greatest interest.

"I think you know very well I haven't. He's probably gone into hiding."

"Don't be so ridiculous!" Bea burst out laughing. "Hide from *you*, Stuart?"

Raul chose that precise moment to appear in the entrance hall, then catching sight of them walked out onto the veranda. "Everyone set?" he asked pleasantly.

"Not until you give me another kiss," said Bea cheekily.

"It will be my pleasure." He smiled at her. "You wanted to talk to me, Stuart?"

Stuart drew himself up to his full six-foot height. "You don't have a shred of guilt, do you?"

Raul looked puzzled. "I'm not sure what for."

"No shame! No remorse, either," Stuart continued. "Cecile was *my* fiancée."

"Stuart, *please,*" Cecile begged.

Raul appeared to think about it. "I really can't be held responsible for your inadequacies as a fiancé, Stuart," he said finally. "However, would it be out of line for me to say I understand your pain?"

"I don't want your bloody sympathy, damn it!" Stuart burst out.

"Right, I'll withdraw it."

"I think that's our cue for departure, kids," Bea suggested dryly. "Kiss me, Raul, before I go."

"He heard you the first time, Bea." Justine frowned, obviously thinking her aunt was just too embarrassing.

"Just because you've lost your charm doesn't mean *I* have, thank you very much, Justine," Bea came back with a snap, moving toward Raul. "You know I always thought Lord Nelson said, '*Kismet,* Hardy.' Not that silly, 'Kiss me.' It wouldn't have set a good example for his men, would it?"

Stuart took no notice of her and pointed a finger at Raul. "You're nothing but a con man," he said contemptuously.

"Really?" Raul's response was outwardly mild, but inwardly he sought to put a rein on his temper. "I'll kiss our beautiful Beatrice—I'm quite sure Nelson said *kismet,* too, Beatrice, then I'll walk with you, Stuart, to the Land Rover."

Stuart declined the offer. "I don't like being threatened," he said, his voice tight. "I don't have the stomach for this sordid mess, either. Goodbye, Cecile," he threw at her harshly, almost running down the steps as though he couldn't bear to look at her a moment longer. "You'll be hearing from me, don't worry."

"WHAT WAS THAT all about?" Raul asked after the Land Rover, driven by Jack Doyle, disappeared from sight. "It sounded very much like a threat."

Cecile sighed. "I think Stuart intends to contact the FBI to see if you're on their Most Wanted files."

Raul's mouth compressed. "He thinks I'm an international criminal?"

"He thinks you're a mystery man," Cecile said quietly. "So do I."

"So what is it you want to know?" Raul went to her, linking his hands around her waist and drawing her to him.

She stared up into his burnished eyes. "It's more what *you* want to know, Raul. You've been asking a lot of questions."

"Such as?" He wasn't surprised she'd realized that. He hadn't been all that subtle.

"The circumstances surrounding my uncle Jared's death."

"Wouldn't anyone want to know?" He gave one of those very European shrugs he had picked up along the way. "It's a tragic story. I'm close to you, aren't I? *Aren't* I, Cecile? Tell me, who thought it necessary to report back to you?"

She felt the hot color rise to her cheeks. "No one reported, Raul. It only came out in conversation."

"Yes?" he prompted, unaware his features had gone tight.

"It was Brad, after the match. He mentioned that your playing style, which very much impressed him along with everyone else, reminded him of Uncle Jared's. Then he added you'd shown a good deal of interest in how the whole tragedy occurred."

Raul forced a laugh he didn't feel. "Forgive me if I don't find that the least bit unusual. Perhaps being a Moreland makes you overly suspicious of people, Cecile, is that it?"

She was still staring at him, overwhelmingly conscious of his sexual attraction for her and because of it, her utter vulnerability. "You may be right."

"Don't you love me a little for saving your life?" he asked gently, bending his head so he could murmur in her ear.

It would have been impossible to suppress the excitement that ran through her...except a shocked voice called from the open doorway.

"Excuse me, am I interrupting anything?"

It was Tara. The poleaxed expression on her face made Cecile feel not only embarrassment but a real prickle of alarm. "Not at all, Tara," she said as Raul with no haste withdrew his arms. "Seeing Stuart off wasn't terribly pleasant."

"Well, it looks like you have Raul to comfort you!" There was more than a thread of outrage in Tara's voice. She looked from one to the other, having realized in a split second what she should have picked up on long before if she hadn't been so stupidly blind. Cecile and Raul Montalvan were sexually involved. No question about it. Tara had never felt so upset and so horrendously jealous. She wanted to pack her bags on the instant and leave. Didn't Cecile have enough? She was beautiful. She was gifted. She was filthy rich. Tara would have given anything to attract Raul Montalvan to her side, but she couldn't compete with Ceci. She'd never been able to. She should never have tried.

Tara gave a little agonized cry at the pity she saw in Raul's eyes. Burning with humiliation, she turned on her heel and rushed back into the house.

Cecile stared after her, heart torn. "Oh, Lord, I have to go to her!" She realized, too late, she hadn't taken her friend's interest in Raul half seriously enough. But then, Tara always had been good at covering her deepest emotions with frivolity and amusing banter. She couldn't bear to see Tara hurt. It was far worse than having had to hurt Stuart, and now she'd done both at the same time!

She found Tara facedown on her bed.

"Oh, Tara, I'm so sorry!" Cecile approached hesitantly, feeling weighted by sympathy and something like guilt.

"I've made a bloody fool of myself, haven't I?" Tara railed, thrashing her slender legs on the mattress.

"Of course you haven't." Cecile went to sit on the side of the bed.

"Is *he* why you broke your engagement?" Tara swung her unhappy face to Cecile accusingly.

"No!" Cecile stroked a damp blond strand from Tara's face. "No, Tara. I would have broken my engagement to Stuart if I'd never even laid eyes on Raul. You said yourself that Stuart and I weren't soul mates."

"And you and Raul are?" Tara lashed out with such dislike and contempt that Cecile drew back. She felt for the very first time that their long friendship was in peril.

"I don't know what you thought you saw, Tara—"

"Oh, come off it," Tara retorted furiously. "Have you been to bed with him? What's he like? Bloody marvelous, I bet."

Cecile stared at her friend's puffy, tear-streaked face in utmost dismay. "I haven't been to bed with him, Tara. And really, it's none of your business, is it? You're my dearest friend. I don't want to hurt you. But be reasonable. I didn't come between you and Raul. I couldn't have stopped him falling in love with you if he wanted to." Cecile tried to put an arm around her friend, but Tara threw it off.

"Who's going to fall in love with me with *you* around?" Tara asked with great bitterness and resentment. "It was the same for years and years until you got yourself engaged to

Stuart. You turn your bloody charm on them and I don't stand a chance."

"I had no idea you felt this way." Cecile shrank from Tara's contorted face. "Who did I take from you exactly?" she asked in bewilderment, searching her memory.

Tara punched the pillow violently. "Oh, you didn't do it deliberately. I know that. But the combination of beauty and big bucks is too much for most guys. It could be the same with Raul. Canny old Stuart—he is a top lawyer, after all— could well be right. Our devastatingly handsome and charming Raul could be a fortune hunter."

Cecile tried to maintain some dignity and control. "Do you honestly believe that, Tara?"

"Ohhh! I don't know what I believe!" Tara made a terrible keening sound. "I'm outta here. I can't stay, Ceci. I know I'm going to be terribly ashamed of myself later, but I think it advisable if I go home now. You won't suffer in my absence, anyway. You've got Raul."

Cecile stood up from the bed, unable to believe this was Tara, her friend, who was mad with jealousy and rage. How long had Tara been harboring such thoughts? She had always treasured Tara's loyalty. Now it appeared she'd been deceiving herself. Tara, like many others, had only been using her. That was the downside of being Cecile Moreland. Envy inspired deep resentment. Even hate.

In the heat of the day Cecile felt chilled to the bone.

CHAPTER ELEVEN

HE WAS A MAN at war with himself.

To be free, even momentarily, of all the myriad agonies going round and round in his head! They were causing him many nights of lost sleep. Raul put down the phone after a brief call from Cecile saying she was coming to see him. She didn't say about what and he didn't ask. Just to see her was enough. But it did leave him to speculate on the nature of this unscheduled visit. They were to have dinner that evening. He had always been aware a man like Joel Moreland had the wherewithal to have him thoroughly checked out. Any good private investigator would be able to establish without too much trouble his mother's background: her maiden name, her marriage to his father, her first husband, then to Ramon Montalvan, her second, who had legally adopted him at age twelve. Further investigation would reveal the young man held responsible for the death of Jared Moreland, one Benjamin Lockhart, deceased, had been his mother's younger brother and thus, his uncle.

Was that it? Was he about to be unmasked as the impostor in their midst? So be it! It would almost come as a relief especially as the results of his own investigation had diluted Moreland responsibility for the terrible downturn in his family's lives. But justice must prevail.

Raul walked out onto the terrace of the spacious Darwin apartment he had recently moved into. The vast Darwin harbor sparkled a deep turquoise in the late-afternoon sunlight. Moreland Enterprises owned the exclusive apartment complex, which featured every amenity, including a fifty-meter swimming pool and a superbly equipped gym, so securing a very cozy place indeed to live had been an easy matter.

What deeply troubled him now was the shift in his position. A gradual letting go. He hadn't foreseen it. He hadn't foreseen Cecile. He couldn't help but see the shift as a betrayal to his family. He had returned to Australia with vengeance on his mind. Revenge on the Morelands had twined itself around his life like a great python twined itself around a tree. He seemed as though he had never been free of its coils. Only, what he had long believed as being the truth wasn't revealing itself to be so. There were baffling aspects to the whole thing. A bigger cast of characters than he or his mother had ever imagined. He was certain his mother hadn't lied to him; they were very close. The truth now appeared to have been buried beneath a mountain of grievances, hearsay and outright misinformation. The more he came to know Joel Moreland the more he liked and respected him. No one could have been kinder or more helpful to him than Joel. He was a grandfather figure with a wonderful combination of wisdom, charm and command, as well as a personal history that was the stuff of Outback legend. Add to that the fact that Joel Moreland had a very tolerant way of looking at the world. He believed now, as he had never done before, that Joel had *not* been the deliberate instrument of his family's ruin. It had clearly been Joel's wife, Frances, but the woman had died, only a handful of years back, thus escaping having to admit to him and then the world what she had done. His family name would never be cleared. He had taken a great gamble coming here. The gamble had not paid off.

They were all dead, Raul thought wretchedly. All the main characters in that tragic tale. Even Frank Grover had met with a horrific end. If Frances Moreland had been prepared to turn her back on a pregnant young woman carrying her grandson, she was capable of anything. He had talked about that with Beatrice, who hadn't held back on what she thought of her late sister-in-law.

"Wicked! What she did was wicked!" Beatrice had said, her tiny face pinched in remembrance. "The sad thing was, Frances was totally fixated on her son. She adored him. She had little time for poor Justine. None of us, most of all Joel, had any idea she was going to change so drastically after only a few short years of marriage. Joel was away a lot—it was always business, business, business. He thought Frances had accepted that's what he did. He'd talked seriously to her about it before they married—so for that matter did I—and she seemed to understand. She was madly in love with him. She clearly enjoyed being his wife and all that went with it. Frances was a beautiful woman, but obsessive, as is sad to say Justine. It's in the genes. As the years went on, Jared, not Joel became Frances's obsession. He became her whole life. Whatever persuaded Daniel's mother to set her sights on Jared, heaven only knows. It was madness! Frances was more than capable of ruining the life of anyone who got in her way. Having a lot of money encourages megalomania sad to say."

A sickening perception but in many cases true. He had longed to question Beatrice about the circumstances surrounding Jared's death, but he knew Beatrice, as shrewd as they come, might be alerted to the quality of his interest and see it as a suspicious intrusion into Moreland family matters.

As for Cecile? It was hardly the scenario he had planned. Cecile had grown into his own personal obsession. She'd woven a web around him, in fact around them both. He knew how much Tara's running off had hurt her. It wasn't hard to realize Tara had, without any encouragement, taken a fancy to him. He couldn't help that. He knew he was attractive to women, but he was no womanizer. Anything but. Once or twice he had divined that beneath the breezy banter, Tara was deeply envious of her friend, of Cecile's stunning natural beauty and very privileged lifestyle. It didn't seem to matter that Tara, from all accounts, had long enjoyed the benefits of having Cecile Moreland for a friend.

In another week Cecile was due to return to Melbourne to her family, to her professional career, to her wide circle of friends. He could understand how being an heiress had complicated her life. Most people would assume, as Joel Moreland's granddaughter, she lived a charmed life. She was certainly free of any worrying financial burdens, but that wasn't the whole story. She'd had to accept she was a target for fortune hunters and supposed friends only too willing to help her spend her money. Tara appeared to have been one such experience. Even if at some later date Tara apologized for her behavior, the damage would have been done. It was sad and disillusioning. But Cecile was strong and she was independent. She could have given herself over to a life of pleasure, yet instead had chosen a serious career working with children in deep distress and dire need like her patient, little Ellie, who appeared to be never far from her mind.

Cecile was a deeply caring person. Even Justine, who couldn't quite approve of him, involved herself heavily in charitable work. He had also learned from a number of sources the extent of Joel Moreland's philanthropy. As Moreland's empire had grown, his endowments to hospitals, medical research centers and a whole raft of charities grew apace.

This wasn't a man who destroyed lives.

CECILE ARRIVED about forty minutes later. He let her through the security door at the entrance to the building, then waited for her at the elevator.

His first glance told him the mystery of Raul Montalvan had been unraveled. He couldn't say he hadn't seen it coming. Neither of them spoke but walked in silence to his apartment, of which there were only two to a floor. Once inside she turned to face him, a cool, grave beauty in a lovely white silk dress, belted at the narrow waist in silver-studded turquoise that matched her high heels. "You deceived me utterly, *Rolfe*," she said. "I suppose I should call you Rolfe from now on…but why?"

"Sit down, Cecile," he responded quietly, but there was a flash in his gold-flecked eyes.

She remained standing as though she intended to have her say as quickly as possible, then leave. "What is your state of mind? Do you hate us so much?"

"What is it you know or think you know?" he countered, steeling himself against hearing her grandfather had had him investigated. Like Cecile, Joel Moreland had gotten under his guard.

"I received this in the mail today." She opened her handbag

and withdrew a long, thickly padded envelope. "It's from my ex-fiancé, Stuart Carlson, God bless him. I'm sure it gave him a lot of pleasure seeing it all compiled."

"May I?" He held out his hand.

She gave a slight elegant shrug. "Why not? It's all about you, anyway. Your entire background, I would say."

"Then I am who I claim to be—Raul Montalvan," he returned curtly, stung by her tone. "In Argentina Rolfe somehow became Raul. So you might apologize for having said I deceived you. I just didn't give you the full story."

"But it's all *about* the full story, isn't it, Rolfe? Tell me, is the fascinating accent assumed?"

"Don't be ridiculous!" he said shortly, opening out the pages.

She visibly trembled and he relented. "Are you cold?" It was eighty degrees outside, but the air-conditioning was set at seventy.

"I'm frozen," she said. "With shock."

Her wonderful eyes surveyed him the way he imagined a woman might look on a hero found to be badly flawed. "Sit down," he repeated. "You're not getting out of here before we talk."

"Is that a threat?" she asked quietly.

"Take it any way you like," he clipped off. "But you know you're in no danger." He waited until she sank gracefully into an armchair, then he bent to reading Stuart Carlson's vitriolic covering page. Apparently simple decency in dealing with his ex-fiancée was beyond the man.

"I was always suspicious of you, Rolfe," she murmured, even though she knew he was too engrossed in what he was reading to focus on what she was saying.

"Well, they certainly amassed a great deal of information!" Rolfe observed dryly some moments later. He refolded the pages and put them back into the envelope, laying it down on the coffee table in front of her.

"Was everything just for revenge?" she asked. "Did you have any *real* feeling for me, or was that only an elaborate pretense? Perhaps you despise me. Perhaps your plan was to make me fall in love with you, then publicly reject me. Anything's possible." Only her pride saved her from breaking down.

"I'm not going to deny I thought about it," he said, his expression dark and brooding. "For about two minutes, maybe ten. I've lived with the hated name of Moreland for most of my life, Cecile. Can you understand that?"

"But what did we do?" she cried in bewilderment.

His anger exploded, made all the more potent because he felt he had disgraced himself in her eyes. "You ruined my entire family," he rasped. "My grandparents were forced off their land. Land they had worked for five generations. My grandfather—I was named for him—had a massive heart attack not long after. My grandmother exiled herself to New Zealand just as my mother and father took refuge in Argentina. All of us exiles. Do you know what that means? It's like having an arm cut off. My father died there in a strange land."

"Yes, and I'm so sorry." Tears sprang to her eyes.

"Spare me the tears," he said harshly, even as his heart twisted. "I don't doubt you're sorry, but Moreland sympathy has come too late. It's my uncle Benjie's treatment at Moreland hands I most deeply hold against you. He was hounded to his death."

"But he was killed in a bar fight. Surely that's right." She had read it in the report.

"Provoked into a fight, I'm certain. There was far more to your uncle Jared's death than you've been led to believe, Cecile. I know you grew up thinking it was a tragedy caused by his heroic response to a young fool's reckless stupidity."

"And wasn't it?" She had always looked on her uncle as a hero who had given his life to save another's.

Rolfe's mouth, generous in its lines, tightened. "There's some evidence Ben was pushed off that fence by a man called Grover, Frank Grover. He was a stockman on Malagari."

Cecile was beginning to feel quite ill. "You can't be serious!" she gasped. "I've never heard such a thing. Why would anyone want to harm my uncle, anyway?"

His tone was quiet but it commanded attention. "Crimes of passion happen all the time. Grover was in love with the same young woman, the housemaid Johanna Mull, who was to bear Jared's child. I was told there was bad blood between your uncle and Grover."

Cecile looked as shaken and baffled as she felt. "I know absolutely nothing of this."

"You don't *want* to know anything," he countered, between clenched teeth. "You *fear* the truth."

Cecile jumped up from her chair. "I don't! Stop it, Raul….*Rolfe!*" she cried, wondering if there was anything straightforward in life. "I can't listen. I'm going."

"That's right, run," he challenged, his expression conveying he thought her response cowardly. "You all ran from the truth. Because of that my entire family suffered. My grandfather was hounded off the family land. All right, it was no Malagari, but it had been in the family for five generations. I lost my inheritance. Nothing to you, I dare say, but everything then to me.

My uncle Benjie, an innocent young man lost all direction and eventually died at an attacker's hands."

Cecile saw the burning anger in his eyes. "You hate us, don't you? You really hate us." Would she ever recover from it?

"I hate your grandmother," he said. "I doubt Daniel thinks very kindly of her, either. She was a cruel, ruthless woman."

"But what has my grandmother got to do with this?" Cecile was so shocked she could scarcely draw breath. "She was kindness itself to me."

"You didn't *threaten* her, Cecile." The word was bitterly emphasized.

"There's no peace anywhere, is there?" Cecile's face was as white as her dress. "It's not safe to trust anyone."

That was the worst of it. She had lost all trust in him. He made an attempt to explain. "I couldn't have shown my hand too early. I had to get to know you."

"You mean you had to infiltrate the family." Cecile struggled to keep her voice steady. "You had to become the spy among us. Learn our secrets."

"Of course," he admitted grimly. "I knew most of them already but I had to be in a position to turn your dire secrets against you."

"So that's all it was, seeking revenge?" She was certain that was so.

"All?" he asked harshly. "My family was publicly condemned. I had to set the record straight. I needed to show you up to yourselves. At the beginning, anyway."

"So what changed?" she asked contemptuously.

"*You.* You turned my head. And my heart."

Abruptly she swung away, the hem of her skirt flaring

around her slender legs. "I'm not taken in by what you say," she said bitterly. "From the moment you laid eyes on me you saw how I could be used in your little game."

"No game, I assure you."

Cecile spun back to face him, seeing his brow furrowed with strain. "How could you dream of making a fool of my grandfather, of all people?" she asked bleakly.

Rolfe shrugged. "I hardly think I did. Or *could*. It wasn't Joel who victimized my family and Daniel's hapless mother, as I believed. It was Joel's wife, Frances, your grandmother. She behaved in a manner I believe your grandfather never could. The female is often deadlier than the male."

Cecile made a huge effort to remain calm, although she was dreadfully upset. "I repeat, I know nothing of this," she protested. "You're a man driven by the demon of revenge, yet you were only a child at the time. It would have been impossible for you to form an adult opinion. Too much was put on your shoulders. You accepted whatever was told to you. Small wonder you've become so embittered. So your family's lives were smashed? Did that mean ours has to be smashed, too? Your accounts settled?"

"There are consequences to our actions, Cecile," he said with the gravity of a judge. "Unfortunately for me most of the people involved in that terrible saga are dead. The truth, the real truth, may never be known. It appears to have gone to the grave with them."

Although she was appalled by his words, she steeled herself against him. "If they did wrong, they don't go free," she said. "Don't you believe in God?"

"Maybe not." He shrugged. "If there *is* a God, He wants none of what's going on down here in this deeply troubled world. Did no one know your grandmother was so deeply implicated in my family's ruin?"

Her hackles rose again. "Where's your evidence?" she challenged him. "Have you got a scrap of this so-called evidence to show me?"

"I've spoken to your own people," he retorted. "People in a position to know some of it. You know that. What I have is a good deal of hearsay, I admit, but I'm certain if I dig deep enough, I can get all the evidence I need. I'm not trying to prove anything in a court of law, Cecile. I'm not trying to sue the mighty Morelands for stacks of money. I simply want acknowledgment of a terrible miscarriage of justice. I want to remove the slur from my uncle's name. I believe him to have been the victim of another man's sinister plot. That was Grover. But Grover's dead—a crocodile beat me to him. Your grandmother is no longer alive. What did she die of?"

Cecile was wrenched by painful memories. "Something horrible," she said. "Does that appease you? It was stomach cancer."

"I'm sorry." Hurting Cecile was hardly what he wanted. "You loved her."

"Yes, I did. I can't believe all this…business you're telling me," she said vehemently.

"When you already know she turned her back on her own grandson, Daniel?"

Cecile stumbled into a chair, burying her face in her hands. "Who told you? I can't believe Granddad spoke of it."

"He didn't, but whoever told me had no love or even liking for your grandmother. And wasn't that the action of a ruthless, heartless woman, Cecile?" He kept up the challenge. "Turning the penniless, pregnant mother of her own grandchild out of the house with nowhere else to go to."

"She gave her money," Cecile said, deeply distressed. "At least she did that. She wasn't a bad woman. Bad things happened around her. I know that what my grandmother did to Daniel and his mother was unforgivable, but I believe she paid for it. Guilt gnawed away at her health, her strength and her mind. There was such an air of desolation about her at different times, especially in those final days. Even *you* would have felt sorry for her. Now you want to heap *more* sins on her head?"

"It's the role I was handed, Cecile. The badness arose out of your grandmother's obsessive love of her son. You're the psychologist. You would have read widely on such things. Your grandmother wasn't getting the love and attention she craved from her husband, so she moved on to the son. You can relate to controlling parents. Forgive me, but you must have discovered that in your own mother. Your grandmother carried her obsessive love to extremes. She wanted to be in control at all stages of her son's life. He certainly wasn't going to be allowed to further his relationship with a housemaid. A suitable young woman had already been picked out for him. Doesn't it all sound familiar?"

"Controlling parents are common," she said bleakly. "You haven't been free of parental conflicts. They must have been forced on you from childhood."

"Never *forced*," he said angrily. "I saw with my own eyes how the women of my family suffered. I had to listen helplessly while my mother cried."

"So you lived with a lot of unhappiness and a lot of rage. You lost your father at a significant stage of your development. Not only that, you lost your mother in a sense when she married another man. There must have been a lot of conflict there."

"My stepfather is a good man," he answered repressively. "It's not my life we're examining."

"Yet it explains this drive for revenge. Great stress was put on you, Rolfe. Stress that no child or adolescent should have to bear. I can't believe you didn't clash with your stepfather in the early days, though I accept your saying he's a good man. I expect your mother talked about the past to you from time to time. The past was never allowed to die."

"Especially as it's true the past never does die."

"So your goal has always been revenge? It must be very painful, then, to have that goal dashed."

"Who says it is?" He gave a harsh laugh.

Cecile found herself wringing her hands. "It couldn't have been as you've said. You didn't know my grandmother."

"From all accounts she ignored her daughter, your mother."

Cecile couldn't return his searing gaze. "You're making it sound worse than it was."

His gaze was unwavering. "You weren't there."

"Neither were *you!*" she shouted, losing all control. She loved this man, yes, *loved* him. Betrayal and all. She would have given herself to him in a minute, offered up her heart and her mind and her body, but every step he had taken was carefully planned to bring her down. He meant to use her, then reject her. Revulsion for her own colossal stupidity, her *weakness,* made her rush to the door where she paused, her back to it. "There's no point in talking about this anymore. I have no intention of letting my grandfather see the letter. I love him too much, though I haven't the slightest doubt Stuart will do as much damage as he can."

"Then shouldn't you tell your grandfather even if it's only to stop Carlson?" Rolfe suggested harshly, moving toward her as though she were a magnet. "I'm sure he could. A word in someone's ear should do it. The senior partner in Carlson's law firm. One would have to be a fool to cross Joel Moreland."

"You're admitting you're exactly that, a fool?" A nonviolent person—violence shocked her—Cecile found herself wanting to push him hard, to pound him, to hurt him as he was hurting her. Naked hostility made her eyes blaze like diamonds. "Worse, you're a—"

She got no further.

Rolfe snapped. He hauled her into his arms, the fire of aggression crackling along his veins. It was impossible to have her so near to him yet so far away. She struggled wildly, but no woman was a match for his strength. She was unable to prevent his mouth coming down crushingly on hers.

Cecile couldn't draw breath. Her blood was seething. It was brutal. It was devastating. It was deranged, because at his first touch, she longed for it. Yes, longed for it. She couldn't get enough of him. Nor he of her. She had the sense of being caught up in a great electrical storm. Energy was sizzling all around them, coming off his body, galvanizing her. The sheer force of the sexual attraction swept her off her feet. She could only follow where he led. He was muttering something into her open mouth—she didn't know what, English, Spanish—but she knew what it meant. He *wanted* her. Whatever his initial scheme had been, he was hoist by his own petard. That gave her a sick satisfaction.

"I hate you," she muttered desperately, as they wrestled and weaved across the room. She was shocked by the sound of her own voice. The weight of passion in it.

"Don't say that." Rolfe tried to subdue her without hurting her. "You have to try to understand."

"Well, I can't!"

"*Won't!* Won't is more like it. You're a coward."

"You should talk!" She was frantic as his hand moved to her breast. He cupped it with his hand, a strangely adoring gesture that further incited her passion.

"You're so beautiful," he groaned, "even when you're fiercely hating me."

They were moving, half stumbling, half staggering toward the master bedroom, the two of them breathing as heavily as though they were involved in a marathon. The tears were spilling down her cheeks. "What are you going to do, Rolfe? Rape me?"

Instantly he backed off, his handsome features drawn so incredibly taut for an instant his face looked like a dark golden mask. "No, no, *never.* Just stay with me a while." He was begging, resting his head against hers in a way that conveyed to her how genuinely desperate he was. No way could she mistake those feelings. They were her own.

She could feel herself melting, her limbs giving way. She could despise herself later, but for now her driving needs were too powerful to subdue. She wanted him with an urgency that could not be denied. If this were the only time she was going to experience sex on the scale of grand opera, she was prepared to do it. She didn't love him any longer, she told herself. She *didn't,* yet he pulled her like the moon pulls the tides.

Her hands were fumbling at the buttons of his shirt. She loved the smell of him, the clean male fragrance of his skin that always lingered in her nostrils. Physically he was perfect to her. She slipped her hand inside his shirt, letting her fingers range over the width of his chest, her nails digging into the golden bronze mat of hair.

"I can't stop now. You know I can't!" His mouth slid across her face, wet with tears.

"All this will stop tomorrow," she warned, doing what she had never done before, or even imagined doing—tearing at a man's clothes. "I'm not worried. It's *safe*. You can't trap me that way."

Now they were inside his bedroom and she was pulling off her beautiful white silk dress, throwing it so wildly it was a wonder it landed over a chair and not on the floor. Her sandals came next. She was straightening to start on her slip, only he stood her back against the wall, lifting her arms high above her head.

"You're as frantic as I am, aren't you? Go on, *say* it," he mocked her, leaning over her, his body pressing into her thighs, drawing the tip of his tongue across her mouth.

"I'm saying nothing," she gritted, though the excited color had risen to her face, making her beauty dazzling.

His tongue was against her teeth, determined to gain entry. "Really?" His voice was a low growl in his chest.

Now he was kissing her without restraint. Fierce and fiery. As though she had given him permission to do with her whatever he wanted. She could hear her half-stifled moans. Her slip came off, her bra, her panties. Sunlight was filtering into the room through the blinds, turning her skin radiant.

"You're exquisite!" he muttered. "And, God, how I want you!" His arms closed around her, then he lifted her without effort and threw her trembling and wildly aroused onto the bed.

"The quilt is turned back!" she said furiously. She kicked at the thick folds at the end of the bed. "Did you have it all planned?"

"I don't think there's a moment that I haven't had it all planned." He turned back to her, stripped naked.

The splendor of his body gave her such enormous illicit pleasure she could do nothing else but reach out to him with hands that were a blend of pleading and intense longing. It was no invitation. Only a painful mime of a woman's ultimate surrender.

"This is *all* there is, remember!" She repeated her warning, acknowledging her own surrender, but determined to salvage something of her pride. "No follow-ups, no tomorrow."

He didn't answer but his expression was eloquent of high scorn. He swooped onto the bed beside her, half poised above her, drinking her in with dark eyes that sparkled with gold chips. Then he began to make love to her with his masterly hands, neglecting no part of her body, until her heart was fluttering in her throat.

She could think of nothing. Her mind went blank as every cell in her body sparked into vibrant life. There was only this mind-blowing sensation. Sensation she never wanted to escape. She felt so ecstatic she was impelled to lift an arm to draw his marvelous mouth down to hers. She was thirsting for it as a woman lost in the desert thirsts for flowing water.

At last!

He might take her for his pleasure. He might use it against her, even blackmail her into going to bed with him again. He might do all of those things, but she could never say she hadn't been party to it. She wanted him, she realized, as much as she wanted life itself.

CHAPTER TWELVE

QUITE UNEXPECTEDLY Cecile had reason for cutting short her holiday with her grandfather and thus putting herself beyond Rolfe's orbit. She was in pain and unsure of her ability to withstand him. Maybe at some time in the future she could confront the issues between them but for now so volatile were her moods she knew she couldn't discuss anything with him without swiftly veering into anger. He had *deceived* her. On the face of it he had *used* her. She badly needed time away from him to work out where she was going with her life. Her mother's phone call gave her the excuse to pack up and go home.

Justine rang that very evening, sounding so unlike herself, so nearly hysterical, for a moment Cecile doubted it *was* Justine on the other end of the line.

"What is it, Mother? Just tell me." She had immediately jumped to the conclusion that Stuart, out of spite, had gone to Justine with his report. Not that it would do anyone any good; nor did she think it could make her mother sound so out of control.

"I need you, that's all!" Justine cried. "I can't go into it now. I want you to come home immediately. You've spent enough time with Daddy. I am your mother, after all."

"Well, of course I'll come!" Cecile felt panicked fearing

her mother might have discovered she was ill. The frightening prospect of breast cancer came to mind. Her mother sounded desperate enough. "I'll speak to Granddad now. His pilot will fly me back to Melbourne."

Which was what happened. Her grandfather exacted a promise from Cecile before she left to ring back and let him know what Justine's problem was. "Such a secretive girl, Justine," he said, also worried his daughter may have received bad news regarding her health.

When Cecile did finally arrive at her parents' palatial home, the house where she had grown up, the maid let her in. She found her mother upstairs in the master bedroom frantically pulling her father's expensive suits off the hangers in the dressing room and flinging them all round the place with furious abandon. Justine's tall slim body was encased in a satin robe, though it was midafternoon. Her eyes were wild and her luxuriant mane of hair, always so meticulously groomed, was a tangled mess. She wore no makeup either, and Cecile had rarely seen her mother without it, even first thing in the morning.

"Mum, what in the world is happening?" Cecile was so shocked she dropped the more formal "Mother" Justine had long insisted was preferable to plain Mum.

"Your bloody father is leaving me, that's what!" Justine shouted, her actions growing wilder and wilder by the minute. "Can you believe it? Nearly thirty bloody years together and the bastard is leaving me for another woman."

"Oh, my goodness!" Cecile sank like a stone onto a pile of her father's clothes that were scattered all over the bed, too shocked to shift them. Whatever scenario she had imagined on the flight home, it was never *this!* Her parents' marriage vows— and she supposed the prenuptial agreement—were set in stone.

"Of course he's had his women," Justine said in a voice filled with the greatest contempt and anger. "He's *always* had his women—and don't try to tell me you didn't know about it," she rounded on Cecile as though Cecile had long been her father's coconspirator. "Howard and I had an understanding—as long as he was discreet. I've never been a great one for sex. Why is sex so bloody all-consuming?" she ranted. "I always found it bloody messy!" She shuddered fastidiously. "But it was understood we would always remain married. Now he tells me he truly loves some bitch of a woman who has worked for him for years."

Cecile released a pent-up breath through her nose. Her mother *never* swore, but she was giving "bloody" a serious beating. Her mind immediately began to range over any number of attractive women who worked for Moreland Mining. It could be any one of them. Married or not. Her father was only in his midfifties, a handsome vigorous, *wealthy* man. In other words, a prize. Would his job still be secure? She doubted it. He could and would be voted out if her mother had anything to do with it. She had the sick certainty her mother would become extremely vengeful now that she knew herself a wife scorned.

"You're not going to believe this," Justine was saying, her body visibly shaking with rage. She picked up a large pair of scissors and hacked through a dozen or more beautiful silk ties.

"Must you do that, Mum?" Cecile implored, upset at such senseless destruction.

"Yes, I must!" Justine started on some long winter scarves. "I bought the bloody things anyway."

"I'm so sorry, Mum." Cecile was tempted to go to her mother and hug her, but she knew her mother disliked physical contact. "I know this is very very painful for you."

"You bet your bloody life it is!" Justine said, slaughtering the sleeves of a dress shirt. "How can I be expected to cope with public humiliation? I have a position in society. Now there's you and your father and your broken promises. Two of a kind, it seems."

"How very unfair," Cecile lamented, unable to bring herself to a more angry response. "You've been speaking to Stuart?"

"I gave him a hearing," Justine said. "I don't have to justify myself to you or anyone. Stuart mightn't be perfect, but he would have made you a faithful husband."

"You don't know that, Mum." Cecile felt too miserable to argue. "It was a painful decision breaking my engagement. I should have done it a lot sooner. This woman we're talking about—she's young, around my age?" Cecile thought that would be the case. It usually was. Men in a desperate bid to recapture lost youth.

"She's *my* bloody age." Justine gave a gut churning screech, seemingly more affronted a *mature* woman could steal her husband rather than some blond bimbo. "He says he loves her. Love?" she cried, tugging a pair of trousers across the carpet. "What does that mean?"

"Sorry, I don't know, either," Cecile said forlornly.

"Bugger you! You had a good man and you sent him packing. I thought what I did for your bloody father all these long years was love. I've fussed over him like he was a bloody teenager. I even laid out his bloody clothes. You know that. I keep a marvelous house. I'm a leading hostess in this town. My garden is admired by everyone. I always look impeccable. It didn't mean a thing! I'm Joel Moreland's *daughter,* dammit! That's why he married me. Don't stare at me saucer-eyed. He married me because I was Joel Moreland's daughter. It wasn't any silly bloody love match. It was for the long haul. Compatibility, companionship, moving in the same circles, having the same goals. Forget this idiotic love at first sight business. That's over before it's begun," she snorted, hacking the trousers above the knee.

"Dad wanted a son, Mum. More children," Cecile pointed out just for the record. "You wouldn't give them to him."

Justine's scissors shut with a snap. "What are you talking about?" She stared at Cecile with a stab of near hatred.

"Don't let's have any more deceptions, Mum." Cecile, her own emotions raw, made a stand. "There was no reason why you couldn't have had more children. You just didn't want them. You've been living a myth all these years. I would have loved a sister or a brother, preferably both. Have you ever thought of that?"

Justine strode over to the bed looking like Lady Macbeth about to plunge in the dagger. "Who told you?" she demanded, attempting to drag more clothes onto the floor. "Don't bother to answer. It was Bea, wasn't it? She never could keep her mouth shut, the wicked old bag."

A small part of Cecile knew her mother could be dangerous, but her face stayed composed. "She's kept it shut all these years. What does it matter *who* told me, Mum? You made a very big mistake there. Dad is a virile, handsome man."

"He's bloody well past middle age."

"He doesn't look it or act it."

"Good one, good one!" Justine yelled, attacking with relish a Ralph Lauren polo shirt that had obviously never been worn. The price tag was still attached.

"Think about it, Mum." Cecile had second thoughts about trying to take the tailoring scissors from her mother. "You denied him more children and you denied him a full sex life by your own admission. Didn't you see that was destructive to your marriage? Didn't you see it was the reason he went elsewhere?"

"Reason?" Justine spat out the word, tossing back her thick tangled hair. "Whose bloody side are you on, anyway? Anyone would think I was a terrible person, instead of a splendid wife and mother."

"I'm not on any side, Mum," Cecile said quietly. "I love you both. But I can't help seeing things from Dad's point of view. Is there no possibility of a reconciliation?"

Justine's face went a life-threatening red. "You can't think I want the bastard back, can you?" she asked with incredulous outrage. "He's betrayed me once too often."

You mean he's actually found someone to love, Cecile thought, but didn't have the courage to say. Not with her mother wielding a lethal pair of scissors. "I'm so terribly sorry, Mum. Sorry for your pain. But you must see you allowed this whole situation to arise."

Justine's face went from a hectic red to chalk-white. "I'll never forgive you for that, Cecile," she breathed hoarsely.

"Oh Mum, *please!*" Cecile took her chances. She jumped up from the bed and crossing to her mother, tried to put her arms around her, but Justine, a strong woman at any time, in a manic phase, tossed her off easily.

"I've given you everything you ever wanted, Cecile. The best of everything! You've never been exposed for a minute to the harsher aspects of life."

"That's not true!" Cecile protested. "In my job I see and hear some of the most reprehensible, most shameful, things in life."

"Well, whose fault is that?" Justine pressed on. "You didn't have to do a bloody thing, as I've told you many a time. You could have helped me with my charity work. The thing is, Cecile, you've been overprotected all your life. I spoilt you terribly."

It simply wasn't true. "No, you didn't, Mother," Cecile said, shaking her head. "I tried as hard as I knew how to please you. I excelled at everything because I knew there was no other way. Yet you continued to bully me mercilessly. When I think about it, you practically hounded me into getting engaged to Stuart, the rattlesnake."

"Stop it!" Justine thundered. "It was *time* you got engaged. You could still finish up an old maid. You're a frail creature under that beautiful face. A natural-born victim. You might be clever, but you've got no common sense at all and no good instincts. Stuart told me all about that bloody impostor you've got yourself in deep with."

"Deep as the *Titanic*," Cecile admitted sadly.

"No good will come of it, mark my words!" Scowling darkly, Justine shook the scissors. "And I thought like a fool I had your promise to stay away from him. Ah, well! You're going to find out the hard way. Stuart was naturally reluctant to come right out with it, but I can read between the lines. You're no more interested in sex than I am."

Cecile laughed, though there was no humor in it. "Put it this way—sex with *Stuart* wasn't all that interesting," she said dryly, having experienced the greatest sex of her life but not about to tell her mother.

Justine narrowed her eyes. "So it's this Raul, Rolfe, whatever the hell his real name is. I just hope you haven't spread your legs for him."

Cecile flinched. "That's my business, Mother," she said, thinking her mother could be as vulgar as the best of them.

"The only thing that surprises me is he's not married."

"God knows how he missed out!" Cecile gave a wry sigh. She looked at her mother, who she believed, deep in her heart, loved her. "Have you forgotten so quickly how he saved me from certain injury, possibly death?"

Justine's smile was terrible to see. "Oh, he's brave enough, I grant you that. A marvelous-looking man if you want to be seduced, but from what Stuart tells me, he's a con man. It's written all over him. He set the whole thing up. Meeting Daddy, then you. He knew he was bound to get you to fall in love with him. Your head has always been in the clouds. He broke every rule of decency, lying to Daddy—"

"He didn't actually lie, did he?" Cecile found herself defending Rolfe, even though her heart was broken. "He is who he said he was. Maybe Raul is actually Rolfe, but his stepfather legally adopted him."

"That much might be true, but the rest is all deception," Justine said with lofty disdain.

"What about the deception in *this* family?" Cecile countered sharply. "According to Rolfe, his family suffered terribly and the person who made absolutely sure they suffered was Nan. Even now I can't believe it."

Justine looked poleaxed. "What in the world are you talking about?"

Was it possible her mother knew no more than she did? "Didn't Stuart hand over a copy of his report?" Cecile asked. "It doesn't tell the whole story, according to Rolfe, but he claims that Nan used all the Moreland clout to ruin Rolfe's grandfather and drive the family off their land."

"Whatever for? I read no report." Justine frowned ferociously, resuming her destruction of a charcoal-gray cardigan. "I don't want to hear all this. It's ancient history, anyway. Stuart told me Raul Montalvan is really Rolfe Chandler. His father, from all accounts, was a nobody who got himself killed playing polo over in Argentina where he presumably went to get a job and make some money. His mother's brother was the young hoodlum who was responsible for the death of my brother—*your* uncle I might point out. This Rolfe, this con man, came back to Australia for the grand hustle. He's in the polo game, isn't he? He breeds ponies. He thoroughly researched his mark. Can't you see that? Once he met you, he counted on your falling into his arms. You have, haven't you, you little fool! You couldn't possibly handle a man like that."

"Maybe not," Cecile admitted, picking up her handbag. "You haven't had a lot of success, either. I was a *fool* to come here, Mother, a fool to try to support you. You turn people away. This is a beautiful big house—you have done a great deal for me and Dad—for which I thank you. You are a wonderful hostess, a stunning-looking woman, but you're cheerless and so is this house. I don't wonder Dad wants to get out from under. I don't wonder he wants to know some happiness in the years ahead. And it's disgusting what you're doing." She indicated with a thrust of her chin the piles of ruined clothing that lay on the carpet. "There's no dignity to it. I think you should stop."

"Stop!" Justine's voice rose to glass-breaking point. She rushed forward, robe flying like wings, and before Cecile knew it was coming, struck her daughter across the face. "How dare you!"

Cecile staggered, slowly righted herself, her distress tinged with relief her mother had dropped the scissors. She couldn't imagine at this point how they would ever make their way back. "But I *do* dare, Mother," she said quietly. "I am sorry for you. I'm very sorry for you, but it's impossible for me to stay any longer. You're not—what was it?—*frail* like me. You're one tough lady. I've no doubt you'll get through this, then make up another cover story. You're good at that. You don't love Dad, anyway. At the risk of another smack in the face, I suggest you don't know *how* to love, Mother. Now, I don't think there's anything more I can do for you, so I may as well be on my way. I'll see myself out."

"You do that!" Justine shouted after her daughter. "You and your father, both of you traitors. *Ingrates!* You might have Daddy wrapped around your little finger, but from this day forth in my book you're disinherited."

"Probably a good idea," Cecile answered coolly from the doorway. "Use some of the money to see a good psychiatrist, Mother. You've got lots of problems. It's about time you confronted them."

FOR DAYS AFTER Cecile returned to Melbourne, Rolfe battled his demons. It was an unexpected twist for someone to make *him* feel really bad, but she had succeeded, a *Moreland*. Now he was far too involved with Cecile not to put away all thoughts of revenge. His dark quest had obsessed him for too long. After that afternoon when they had made such sublime love he had discarded all his old hatreds like so much broken furniture held for too long in an attic. History hadn't been kind to his family. It hadn't been kind to the Morelands, either. He had to look to the future.

There *was* no future without Cecile. No future that offered such glorious promise. But what could he offer her? Well, he had worked hard and put away enough. Wealth didn't automatically bring happiness, anyway. More often, it was the reverse.

Finally he made up his mind what he should do. He would go to Joel Moreland and make a clean breast of everything: his background, his dark intentions, his once all-consuming quest for revenge. He would tell Joel Moreland what he had managed to find out. Joel Moreland, because of his grandson Daniel's sad story, already knew what his late wife, Frances, had been capable of. He had to lay it all on the line. Make a full confession. He had hated deceiving Joel, anyway. He would tell Joel everything save his love for Cecile. That was a secret he intended to hold close to his heart.

She had gone away without a word to him, no parting message. He knew she was shocked at his deception. He knew she no longer trusted him, and trust was very important to her. It would be a long road back to regain her confidence. But what they had shared that tumultuous afternoon, the glory of it, continued to warm him, heart and soul. It gave him the courage to confront the Man with the Midas Touch.

WHEN HE ARRIVED at the Moreland mansion, the house manager, a pleasant, competent man in his late fifties, showed him into the garden room at the rear of the house. A large collection of tropical orchids was in spectacular bloom, many he was familiar with from his mother's extensive collection. Great luxuriant ferns suspended in baskets from the huge beams that supported the soaring ceiling drew the eye upward. It was a beautiful room. Joel was sitting at a large circular glass-topped table surrounded by papers, enjoying a cup of tea, but he rose and held out his hand.

"Raul, how nice you've come to keep me company."

The welcoming smile made Rolfe feel even more sick at heart. How long would the smiles last? "How are you, sir?" His nerves on edge, he slipped back into formal address.

"Missing my beautiful Cecile." Joel sighed. "Apart from that, I feel like a million bucks. And you, Raul? You look a little tense. Sit down, sit down. Would you like tea, coffee, a cold drink?"

"Nothing, thank you, sir."

"You're very formal today." The remarkable eyes scanned him. Eyes that took in everything about a person.

"I hold you in the greatest respect," Rolfe answered gravely.

"So what's on your mind?" Joel asked. "You've obviously got a problem. I suspect you're missing Cecile, too?"

Rolfe's face went taut. "I doubt she's missing me."

"Oh? I thought you two were madly in love?"

Rolfe's expression registered his shock. "I beg your pardon, sir?"

"I've got eyes, my boy!" Joel scoffed. "You must remember I'm Cecile's granddad. I know every expression that crosses her face, every little inflection in her voice. She's the closest person in the world to me. Closer than my daughter, who has never forgiven me for neglecting her with my absence. Closer even than my grandson, Daniel, so new to me. But I love all three. So you could say Cecile is an open book to me."

"Then you must have sensed she's finished with me now?" Rolfe asked somewhat grimly.

"Well, I knew something was wrong," Joel acknowledged. "There was the trauma of the broken engagement, but then there has been another major concern. You'll find out soon enough. My daughter, Justine, and her husband are splitting up after thirty years of marriage. I understood that was the reason Cecile hurried off home."

"I never knew," Rolfe confessed, feeling more and more rejected. "I had thought Cecile's parents' marriage was rock solid."

"Well, it might have appeared to be. It was certainly no battlefield, but sadly at the end of the day it has no real meaning. In many ways Justine and Howard led isolated lives. Howard devoted himself to the business. I have nothing but praise for him in that regard. My daughter devoted her life to being the perfect wife, and in many respects she was. But one reaches a stage in life when all the old ambitions take a back seat. People as they age begin to think very seriously about the quality of their emotional life. Making money, keeping it intact is no longer as important as it once was. I would have traded everything in the blink of an eye for the life of my son. That was not to be, but I have Daniel, for which I daily thank God. My daughter Justine is understandably devastated, but I'm confident she'll slam down a few barriers and regroup. She has never suffered from loneliness you see, or introspection."

"So it was Cecile's father who wanted to leave?" Rolfe remembered Howard Moreland as being an uncommonly attractive and charming man.

"Apparently. There's another woman, of course. There always is. But this woman—it's not a case of Howard leaving my daughter for a much younger woman—must be able to make my son-in-law happy. Cecile flew home to be with her mother, but that wasn't overly successful, she tells me. Justine is quite capable of doing Howard a lot of harm. I'll get drawn into it fairly soon. So will you."

Rolfe gazed unseeingly around the beautiful plant-filled room. "Not when you hear what I have to say. There are things about me, Joel, you don't know."

"Why don't you go ahead and tell me," Moreland invited briskly, then held up a staying hand. "I think I will get a fresh pot of tea made and some coffee, maybe a few sandwiches?" he suggested. "You look like you need a bit of bucking up. I'm happy you've come to me with your problems, Raul. I'll help you in any way I can."

Would he be happy afterward? Rolfe thought. Having made his decision, he had no option but to launch the missiles that would shatter Joel Moreland's good opinion of him. He suddenly realized that the man's opinion mattered a great deal.

Rolfe began to speak in a low measured tone. He started from when he first arrived in the Territory. He didn't attempt to tone down his reason for returning to the place of his birth. He had meant to cause the Morelands pain....

He was not interrupted. No matter what the revelation, Joel Moreland never said a word. He waited until Rolfe finished speaking before sitting back in his chair, removing his glasses and rubbing the bridge of his nose.

"Revenge never works, Rolfe, does it?" he said finally, in a quiet musing tone. "Rolfe suits you better than Raul, by the way. Hate is corrosive. It eats away at the soul. I've firsthand experience of that—not so much myself, hate doesn't seem to be part of my nature—but I've seen it become an integral part of the lives of so many others. First of all I must tell you not all of this comes as a surprise."

Rolfe pulled upright in his chair. "I should have known."

"Yes, you should," Joel agreed. "I had no intention

whatever of doing any check on you if that's what you're thinking. I liked you, that's all there was to it. I took to you on sight. My instincts have never let me down. I could see Ceci was attracted to you. But I have many contacts in the international world of polo. You must realize that."

"Of course." Rolfe had allowed for the fact Joel Moreland might check on him. He had taken the chance.

"I sell many of my polo ponies overseas, including Argentina," Joel explained. "However, it was sheer chance that drew me into conversation with a South American buyer, a Brazilian actually, who knows your stepfather, and has in the past done business with him. I had accepted you were who you said you were—Raul Montalvan. I mentioned your name in passing. When this man told me something of your story, which he'd had from your stepfather, my heart went out to you. I heard how your father was killed, how your mother was left virtually a penniless young widow in a strange country with a young son to rear. How she later married Ramon Montalvan, an excellent man. I received quite a shock when I further learned your mother was an Australian, as was her late husband and of course, you. I hadn't been expecting that at all. After that, I made my own inquiries. I felt in my bones—some presentiment, some fragment of memory— there was a connection. Possibly it was your father's name. I vaguely remembered him as being a promising polo player. It was easy to fill in the rest."

"Dear God!" Rolfe leaned forward and buried his face in his hands. How long had Joel known? How could he still smile?

"My son's death overwhelmed me," Joel said. "You must understand that. You, too, know all about grief. I was desolate. For a time all the life drained out of me. My success, my position in life, meant nothing, though I was forced to keep going. So many people, towns, depended on me for their livelihood. I know now my wife, Frances, was the cause of great unhappiness, great hurt and great wrong. I should have been more aware of what was going on, so I, too, bear the burden of guilt. I can only plead I was adrift in a nightmare and ask for forgiveness. I had such grand plans for Jared. Plans that differed from my wife's. One of her pet objectives was to marry him off to some young woman suitable in her eyes and one I imagine Frances thought she could control. Instead all my son got was a marble headstone. I have arranged that fresh flowers be laid on his grave every day that I live."

"My uncle Benjie didn't get that," Rolfe pointed out quietly. "When did you first know?" He looked into Joel Moreland's eyes. "You gave no sign. You never told Cecile, obviously."

"I think I'm a good judge of men, Rolfe. I held my tongue, waiting to see what you would do. I've gone further. It's something I felt I should do. I've bought back your grandfather's property. It's very run-down, but it's yours to do whatever you like with. Work it, put a manager on it. I don't imagine you want to sell it."

Rolfe looked back in a daze. "But surely…" He could get no further, spearing his hand into his hair in distraction. Whatever he'd expected of today's traumatic encounter it wasn't this.

"I've made other investigations into my son's death—far too late—though nothing will bring Jared back or your uncle Benjamin. It seems appalling to me to malign my poor Frances—I know she passed many many unhappy years—but she held to denying her own grandson until she was on her deathbed. She carried the secret of how she had imperiled your family to her grave. I ask you to forgive her. To forgive me. On the level of family, Frances was obsessive to a cautionary degree. She adored Jared. That he fell in love with one of our little housemaids and got her pregnant goaded Frances beyond endurance. Then Jared was killed. I knew my son. I'm absolutely certain he had no idea Johanna was carrying his child. If he had, he would have married her and I would have stood beside them both. Your family had the great misfortune to face a bereaved mother's wrath. It falls on me, Rolfe, all these many years later, to make retribution. I ought to have known. With Johanna and my son, I was too involved with my business affairs to notice a romance going on right under my nose. When Jared was killed I was like a man in a coma. I functioned on one level but not on another. That's not much of a defense, I know."

"I think it is, sir." Rolfe's voice was both gentle and understanding.

"You've suffered greatly, haven't you, Rolfe?" Joel asked, looking into the younger man's dark eyes.

Rolfe shrugged off the many blighted areas of his life. Something so far he had been totally unable to do. "Not in any material sense," he said. "My stepfather, Ramon, is a generous, good-hearted man. He adores my mother and because of her he tried very hard with me. Gradually I settled down, though for a long time I was pretty wild. For the last five years I've been in charge of the breeding program of our polo ponies and their training, as you now know. Horses are my passion. I have a special way with them. Ramon thought so, too."

"Horses are my passion, as well," Joel confirmed. "I understand from my Brazilian friend, you were gaining quite a reputation. I've been told your stepfather is particularly proud of your ability to turn out the finest polo ponies. I've checked the sales for the Montalvan estancia. Top prices."

For the first time Rolfe smiled. "It's a great satisfaction to my family—my Argentinian family—I've been so successful, but it wouldn't have happened without my stepfather. It was Ramon who gave me the opportunity and authority over others much longer in the business. If he hadn't, perhaps I would be dead on the polo field like my father from a fatal kick in the head."

Joel visibly shuddered. "Don't say that, Rolfe!" he implored. "Has what I've said given you any peace at all?"

Rolfe looked away, much moved. "I thought you'd brand me an impostor, a fortune hunter, someone utterly untrustworthy."

"Well, there are such men about," Joel said dryly, "but I was and am still prepared to put my trust in you." He put out his hand.

Rolfe took it. "I can never thank you enough for the kindness and understanding of your response. It means a great deal to me. I know I've lost and deserve to lose Cecile's trust. In her beautiful eyes I'm a badly flawed man."

"Then you'll have to work to persuade her otherwise, won't you?" Joel told him bracingly. "I can say it now, but I wasn't happy about her marrying Stuart Carlson. I didn't think I had the right to interfere. Although before you appeared on the scene, I was getting around to it. My daughter Justine is a very strong-minded woman like her mother before her. She has always tried to deny Cecile complete freedom of action. Stuart was *Justine's* choice."

"Carlson had his own dossier compiled on me." Rolfe brought it out into the open.

"Did he now!" Joel whistled softly. "I think I'll have to persuade him to burn it. Not that there could be anything in it to actually discredit you in any way, which obviously was what he hoped. Cecile knows about this?"

Rolfe nodded. "He sent it to her. She thinks the worst of me."

"He sent it to her, did he?" Joel Moreland's voice filled with contempt. "Tells you what sort of man he is. Give Cecile a little time," he advised. "My granddaughter is not the sort of woman who likes to think the worst of anyone. She has a compassion-ate heart. That's why she's so successful with her little patients. She's compassionate and she's clever. She comes up with breakthrough ideas. She's very highly regarded by her peers. She has the gift of healing."

"I don't doubt that for a moment," Rolfe said with deep fervor. "She healed me."

IT WAS EARLY AFTERNOON some three weeks later. Cecile was sitting at her desk, looking at Ellie Wheeler's drawings. Cecile, who thought she was beyond being shocked, was brought to the edge of actual nausea. Since returning to her practice, she had made special time for Ellie, fitting her into her very busy schedule to the extent she was starting earlier and finishing late with many a lunch break missed. But what did that matter? Ellie was in need of intensive therapy. Ellie's mother had brought in the girl originally because Ellie's latest school had insisted on Ellie's getting counseling. There would have been no counseling otherwise, Cecile knew. But as hard as she tried, she hadn't been able to make the breakthrough she was seeking, although they were doing a lot better now that Cecile had confined Mrs. Wheeler to the waiting room. Mrs. Wheeler had been adamant she be allowed in, but Cecile had quietly said no. Ellie was a very difficult child, physically abusive to her mother, to her schoolmates and of recent times to her younger brother. Both parents—Cecile had met the father once—to all appearances were good caring people, patient and understanding. But they were almost at the end of their tether, now that Ellie had begun attacking her brother. Ellie was under a two-week suspension from school. her previous school had asked for her to be removed—because she had spat at and kicked the male sports master when he attempted to help her tie up her shoelaces. Ellie had been deliberately dawdling, holding up the class. "A small fury!" was the way the teacher described her during the attack. "She even punched me!"

Ellie, despite her angelic appearance, beautiful blond hair and big blue eyes, acted as much like a little devil. Cecile had tested her for a number of personality disorders, as well as ADD and autism. Her behavior didn't match any of those. Previously Ellie had been considered of exceptional intelligence—her father was a doctor, her mother a music teacher—but at her new school Ellie had gained the reputation for not only being highly disruptive and aggressive, but downright stupid. Many teachers along the way had tried to help her, baffled and challenged by the child. Because of her looks, other children had tried to befriend her, only to be met with bites, scratches and hostile rejection.

"Is she psychotic?" Dr. Peter Wheeler, Ellie's father, had asked in his pleasant cultivated voice, his gray eyes behind dark-framed glasses deeply concerned.

"She wasn't always like this," Marcie Wheeler added, sounding so close to tears her husband had grabbed for her hand.

ELLIE WASN'T STUPID. Far from it. Cecile had divined that from the moment she had met the child. But Ellie was emotionally disturbed. There had to be good reasons for why the child was acting so badly. Cecile knew there was a lot going on behind the either perfectly blank or wildly mutinous little face. Just those two expressions. With her mother present Ellie was given to extreme temper tantrums that her mother appeared totally unable to control. Now that Cecile was working with the child alone, Ellie's behavior had settled closer to normal, and the way she swiftly solved puzzles showed an exceptional intelligence at work. She was even allowing Cecile to come close and she was directly meeting Cecile's eyes, something she hadn't done until that very week. Cecile knew she had been under close scrutiny by the child, and thankfully she appeared to have passed whatever tests Ellie had set. To gain the trust of a child was great progress. Cecile had been quietly thrilled.

Now *this!*

Of course she had considered this possibility, but rejected it. Dr. Peter Wheeler had been described on all sides as a good caring man and a fine doctor. He had certainly come across that way. Cecile had focused all her analyzing powers on his mannerisms, expressions, body language and his account of his troubled little daughter's history. Here was a devoted father.

But my God! The reality could not have been more different! And the mind-blowing arrogance of the man allowing counseling to go ahead! Of course the school had insisted on it and Ellie was fast running out of schools, but there was so much to *hide,* so much that didn't bear examination. Yet Peter Wheeler obviously thought he had such control over his child, or Ellie was so much in fear of him—she would have been threatened with punishment should she ever speak the unspeakable—that the whole sordid story would never see the light of day. Her father's power over her was central to her life.

Only, Ellie had broken free! Dr Wheeler hadn't allowed for Ellie's intelligence and courage. She was a remarkable child whose range of behavioral problems had not as yet progressed beyond the problems of other children Cecile had treated who were not the victims of sexual abuse. Ellie was truly a fighter. Cecile took a shuddering breath, thinking that because of her, because she'd been away, this brave little girl had been left longer in hell. Drawing had long been used as therapy when dealing with emotionally disturbed children. Ellie's drawings to date had been a series of wild interlocking circles always in black and charcoal signifying, to Cecile's mind, that Ellie regarded herself as being in a prison. Some days the strokes suggested barbed wire.

Now *this!*

Ellie had sat quietly while she had been drawing what could only be described as a sexually abused child's cries for help. Sexual abuse was routinely considered early in therapy, but Ellie had been positively brilliant in hiding what had been happening to her and was probably still happening. So much for the slowness or the stupidity! Tears sprang to Cecile's eyes as she took the colored drawings in hand. Here was a child with long curly blond hair, big blue eyes and *no mouth*. Tears splashed from her eyes to the floor. Another showed the same child in bed with a tall figure with huge black wings like a bat looming over her. Another showed the child locked in a forest with a woman—her mother?—running away from her to the extreme edge of the trees.

"Do you see?" Ellie came around the desk to whisper, a terrible sadness seeping out of her eyes. "Do you see what's been happening to me?"

Cecile lifted her head to meet the child's eyes. "Yes, I see, Ellie. I want to tell you you're a very brave girl. I'm proud of you."

"Are you?" Ellie's voice showed a tiny burst of pleasure. "I wanted to tell Mummy, but I knew she wouldn't listen. She's afraid to say anything to Daddy. We all have to be very careful around him, even Josh. He loves Josh. He doesn't love me. He tells me he loves me, but he's killing me. He wants to kill me."

Cecile didn't admonish the child. She didn't murmur, "That's a terrible thing to say about your father, Ellie." She remained silent, listening for what else Ellie would say.

There was more. A lot more, utterly conclusive as far as Cecile was concerned. And it had to stop *today!* For a ten-year-old child to so graphically describe tearing, searing physical pain, the things that were done to her body. The landscape of a man's body. The *weight* of her abuser. It was all being taped. Cecile's gentle voice encouraged the child in telling her appalling tale, without ever leading her. This was Ellie's terrible story. Ellie had to be protected.

But first there were procedures to be followed. Children's Services. She was well acquainted with the people there. One woman in particular, a woman of enormous understand-

ing and sensitivity. Cecile picked up the phone, after telling
Ellie she needed to talk to her mother.

"Do I have to stay there?"

"No, dear."

Ellie looked relieved, though there was still profound fear
in her eyes. "She won't believe me. She'll tell Daddy."

"You want this to stop, don't you, Ellie?" Cecile asked
quietly.

"Oh yes! Will you help me? I don't want to go home. I
don't ever want to go to bed. It's not my fault."

"Never!" Cecile shook her head, taking the trusting hand
the child held out to her. "You must never ever blame yourself."

"Daddy said he'd kill us all if I told."

Such sickness of the soul! It seemed almost inconceivable
Dr. Peter Wheeler, who presented so well, was the father from
hell. Cecile would never have guessed such a depth of de-
pravity in the man. She was stunned he was a doctor. And
alarmed. Other children could be under threat. "That's not
going to happen, Ellie," Cecile said, radiating comfort and
quiet authority to the child. "You have *me* to help you. *I* have
the support of kind people who devote their lives to helping
children like you. It will be safe for you to talk to them and
I'll be there. You and your mother *and* Josh are going to get
help. I promise."

Only it wasn't that easy. Ellie's mother at first called her
child "a lying little monster" and refused to believe what Ellie
had said. "She's made it all up. She's not stupid. She's cruel
and cunning and a shocking little troublemaker. She's trying
to come between me and my husband. Peter's a *doctor!* A
man who cares! He's a saint!"

"He'll get the opportunity to prove it, Mrs. Wheeler," Cecile said, keeping all trace of revulsion out of her voice. "Children do lie. They make certain things up. They can even fool experts, but I'm prepared to believe a medical examination will prove Ellie is telling the truth. No child I've ever spoken with, living in the suburbs with a saint for a father, could describe so graphically sexual abuse. Ellie has a great deal of courage. I'm wondering if *you* knew about it and kept quiet?" Cecile, though sickened, gave the woman a chance. "You were too frightened to get help? I understand how that can happen."

Understand but never never condone.

Cecile played back the tape of Ellie's story, while her mother cried convulsively, the bitter tears streaming down her face as she listened and stared at the drawings. "Where is she, my little Ellie?" she asked finally, looking beaten into the ground. "Will she ever forgive me? I'm not a mother at all. I'm a gutless coward who has lived at my husband's mercy, but not anymore! Tell me what to do."

CECILE RETURNED to her apartment that evening feeling utterly drained. Damning evidence of sexual abuse had been found during Ellie's medical examination, conducted by a kindly woman doctor Cecile and her colleagues often called in. Josh had been picked up from school by the police. The family had been taken to a safe house, pending charges being laid. "We'll never be safe," Mrs. Wheeler had murmured fearfully to Cecile at the last moment, her shoulders hunched in strain. Her two children stood quietly a little distance away, hand in hand. "There's *no* safe place."

"You'll be safe if he's in jail," Cecile told her, placing a hand on the woman's shoulder, feeling the rigidity there. "Your husband can't get away with this anymore, Mrs. Wheeler. You have to be strong for your family."

"He was such a sweet man," Marcie Wheeler confided in the voice of the lovesick teenager she once had been. "He was hurt badly in a car accident five years ago. Do you think it was that? Something twisted his mind?" she asked hopefully. Eyes as blue as her daughter's appealed to Cecile. Marcie Wheeler was a very pretty woman.

"I can't help with that, Mrs. Wheeler," Cecile said flatly, shaking her head, "but I *can* help you."

AT HOME Cecile played back her phone messages, which included one from her father confirming their lunch date for the following week. Soon after her disastrous confrontation with her mother, she had conceded to her father's plea to meet the new woman in his life, Patricia Northam. Patricia had a beach house on a beautiful stretch of the Mornington Peninsula, which Cecile discovered was set in native bushland with a wonderful view of the sea. The two of them were waiting to greet her at the front of the cottage, their arms entwined.

Her father looked ten years younger and an altogether different person. She'd rarely seen him out of his tailored business suits and his expensive smart, casual clothes. But here he wore an ordinary pair of cargo pants, a black cotton T-shirt and canvas trainers on his feet. The woman tucked beneath his arm looked as fragile as a china doll. She had very curly red hair that reached past her shoulders, unlined skin warmly sprinkled with freckles and eyes as blue as the sparkling sea. As casually dressed as Cecile's father, she wore espadrilles on her feet; even with the wedge heels, she was tiny. She couldn't have looked more different from Cecile's mother. Her father had always appeared to admire the "glamour girls," tall, confident women as well-groomed as racehorses, always dressed in the height of fashion—like Justine. Patricia, or "Patty" as he called her, was a big surprise. She was fresh and natural, quite without artifice.

Her father had come forward to give her a hug and kiss her cheek, thanking her a little awkwardly for coming before introducing Patricia. This was accompanied by a loving look Cecile had never seen when he looked at her mother. Cecile had expected the meeting wouldn't be all that easy for any of them, but she found herself warming to Patricia despite her loyalty to her mother.

Cecile learned Patty's invalid mother had died several months back. Patty had been devoted to her, never marrying. Her mother had left her the cottage and their Melbourne apartment.

"She's led a life of service," Howard had told Cecile quietly. "Now I want to look after her. Your mother never needed looking after. She never needed me except as the obligatory husband. She actively discouraged me from playing a larger role with you. But that's all over. I want us to be close, Cecile. You're my daughter, my only child. I never wanted to hurt Justine, but I think you'll find it's mostly her pride that's been stung."

Cecile hadn't had the heart to comment on the hatchet job her mother had done on his clothes and he didn't mention it, either. Her father looked and acted a different man, more *real* than she had ever seen him. He had resigned his position as Moreland Minerals' CEO. "Joel never asked for my resignation," he told her. "Your grandfather knows how long and hard I've worked for the company, but we both agreed that my staying on would be nigh on impossible with your mother on the board. So, I'm taking early retirement. I intend to enjoy what's left of my life, Ceci!"

Cecile had found it hard to blame him.

She moved to her bedroom and quickly changed out of her elegant gray suit, hung it in the closet, then deciding to take a quick shower, walked into the ensuite bathroom. She brushed her teeth first in an effort to get the taste of evil out of her mouth. She wasn't surprised to see her hands were shaking. The whole Ellie episode had upset her tremendously, although Ellie was far from being the only sexually abused child she had treated. Ellie, however, had been very much better at keeping her dark secret padlocked.

Beneath the shower she allowed herself to weep for all the abused children of the world. The tears streamed down her face. Jets of water washed them away. This was her private place for crying. No one had to know about it. Sometimes her job made her very emotional. She knew she had to guard against it or go to pieces, but children like Ellie made that very difficult.

Afterward she rubbed a deliciously scented moisturizer over her face and body, as though the aroma and the massage would help her relax. There was no way she could banish her sadness, but she was feeling a little better. She had done as much as she could do. The authorities had to do the rest. Lack of faith in Marcie Wheeler had crept over her slowly. She had confided this lack of faith to her good friend Susan Bryant at Children's Services. Susan, ten years older and very experienced, wasn't particularly surprised. "Usually the mothers know about the abuse," Susan said, "but they're so emotionally battered themselves they can't bring themselves to do a thing about it. For all we know the good Dr. Wheeler could have been abusing *her,* too. I wouldn't be in the least surprised."

The fact Susan had picked up on Marcie Wheeler's vulnerability made Cecile feel easier. It would be dreadful if Ellie had to be taken from the only parent that was left to look after her.

Dressed in a cool ankle-length caftan, she poured herself a glass of white wine from her refrigerator. She felt incredibly lonely. Something she had never really experienced until she banished Rolfe from her life. He'd opened a door onto a rapturous world for her. He had been *everything* to her, so his deception had left her shaken to her core and accusing herself of every kind of weakness, so much so that when she had first arrived back, she doubted her ability to pick up and go on with her stressful job. She'd refused to take his calls, though she'd played his messages over and over just to hear his voice. He'd begged her to allow him to see her, but her underlying fear was he was still using her and would continue to. He had seen himself as an avenger on her family since his childhood. Powerful obsessions didn't disappear overnight.

If ever!

She had spoken to her grandfather many times. On one occasion he confided he bought back the old Lockhart cattle station, which was very run-down, and deeded it over to Rolfe.

Could that have been one of Rolfe's goals? The loss of his own inheritance had plagued him. He'd told her so.

"Not that it could possibly compensate him for what he

and his family suffered," her grandfather had offered as a reason for his generosity.

Quite simply Raul Montalvan or Rolfe Chandler, whatever he in his heart called himself, had won over the Man with the Midas Touch. No mean feat! It had been a coup on Rolfe's part to go to her grandfather with a full confession. Her grandfather was a decent, highly principled man. He had wanted desperately to make amends for the sins of her grandmother.

And as for her, she had fallen madly in love with him, or at the very least been engulfed by powerful emotions, at their first meeting. Whether it was possible to trust him again she was a long way from deciding.

She was drawn to the kitchen to make herself something to eat—a light pasta with ricotta and prosciutto? She had fresh herbs growing on her balcony—chives, basil, coriander, mint, dill and fiery little chillies—but she couldn't be bothered cooking a sauce. The loud buzz of her security monitor startled her. Who could it be at this hour? She wasn't expecting anyone. Her friends always rang before they called. Maybe it was a mistake, a visitor wanting someone else. It happened.

She checked what she was wearing. Perfectly presentable to go to the door if she had to, in fact, very pretty if a bit on the sheer side.

She walked the few steps to the wall-mounted monitor and saw a messenger wearing a cap with a logo on it. She couldn't read what it was. He was holding a bouquet of flowers so big they obscured his face.

Well, well, life was indeed surprising! "Yes?"

"Delivery for Ms. Moreland."

"Thank you. I'll let you in." She pressed the button to release the security door. Was it possible the flowers were from Rolfe? She couldn't help the involuntary rush of hope, then chided herself not only for the feeling, which clearly betrayed her ambivalence, but for being stupid. He didn't even know where she lived. What an exercise in futility it was trying to clear all thoughts of him from her head. It was becoming more and more difficult, not easier, with the passing of the days and weeks. The flowers could be from a longtime admirer of hers, Adam Dahl, who'd begun ringing her since her breakup with Stuart had become common knowledge. The bouquet looked enormous. Adam always had been one for going over the top. She had already accepted one of his invitations to dinner. No reason why she couldn't. She was a free woman.

No, that was far from true. In her present mood and state she felt she would never be free of Rolfe.

A faint sigh on her lips, Cecile opened the door, startled to see the messenger already there. He must have stepped straight into the lift. She felt a momentary pang of anxiety. Wasn't it too late for a delivery? Although it *was* Friday, late night shopping.

She put out her hand to take the bouquet, but before she had time to think what was happening, the messenger shoved her back forcibly into the entrance hall of her apartment, shutting the door behind him. She gave a tiny shriek of alarm.

"Afraid, are you?" Peter Wheeler snarled, pitching the bouquet violently across the living room where it fell in a scatter of tall, bloodred gladioli and silver wrapping paper.

Through her fear, Cecile managed to think hard. "What are you doing here, Dr. Wheeler?" she demanded, succeeding in her effort to keep her voice from sounding too panicked. "I'm expecting a friend to drop by any minute now."

"Dressed like that?" He ran his eyes over the contours of her body, revealed by the sheer fabric. He showed not the slightest interest in her. Oh, no, this was a man who liked *little* girls! He wasn't wearing his glasses. She suspected now they were mostly for effect. His eyes were cold and hard like dull gray pebbles that gave back no light.

"I assure you he *will* be here," Cecile said with a show of confidence. "If you have any sense at all, you'll go."

"Go? Where do I go?" he asked in furious frustration. "Thanks to you, the police are out looking for me."

"Then shouldn't you be giving yourself up," Cecile retorted. "They *will* find you."

"They'll find you, too," he said, with a peculiar sliver of a smile.

Cecile felt a sickening sensation in the pit of her stomach. "You're threatening me, are you?" Her voice was absolutely steady. "It's not a good time for you to do it. My friend is a lawyer."

"Then the one thing you must not do is warn him," Wheeler said, not taking his eyes off her. "I don't want to punish him. Just you. You've ruined my life. I face jail. I face the loss of Ellie. You wouldn't know, you sanctimonious bitch, but I *love* her." His face twisted in genuine anguish.

Cecile felt bile rise to her throat. "Love?" she exploded, thinking she would be forever haunted by what Ellie had told her. "You mean you've been abusing her for a very long time. You're a sick man, *Doctor* Wheeler. But you couldn't help yourself, could you? You will wind up in prison, though. I wouldn't want to spend any time there, a man like you, a pedophile. A man who's preyed on his own little daughter. The other prisoners will—"

"Shut your mouth!" Wheeler threw a savage punch, but Cecile was too quick for him. Adrenaline pumping, she ducked and picked up a vase, then hurled it as hard as she could—not at Wheeler but at the etched-glass partition in the entrance hall. It broke into great shards with a loud shattering sound. The apartments were pretty soundproof, but someone might hear something and come to investigate.

Cecile was thinking rapidly. Where was her mobile phone? Damn it, it was still in her bedroom, though she had taken it out of her bag. Joyce Walden, a widow in her early seventies, lived in the adjoining unit. Joyce was inclined to be nosy, which would help, though her sliding glass doors to the rear terrace would be shut with the television and the air-conditioning going full blast. She wouldn't want Joyce to be drawn into any danger, but she could shout, "Call the police!" should Joyce take it into her head to knock.

She began to yell, "Help!" at the top of her voice, but Wheeler sprang at her, a big strong man bent on shutting her up.

And then what? Cecile thought. Would he kill her? How had he found out where she lived? Why hadn't he already been picked up by the police?

"You stupid bitch!" His fierce open-handed slap connected just enough to send her sprawling backward. She fell onto a sofa, where he leaned threateningly over her. "Don't try that again or I promise you you'll be sorry."

"Who told you where I lived?" She threw up her chin, determined not to show fear. He'd had enough of that from his wife and poor little Ellie.

"Easy," he sneered. "I followed you to this building weeks ago. You were trouble right from the beginning. Ellie liked you.

She's never liked anyone else. Her bloody fool mother actually rang me to tell me to run. Can you beat that?"

"Your *wife* tipped you off?" Cecile thought of Marcie Wheeler with disgust and pity.

"She loves me, don't you know?" he crowed with sickening triumph.

"Then she is indeed a bloody fool," Cecile said with the utmost contempt.

His face turned to granite. "I told you to shut up. You can't, can you? You're the psychologist, trained to keep people talking. But this should do the trick." With that weird smirk on his face, Wheeler withdrew a syringe from the inside pocket of his bomber jacket. Cecile saw it contained a colorless liquid.

Her throat went so dry she had difficulty speaking. "What do you think you're going to do with that?"

"Shut you up of course. For good. Only fair, don't you think? You ruin my life. I finish off yours."

"Before you do, what I want to know is this. Indulge me, can't you? You have the upper hand. If your wife warned you, why didn't you simply run? Make your getaway. You can still do it. Isn't that more important than killing me? Getting away?" If she *could* keep him talking, humor him in some way, maybe she could make a break for it. He hadn't locked the door to the apartment, only closed it, before moving into the living room.

"You want to see Ellie again, don't you?" She hated using the child's name, but that was the only connection she thought might work. "Can't you tell me how this first happened? I want to hear. I'm used to listening. What destructive impulses drove you? Or were you forced into it? Were

you so unhappy with your wife—the sex was so inade-
quate—you turned to the child? How did you keep your
secret from your wife, or did she know? Evil is completely
foreign to a moral man. Aren't you a moral man, Dr.
Wheeler? Were you the victim of sexual abuse? Please—help
me to understand."

He paused, his face twisted as though he really sought to
pinpoint the time when his pedophilia began to manifest
itself. He was as pale as a ghost and there was a small involuntary twitch on the left side of his mouth.

"It's all right, you can trust me," she said in a calm, quiet
voice.

"I didn't feel that way about other children, other little
girls," he said, a vein pulsing in his temple. "It was only Ellie.
She was so affectionate with me, kissing me and sitting on
my knee. You know all about what bloody Freud had to say.
Fathers, daughters, mothers, sons. I fell in love with her."

"Didn't that scare you out of your mind?" she asked with
no vestige of pity.

"Yes. I *hated* myself, but I couldn't stop it."

"You didn't seek treatment, a way of fighting back?"

"God Almighty, who could I tell? You? I have a reputation in this city. Who could I have gone to?"

"You know perfectly well the code of confidentiality. You
could never have been at peace. What you were doing was a
crime. It was your God-given duty to keep your child safe."

"Damn it, I didn't *hurt* her," he shouted. "I loved her. I
wanted her."

"Pig!" Before Cecile could consider the lack of wisdom
she spat out the word.

"Ah, I see." He shook his finger. "You were playing for

time." He turned away, holding the syringe up to the light. "I'm a doctor, remember? I should know what you're up to. You were hoping to make a dash for it. It won't happen. You've destroyed me. I have no career anymore. And I'm a *good* doctor," he declared with desperate pride. "My patients love me. When they wake up and read the newspapers they won't believe it. There's been some terrible mistake. Not Dr. Wheeler! It can't possibly be *him.* There's only one way out for men like me," he said in quite a different voice.

"You plan to shoot *yourself* up, as well?" Cecile asked with contempt. "What is it in that syringe?"

He threw back his head and laughed. "A lethal dose. You have to be punished for making this happen. You understand that, don't you? I'm not a natural-born killer."

"You're natural-born scum!" Cecile, who had been pretending the near paralysis of acceptance, was on her feet very fast indeed, screaming, "Police! Police!" Surely to God someone would hear her! Even if they didn't, Wheeler had become very agitated, his bloodless skin blotched now with red.

Please God, let him forget me and run!

He didn't. He came after her. Cecile picked up the stainless-steel coffeepot on the stove, prepared to throw it. He intended to kill her. In her own apartment, of all places, with its excellent security system. How could she have been so careless to open the door to anyone? Assumptions could be very dangerous. His voice had been distorted, the bouquet of flowers had all but covered his face. She wondered how many other women had been taken in by such a ploy. A lone woman should never be so trusting. She would never see her family again. She would never see the one man she had ever loved. Life was beyond her frail understanding.

The extent of the man's breakdown was carved on his face. It resembled a devilish mask. He looked horrible, quite mad, worlds away from the calm, caring professional who had presented himself at her office.

The energy was draining out of her as the demands on her nervous system had to be met. She hurled the pot, realizing she could throw as many things as she could lay her hands on, but in the end he would overpower her and a terrible sequence of events would ensue.

Still, she had to fight. She didn't have to sit down and wait. As a last resort, fearing the use of such a weapon, Cecile reached into a drawer and pulled out a wicked-looking carving knife, knowing he might well end up using the knife on her, instead of the syringe.

"Hey, hey, hey," he chided, skidding on drops of water that had fallen from the coffee percolator and reaching for the counter to steady himself. "Put that down."

"I'll carve you up if you come near me," Cecile gritted, her eyes glittering brilliantly.

"No one is coming to rescue you, my dear." He laughed. "It's just you and me. It will be bloody easy just to end it!"

CHAPTER THIRTEEN

ROLFE CHECKED into his Melbourne city hotel around 5:30 p.m. He had been traveling most of the day, so he had a quick shower and changed his clothes. It was coming up to a month since he had seen Cecile. A lifetime, when he missed her so badly. He had given her a breathing space, but the urge to come to Melbourne to confront her had been building so powerfully he had surrendered to its demand. He realized the very fact her grandfather had bought back the old Lockhart cattle holding and presented the deed to him would work against him. She would think of it as a continuing con, though he doubted a true con man could put anything over Joel Moreland. Joel knew a great deal of life. He had learned even more from the revelations following the death of his wife, Frances. The discovery he had a grandson called Daniel had made him more deeply understanding of the way Frances Moreland had turned the cool ruthless eye of an enemy on his own family.

Cecile hadn't even been born at the time all this was happening. She couldn't know. She wasn't ready to face it, anyway. It would seem too incredible to her. And why not? From all accounts, Frances Moreland had been a loving grandmother to her. Cecile's thinking would be that had he taken her into his confidence early, it would have validated any *real* feeling he had for her. Instead, by not doing so, he had grossly deceived her. On top of her broken engagement and her parents' marriage breakup, little wonder she had retreated into her shell. Finding out he'd been born in the Northern Territory and not in Argentina would have come as an additional bolt from the blue. Nearly twenty years spent in that country and he could have fooled anyone. His Spanish was Ramon's, the cultivated upper class.

Joel had advised him not to put pressure on Cecile, but he didn't intend to make any demands. It was more she couldn't be allowed to lock him out. That prospect was too grim. What they had shared had affected her as powerfully as it had him. He would stake his life on that. It was a miracle to find bliss in being with another human being. Having experienced that miraculous connection, he couldn't bear to lose it. He had to convince her he was someone on whom she could depend. Someone who most deeply and truly loved her.

He had no intention of returning to Argentina except to visit. His life was here in the country of his birth. His life was with Cecile, if only they could talk through their problems and reach an understanding. He had hesitated about ringing her. He knew she wouldn't answer, but at least she would hear his voice. Tonight he reasoned it would be better to simply arrive on her doorstep rather than alert her with a phone call. It was almost a pity it wasn't pouring rain, though he had heard on the radio a late storm was forecast. She might feel sorry enough for him to let him in. Perhaps even the shock of having him on her doorstep would gain him access for a little while?

In the end, sick of indecisiveness, Rolfe took a cab to

where she lived. Her address wasn't listed in the phone book, but Joel had given it to him. Joel was playing Cupid even as he was trying to play negotiator in his daughter's marital crisis. One way or another Joel was being kept very busy.

Rolfe was paying off the cab driver when he saw a messenger carrying a large bouquet of flowers approach the front entrance of the elegant, up-market building. For some reason, a hunch, he thought they might be for Cecile. Perhaps her ex-fiancé was trying to get back into her good graces. He waited at the curb for a few moments watching the messenger press one of the numbers, then say in a crackling sort of voice that carried on the still air, "Delivery for Ms. Moreland."

For an instant Rolfe considered arriving with the flowers, then rejected that as not a good idea. He waited until the messenger was well inside the building before he made his own approach. He was lucky. Two attractive young women were on their way out. They greeted his arrival with bright faces and bold, assessing "Hi's!" He smiled back, as though he found them equally interesting, then walked with cool confidence inside as though he was either a resident or visiting one. Obviously they hadn't judged him any sort of a security risk.

The lift was sitting at the ground floor. Why hadn't the guy delivering the flowers come down in it? He'd had ample time to hand over the bouquet. Rolfe stepped into the empty lift and pressed the button for Cecile's floor, fully expecting to see the messenger up there waiting to get in. Instead an elderly lady was hovering in the quiet hallway, looking very agitated. When she caught sight of Rolfe, she pressed a finger to her lips indicating she wanted him to be quiet, then beckoned him to an alcove with a tall plate-glass window giving an expansive view over the park opposite.

Rolfe followed, though his reassuring smile had vanished. What was she going to tell him? His face tight, he looked down at her.

"Are you visiting Cecile?" she asked, pointing an arthritic hand at Cecile's door.

"Yes. Is anything the matter?" He wanted her to get to the point.

"I don't know," the woman wavered. "I heard a crash. At least, I thought I heard a crash. My television is on. It's one of my favorite quiz shows, but it's rather noisy. Then I thought I heard Cecile shouting."

Rolfe waited for no more. Fear clamped into him like a steel claw. "Call the police," he instructed. As the old woman scurried back to her apartment to do so, Rolfe considered his options. Knock? Call out her name? Instinct warned him against doing that. He had seen the messenger delivering flowers to her apartment. The messenger had come up. He hadn't gone down. So where was he? Rolfe stood in absolute attention, his ear pressed to the heavy door.

No sound at all from inside. Very cautiously he gripped the doorknob, immensely relieved to feel it turn. What a godsend! He opened the door slowly, his nerves strained against making the slightest noise. One look at the shattered glass partition was enough to make his chest heave. Carefully he sidestepped the shards. Gladioli as red as blood had been tossed all over the floor.

So he *was* here! Kidnapper, rapist, psychopath? Rolfe suppressed a powerful urge to shout out a threat. The police might arrive soon but they would be too late to save anyone who had hurt Cecile from getting pulverized.

There was no one in the living room. He couldn't as yet

see into the kitchen. He dropped into a crouch to inch his way silently across the thick carpet to a position behind one of the sofas. Now that he had a clear view, he was able to see there was no one in the galley kitchen, either. Where had he taken her—the bedroom?

Rolfe's blood ran cold. He stood upright, quietly removing the leather loafers he was wearing before moving cautiously down the hallway.

Still no sound, but he was absolutely certain he wasn't alone in the apartment. He paused for long moments, not daring to draw breath, then he heard a man's voice say tauntingly, "I don't think your friend is coming, my dear. I don't think anyone is coming."

Aren't I, you bastard! Rolfe swore in silent fury, his strong features compressed into granite. He had no fear of confronting another man, even a dangerous, violent man with a weapon. He just had to be very very careful and as silent as the mountain lions of Argentina. The one thing he didn't have was the luxury of time. He wasn't even certain Cecile's elderly neighbor had done as he'd instructed. She'd looked almost too frightened to speak coherently over the phone.

"Do you really think you're going to get away with this?"

His heart leapt at the sound of Cecile's voice. *Thank God!* His hope grew. She sounded quiet, controlled, even quite extraordinarily patient. Patient with a madman?

Then came the man's laugh. An ugly unnatural sound. "Well, *you'll* never know, my dear. Don't struggle. It's quite useless." The voice became pleasant, even admiring. "I have to confess I'm rather impressed with you, Ms. Moreland—"

Rolfe waited no longer. His body poised to lunge, he

inched his face around the bedroom door. The man's back was to him. His right arm was raised. In his hand was a syringe filled with a clear liquid.

Electrified, Rolfe lunged. He landed heavily on the man's back just as Cecile either fainted or slid deliberately to the floor.

"The police will be here soon." Rolfe let out a loud menacing growl, putting all his strength into the lock on the man's wrist. "But not soon enough for you, pal." The man struggled ferociously. He was strong, but Rolfe was stronger. He was also fueled by fury. The syringe fell harmlessly to the floor. Rolfe twisted the man's arm behind his back, increasing the pressure till the fake messenger cried out in pain.

"You're pulling my arm out of its socket!"

"Is that so?" Rolfe allowed himself a harsh laugh. He wrestled the guy to the floor, straddling the man's body, forcing him to lie still.

Cecile hadn't fainted. She had engineered a way to get clear of the syringe. She was up in a crouch now, her face paper-white.

"We need something to tie him up, Cecile." There was an urgent command in Rolfe's voice. All of his considerable strength was given over to controlling her attacker, whose breath was hissing like a steam train as he struggled to get free of Rolfe's hold. Rolfe banged the man's head hard on the floor, just barely resisting the urge to keep going. That quietened the man a little, but soon he resumed his struggle.

Of all things, Cecile put a child's skipping rope into his hands. She swiftly fell to her knees bending over the man's head with a glass water jug. There was no water in it, so presumably she intended to clobber him with it if he got out of control.

"You know him?" Rolfe grunted, binding the messenger's two hands very tightly behind his back.

"Yes." Cecile's voice was ragged. "He's the father of a patient."

"Is he now?" Rolfe stood up, delivering one sharp kick to the ribs of the would-be murderer, who bleated piteously. "Stand away from him, Cecile. He's not going anywhere."

"You'll answer for this!" Wheeler moaned, turning his head to give Cecile a black, betrayed look. "There was no abuse. Ellie was lying. That's what she is, a little liar."

"*You're* the liar, Dr. Wheeler," Cecile said. "Long term abuse has been confirmed."

That appeared to astound him, though why it did Cecile was at a complete loss to know. Wheeler began to bash his own forehead against the carpet in intense frustration. "She *belongs* to me," he cried as though offering the perfect defense. "She's my own flesh and blood. It's my *right* to do to her whatever I want."

"God Almighty!" Rolfe was filled with revulsion. "Shut up!" He directed another kick at the man's ribs. He turned to stare into Cecile's brilliant eyes. "What *is* this guy?"

Contempt was etched into her expression. "A pedophile. A monster. My little patient, Ellie, is ten years old. His *daughter!*"

"You sick bastard!" Rolfe began to flex his powerful right hand, punching it into his left palm like a boxer. "And what did you intend doing to Ms. Moreland?" he asked with quiet menace.

"He was going to kill me," Cecile's voice was toneless, but her whole body was shaking. "He was going to jab me with that syringe. God knows what it contains, but he told me it would have done the job. I think we can believe him. As a doctor he has access to drugs. The police will be wanting to take the syringe into evidence."

"For God's sweet sake!" Rolfe groaned. He moved toward her, feeling in some ways she was handling the shock better than he was. "I arrived in the nick of time, then."

"Funny you should say that!" She gave him the faintest little smile before crumpling slowly to the floor.

THERE WAS A WHOLE LOT of noise outside. Rolfe laid Cecile on the bed, welcoming the pounding on the door. It was followed up by the crunch of glass being trampled under heavy boots. There were loud identifying shouts of "Police, Police!"

"In the bedroom," Rolfe yelled back. "The woman's safe."

Their weapons drawn, two police officers responded, inching their way along the hallway, much as Rolfe had done, the first officer's nose rounding the door frame of the bedroom, neither man prepared to trust an anonymous voice.

"Clear!" One notified the other.

What they saw was a young woman lying on the bed, moaning softly, a young man standing beside her, his hands up and turned palm out in the universal gesture of no threat, another man trussed up on the floor. The trussed man was bawling like a baby.

ROLFE WATCHED as the police car carrying Dr. Peter Wheeler drove away. It was well over an hour later. The streetlights were on. A storm was threatening. He and Cecile had given their statements. Wheeler would have attempted murder added to his list of charges.

"That should put him away for a long long time," Rolf observed with intense satisfaction. "Suddenly your little patient has a future free of fear."

"They'll have to keep an eye on the mother," Cecile said, feeling oddly numb. A policewoman had made her a cup of tea with lots of sugar. She had drunk it even if it had been sickeningly sweet. "I wouldn't be in the least surprised if Marcie Wheeler rolled up to prison every month for a visit. Why is it certain women are drawn to evil men like moths to a flame? I would never have guessed at that hidden evil when I met him. He seemed so caring, and he *was* a doctor!"

"Plenty of doctors are murderers," Rolfe commented, "the infamous Dr. Crippen for one. People who knew him described him as a pleasant man who wouldn't hurt a fly." He moved back into the living room, shutting the sliding glass doors. It was hot and humid outside—a thunderstorm was building—but inside the apartment it was pleasantly cool. "How do you feel now?"

She let her head fall back against the sofa. "Shaky, whereas you're a rock."

"Don't you believe it!" He sat down on the white upholstered sofa opposite her, a marble-topped coffee table the barrier between them. "I'm still in a rage. I wanted to beat that guy to pulp."

"I thought you were going to," Cecile murmured dryly, laying her head back again and closing her eyes. "His wife warned him, you know. She told him to run. I can't believe it. I mean I *can* believe it, but I'm shocked out of my mind. I'd be dead by now if you hadn't arrived."

"When you feel better, maybe you can say thank-you," he suggested lightly.

"Maybe." She rubbed her arms.

"You're not cold, are you?" His eyes ranged over her. She was still very pale.

"A little. It's just the shock. There are shawls on one of the shelves in the walk-in wardrobe. Could you pick one out for me?"

"Sure." He stood up at once. "Do you want to lie down?"

"I think I can hang in there for a little while yet."

Rolfe rummaged through the shawls and picked one out— long black and fringed, lavish with amethyst, blue and emerald scrolls. The label said silk, but to him it looked and felt like velvet.

"This do?"

"Perfect." She went to take it from him, but he arranged it around her shoulders. "Thank you." She waited until he'd resumed his seat. "In all the excitement I forgot to ask how you knew my address."

"Does the word *granddad* mean anything to you?"

"Of course!" She gave a little click of her tongue. "What exactly does he think he's playing at?"

"One of the oldest games in the world. Cupid!"

Cecile frowned at the levity of his tone. "Granddad has been very successful at just about everything he's attempted, but he'll come a cropper here. I'm finished with you, Rolfe. I thought I'd made that abundantly clear."

"You'd better not say that," he warned. "You might need me. I seem to get to you faster than anyone else."

Cecile exhaled a long breath. "And I'm grateful, but you've lost all your power over me. I can't trust you. Trust is very important."

"Can't you give me a chance?" He leaned forward,

speaking as persuasively as he knew how. "I don't make a living out of lying to people, Cecile. I'm not the hustler you seem to believe I am."

"I'm past caring, Rolfe." She shook back her long hair, but it kept sliding over her shoulder. "You've got a lot to answer for. I let you make love to me."

"You *gave* yourself to me completely," he corrected, his gaze dark and mesmeric.

"And it was wonderful! The only thing missing was the all-important trust I'm talking about."

His eyes stayed on her. So beautiful! The fairest of them all. She was wearing a loose turquoise caftan of some almost sheer material that clearly displayed the contours of her body. The silk shawl twisted around her made an exotic contrast. Her skin shone luminous under the lights. Her eyes sparkled. Yet she looked fragile. And why wouldn't she with a maniac bursting in to kill her?

"Don't let's talk about it now," he said quietly. "You need a chance to recover from your ordeal. So do I, for that matter. The bastard's strength was unbelievable."

"He was the one facedown on the carpet," Cecile pointed out dryly.

"Yes, in the end and blubbering like a baby. Why is it those who inflict the most pain on others have such a low pain threshold themselves?"

"Bullies and cowards," Cecile said, her voice racked with emotion. "That little girl has lost something irretrievable. She's lost—" She broke off, unable to go on.

"You'll help her. You've already helped her." Rolfe offered swift consolation, wanting to go to her, but knowing he had to hold back. He had to wait until she came to him. He had visions of tenderly peeling off her clothing, entering her body, feeling her surge up against him. He wanted her to beg him to make love to her. Would that ever be again?

"Don't tear yourself to pieces," he went on. "I know it can't be easy but you know you have to maintain your emotional balance just to function. How about I make us something to eat?" he said in a brisker tone. "You can't have had anything. Neither have I."

For the first time Cecile gave a real smile. "Seriously, can you cook?"

He gave his elegant shrug. "Not terribly well, now that you mention it. In my stepfather's house there are lots of servants."

"Speaking of which, what name are you going to call yourself from now on?" she asked with cool sarcasm.

"Rolfe Chandler," he confirmed. "When I go back to Argentina to visit my family, I'll be Raul Montalvan. I never lied to you about that."

IN THE END THEY SHARED what Cecile had originally intended to have for dinner, the light pasta with ricotta and prosciutto. She let Rolfe handle the pasta. Lack of experience in the kitchen or not, he was characteristically adept. She prepared a green salad, tossing it in a Thai chilli dressing. Rolfe opened a bottle of very good shiraz, which they continued to drink long after the meal had ended.

"You've got your color back," he said, greatly relieved. "You seem more yourself."

She shook her head. "Don't be misled. I'm still very angry with you, Rolfe. It's just I'm not up to showing it tonight. You did save my life."

"I'm getting used to it." He smiled ruefully. "Would you like coffee?"

"If you can find the percolator. I hurled it at Wheeler."

"It's okay. Our nice policewoman retrieved it and she cleaned up the glass."

"She *was* nice," Cecile reflected. "I'll remember her name. Coffee beans are in the fridge in a canister. Grinder on the bench." She sat back trying to compose herself. A hot prickle of something like shame ran through her. She remembered all the nights of lying awake congratulating herself she'd found the will to finish with him! Oh, frail resolve! Desire crackled in the atmosphere, turning the air inside as electric as outdoors.

AT AROUND TEN-THIRTY, the storm that had been threatening for the past few hours finally broke over the city with the usual spectacular display of pyrotechnics.

"You can't stay here," she warned him, beating down her tormented longings.

"I know. But you can't toss me out until it's over," he argued. "You're going to be all right?"

"Of course, but I can't guarantee not having a few nightmares." They were back to sitting on opposite sides of the coffee table. A squat crystal vase was atop it, filled with the beautiful full-blown heads of yellow roses. The perfume was so heady Rolfe could taste it. "I'll never let anyone in like that again," she said with a shudder. "I couldn't see his face. I saw the flowers. That put me off my guard."

"Who would the flowers have been from?" he asked, keeping his eyes on her beautiful face, the beauty she wore so lightly.

"Strangely enough my first thought was they might be from you. Then I realized—I *thought*—you didn't know where I lived. I'll be having a word with Granddad. He doesn't usually interfere. This incident can't fail to get into the papers."

He nodded, already seeing the big black headline: Moreland Heiress Threatened By Crazed Sex Offender. "The press have gathered down on the street. I don't know if the police made any statement there and then. Someone tipped them off."

"Someone always does." Cecile shrugged.

"I suspect a couple of reporters will hang around hoping you'll drive out of the building. Your phone would have been ringing, only you're not listed. Is there any other way out, a back street?"

She shook her head. "You *can't* stay."

"Why not?" His eyes flowed down her throat to her breasts.

"Because we'd only sleep together," she said harshly.

"Is that so bad?"

His voice was so filled with tenderness, it shook her badly. She'd seen his face when it was taut with passion. The expression he wore now was incredibly *sweet*. It reached for her, attempted to gather her close. He had an excess of sexual power and he was bringing it to his service right now. Only, she was committed to fighting temptation.

"*Now,* Rolfe." She leapt to her feet. "Go *now!*" She had to spare herself this dangerous dance of seduction. Remember how he had deliberately deceived her.

"Okay, okay. No need to get agitated." He hunted up his jacket, shouldered into it. "You're so cruel. It's still raining."

"I'll lend you an umbrella." Her voice was brittle.

"No thanks. I expect it's like something a model on a catwalk might carry. Is there a cab rank handy or do I need to call one?"

"I'll call one," she said, then visibly jumped when the sliding doors to the terrace lit up brilliantly from a flash of lightning.

"Oh, sit down again." She waved him back helplessly as a great rolling thunderclap followed. "Why did you come here?"

"Thank God I did."

"And I can't wait for you to leave." She made to retreat to the safety of the sofa. But he caught her arm.

"I want you so badly," he told her passionately. "I want to put my arms around you. Comfort you. May I?"

"*Don't*, Rolfe!" Her voice was pitched high. "When the storm is over, you must go."

"I *long* to hold you."

His voice was the perfect instrument for seduction. "Oh, spare me the razzle-dazzle," she said angrily, throwing back her head and exposing her long elegant neck.

Immediately he released her. "No razzle-dazzle, only truth. What's the number of the cab company? I'd walk back to the hotel if I knew which way I was going."

Cecile put a hand to her temple. "Just a moment. I have to look it up. I rarely take cabs." She was desperate for him to go yet the price of maintaining her self-respect appeared to be desolation.

Her face reflected her tormented feelings. So did the agitation of her movements.

"Come here to me," he said.

How could gentleness be so deeply erotic? Her willpower was fading under the impact, her body thoroughly aroused. She was baffled and beaten by the complexity of her feelings. She had sought respite from him. But she couldn't lock him out.

He had only to look at her, smile at her, speak to her with his voice flowing like honey. She couldn't, however, let him touch her. But oh, that *sinking* feeling!

She laughed, a trembling little laugh. "You never give up, do you?"

Her beauty swept over him, her vulnerability. "Not on you," he said. "One kiss, the price of having saved your life. *Then* I'll go."

She saw the little flames leaping in his eyes and caught her breath.

First he buried his face in her neck, then he kissed her. The now familiar languor stole into her limbs. It wasn't a gentle kiss. It was the kiss of a man who had known and possessed every inch of her body. That knowledge alone was an unbreakable bond between them.

Instantly she was drenched in desire. It flowed from him to her. In a way it was a revelation. She had never really known what it meant until he had first made love to her. Now she would never have to wonder again. The composed mask she wore had been stripped from her. All for *him.* Her mouth opened to greet his questing tongue. Her fascination for him was overwhelming. She had no defense against it, however hard she tried.

She couldn't resist him or his touch. There was a kind of fear in it, the fear of loss of self. It was as though she had lost all choice. His hands were moving loverlike across her shoulders and down her back while she fell into a thrilling reverie, letting him do what he liked, moving her this way and that, molding her body to his. She slid her arms beneath his jacket, locked them around his waist, feeling his powerful erection settle against the slight curve of her stomach. What an instrument of pleasure and torture that was!

Briefly he lifted his mouth from hers, staring down at her. "If we start this, I'll *never* leave."

"Well, we *have* started it, haven't we?" she answered with a little twist of bitterness. She wanted to hurt him as he had hurt her. She still wondered if she was part of his plan, but the most primitive sexual excitement had taken hold of her and transformed her into someone else. His for the taking. Was it any wonder she was frightened?

THEY WERE LYING NAKED together on the bed, while the storm raged outside the shuttered doors as if trying to get in. She was spread out beneath him, arms and legs, toes and soles of her feet sliding across the smooth surface of the bed linen. His palms sought the creamy undersides of her breasts, lifting first one dark pink nipple then the other to his mouth. The horror of the early part of the night was obliterated by the flames of passion that now enveloped them like a great bushfire.

"Forgive me," he whispered into her ear.

"No." He had exposed her to too much pain, too much self-doubt.

"I'll keep doing this to you."

She had opened herself wide to him. Now she cried out as the pleasure mounted too high to be checked.

"Are you going to thank me for saving your life?" He didn't say it was one of the worst moments of *his* life.

"Thank you," she gasped, while outside the storm howled.

"No, no, you mustn't come yet." He taunted her softly, continuing his ministrations that excited her to the point of tears.

She was shaking all over, her body flushed, but she wasn't going to beg.

Then when she thought she couldn't stand the shattering ecstasy a moment longer, he moved his hand away and began to thrust deeply into her. In and out. Back and forth, his penis growing so big it seemed to fill her right up to her throat. Swiftly she caught his rhythm, reveling in the ease with which they fitted together. Groups of muscles clenched and relaxed. Their movements were as smooth as oiled pistons, moving smoothly together until they fired. He lifted her legs high and her fingernails dug into his powerful shoulders. It was excruciating torment and it made her eyelids flutter and her heart pound madly. How much more did he want of her? What part of her body was he trying to reach? Her penetrated womb throbbed with heat as if his penis had put a brand on it. The small of her back strained to arch up from the bed, fell back as his mouth swooped on hers again. She had the crazy sensation she was flying…her flailing arms were wings…the whole world was vibrating…

Rippling sensations began deep in the cave of her body, slowly at first, then gaining strength and speed. She tried to control the onward surge, but it was hopeless. Ah, the power of the flesh! The will was as nothing. It was hopeless to control this tumult or contain it. She had to go with the tide until the tumult subsided. Her heart was hammering. Inside she was convulsing. Rolfe loomed over her, his own orgasm powerfully fierce.

A cry gushed from her mouth. His name?

Tears slithered down her cheeks.

Faster and faster they rocked. It was a mating dance designed by nature to bring forth new life. Pleasure soared to the highest point she had ever reached.

She was split open.

Then....release! Deep internal shifts began that took long....long...minutes to shudder into calm. Minutes more for the heart to settle.

Utterly spent and dangling one arm over the bed and one across Rolfe's chest, Cecile in her mind's eye had a sudden vision of a perfect little boy with golden blond hair and eyes of velvety brown. Rolfe as a child? There were wildflowers all around him. She knew those flowers. They were the yellow and white paper daisies that carpeted the Red Centre after rain. She could hear him laughing. Such a merry laugh, full of security and happiness. What kind of vision was that?

SHE WAS DREAMING. She was in an abandoned building, a hotel or a derelict apartment building. She could see numbers on the doors although it was very murky with deep shadows. Some numbers were hanging upside down. One of them was hers: 24. A crashing sound came from behind her. Something heavy. A fallen beam? She knew the building was condemned. Then the sound of pounding footsteps. Someone was coming after her. She began to run, too, her heart beating violently in her chest, but the faster she ran, the farther away the end of the corridor grew. There was a terrible sense of danger all around her. Those heavy footsteps belonged to a killer. *Her* killer. She called on all her strength, but she could hardly breathe. There was a bad stitch in her side. He was coming after her, deadly in pursuit...

Help me!

"CECILE!"

She awoke with a great start. A bedside lamp was on. Rolfe was holding her shoulders, staring into her face. "It's okay," he was saying. His face and voice were full of concern.

"You're quite safe. I'm here with you. Cecile, wake up!" He shook her gently.

She responded more fully, throwing an arm over her eyes. "Oh, God, I was having a nightmare. It was dreadful."

"I know." His hand curled around her bare shoulder.

"I was running through a derelict building. One of the doors had the number of my apartment on it. Aren't dreams strange? Someone was coming after me. I was running fast but never fast enough. It was so *real!*"

"They always are." His arm beneath her, he settled his body alongside hers, savoring their closeness as if at any minute it might be over.

"What time is it?" She was immensely grateful he was there with her. He was so strong and *physical*. A man of action.

Rolfe glanced at the digital clock. "Three-thirty. Breathe deeply." He began to breathe with her as if to show her.

After a while her heartbeat quietened. She was feeling better, though the terror of the nightmare clung to her like a fume.

"Would you like a drink of water?" he asked, stroking her blue-sheened hair back from her face.

"Yes, please." She swallowed on a dry throat.

"Okay. I'll be back in a moment." He slid out of the bed, as gloriously naked as a sculpted work of art.

When he returned to the bedroom, she was propped up against the pillow. "Thank you." She drank thirstily. He had water from the dispenser on the refrigerator door, so it was deliciously cold. "The storm's over?"

"Long over," he said.

"And you're still here."

"It seems so." He walked to the sliding glass doors with superb unselfconsciousness. "The moon is riding high in a cloudless sky," he told her, opening the door wide so she could breathe in the rain-washed air.

"The odd time, I have the feeling I can't do without you, Rolfe," she told him.

"And this is one of those times," he answered dryly, coming back to the bed and stretching himself out alongside her.

She turned on her side to stare into his gold-flecked eyes. There was hunger in them. Hunger renewed. She wanted to hold her tongue, especially at this time, but she found she couldn't. "I can't put aside the fact you deliberately deceived me, Rolfe," she said heavily. "Surely you see it was a deception of some magnitude. You made a fool of me. Made me suffer. I can't forget that."

His response was simple, "You're going to have to."

"Or you'll depart for Argentina?" she asked, a war waging inside.

His handsome face tightened as he stared back at her. "I've come *home*, Cecile. Home where I belong. It was a dream I never abandoned. Thoughts of my return have been with me practically my whole life."

"Along with thoughts of revenge. They never left you, either. Was revenge at the heart of it?"

His eyes glittered with a kind of vehemence. "It was part of it," he admitted grimly. "But far more important, more important than even I realized until I came back, was the love of *my* land. It's not just the aboriginals who have it. The white man can have it, too. The red desert sand is in my bones. When I die they can scatter my ashes to the desert winds. I can think of no better end."

"Please…." Cecile reached out impulsively to stop his mouth. "You have a long life ahead of you. I don't want to hear you talk about dying." She visibly shivered.

"We all die, Cecile," he said, lifting the sheet around her. "The price of having any life at all. You asked if I'd return to Argentina. The answer is certainly. Argentina is my second home. My mother is there. Ramon, my stepbrother and sister. But it will only be for visits."

She lay back. "How would you describe your mother?" she asked, staring up at the plastered ceiling.

He answered instantly. "A beautiful woman inside and out. I love her dearly."

"Did you have problems when she married your stepfather? You were still a boy, not an adult. Even adults have problems when a much-loved parent remarries. You'd lost your own father in terrible circumstances."

"What is this, a therapy session?" He loomed over her so she could see clearly the fine grain of his dark golden skin and the glinting blond streaks in his thick mane of hair.

"Well, you *are* lying down," she pointed out. "In *my* bed. How did you get here?"

"The same way you did," he said crisply. "You wanted me as much as I wanted you. *Want* you," he amended, hunger still spilling out of his dark eyes.

She shielded her face from it with her arm.

"The lamp too strong?" he asked with a measure of sarcasm.

"No, leave it on. Is *want* what holds us together?"

He didn't answer for a minute, settling himself back. "A lot of people would think the way we want one another is more than enough. But no, I don't just want your body,

Cecile, though it gives me unbelievable pleasure. I want your heart and your mind. You're more real to me than any other woman I've ever known."

"So why didn't you *talk* to me," she demanded, engulfed by a kind of desolation. "I would have listened. I would have listened to everything you said. Even though you've had much to say about my family that's really bad. Your story wouldn't have fallen on deaf ears. You know that now from my grandfather's reaction. Granddad is a wonderful man."

"I know that now," he said. "I didn't know it before. Your grandmother's role in our downfall was all new to me." And to my mother, he thought bleakly, almost ready to reveal to her the true story.

"Well, Granddad tried to make amends by buying back your old property," Cecile retorted. "It's *yours* now. You have your inheritance back. So one of your objectives has been fulfilled." Even after their sublime lovemaking she was unconvinced he wanted her for herself alone.

It must have been the worst thing she could have said because he suddenly caught her chin with strong fingers and dropped a punishing kiss on her mouth. "Time to go, I think," he said in a clipped voice. "I've got enough scars without your adding to them, Cecile." He slid out of the bed and squared his shoulders.

She raised herself on one elbow, a whole range of emotions running through her so fast she couldn't grab hold of a single one. "But it's the way of things, isn't it? Each of us hurting the other." She stared at him, following each swift decisive movement as he pulled on his clothes.

Rolfe waited until he was fully dressed before he looked back at her. Her black hair was tumbling down her back and brushing her shoulders, accentuating the magnolia texture of her skin. Her eyes were pools of light. Her delicate breasts and her body down to her waist were fully exposed. He couldn't help the leap of desire, but he choked it down. "I deeply regret I've hurt you, Cecile," he said in a voice she thought had no apology in it, "but I'm not going to spend the rest of my days apologizing for what I failed to tell you," he confirmed. "I didn't, however, *lie*. You must have learned other things about me. A few good things, surely?" he questioned with a trace of bitter challenge.

She drew herself up, trying to reach for her kaftan to cover her. "I can't...I don't deny I—"

He cut whatever she was trying to say short, shouldering into his jacket. "Don't get out of bed," he said, already on the move. "I can see myself out."

CHAPTER FOURTEEN

THE PUBLICITY THAT FOLLOWED the arrest and charging of Dr. Peter Wheeler on two counts, one of attempted murder and the other of incest, combined with the fact it was the Moreland heiress, Cecile Moreland, who had been the victim of the murder attempt in her luxury apartment, caused Cecile to want to take flight until the worst of the media coverage had died down. Her family hated publicity. Now they had plenty of it. Her face and her life all over the newspapers. She wouldn't look at a newspaper for days on end in case it carried yet another photograph of her. So many on file? Why was she always smiling? This was a dreadful business that was being reported. Surely they didn't have to pick photographs where she was smiling, did they? The only plus for her was that she and her mother were talking again. In fact, her mother had rushed to be with her, shocked out of her mind such a thing had happened to her daughter.

"I've told you, I've warned you, Ceci, you're in a dangerous profession." Justine had sobbed. Something she never did. "Thank God for Rolfe! How we owe him! Where *is* he?" She looked around wildly as if he were hiding away in the apartment. "I have to thank him personally. You could never, never, have faced that maniac alone."

A lot of people arrived. The apartment was jammed with them. Relatives, friends, colleagues. Justine stared at the crowd for a few minutes, counted heads, then organized lavish refreshments from one of her innumerable sources. She didn't appear in the least heartbroken over her marriage breakup, Cecile thought. She looked in her element, taking over. Her daughter needed her. That was all that mattered to Justine.

Her grandfather sent the Learjet for her. Her mother tagged along, saying she couldn't bear to have Cecile out of her sight. They returned to Darwin where the population respected the family's privacy. At the weekend they would go on to Malagari where Cecile felt her happiest. She had advised the police of her whereabouts. Her senior colleague, Susan Bryant, would be taking over Ellie's counseling. Children's Services would be conducting routine checks on Marcie Wheeler and her children, though Mrs. Wheeler had notified everyone concerned of her intention to move permanently to New Zealand where she had relatives. Cecile was pleased to hear it. She and Ellie and Josh would be out of harm's way. Mrs. Wheeler further told Cecile when they spoke she never wanted to lay eyes on her husband again. "What he could have done to you and it was my fault!"

Cecile couldn't bring herself to pat the woman's hand soothingly and deny it. Marcie Wheeler had acted very foolishly indeed. Much as she appeared to hate the thought—and who could blame her?—she would have to sight her husband when the case came before the court. She would have to be strong. So would Ellie.

"He doesn't scare us anymore," Marcie told Cecile earnestly. "He deserves to be behind bars. Ellie is so much better you wouldn't believe. We're going to make a fresh start."

Wherever they went Ellie would need further counseling. Possibly for years. Cecile made sure Marcie Wheeler fully understood that.

IT WAS THEIR FIRST NIGHT home in the Moreland mansion. Cecile was preparing for bed when clearly her mother was ready for another heart-to-heart. "What's she like, this Northam woman?" Justine asked, studying her beautifully manicured nails. She was sitting in a Louis armchair, looking very much like she'd used up most of her olive branches. The worst of the scare was over. They were safe with Daddy now. Justine wanted to get down to business. "I know you visited them at her beach shack…" Her quick glance was accusing.

Was there anything her mother *didn't* know? "Actually it's quite spacious. I'd be happy in it."

"You'd be happy anywhere Rolfe was around," Justine scoffed. "Where is he, by the way?"

"The last time I spoke to him he was still in Melbourne," Cecile evaded.

"Don't worry, he'll be back. You're making a huge effort to play it down, but I know you. Now, to get back to your father. Gilly Massingham saw the two of you having lunch. She said he'd put on a lot of weight."

"Nonsense! He looks great, Mum," Cecile said. "Just great!"

"Really!" Justine raised beautifully shaped eyebrows. "He's a great-looking man. She's in it for the money. Not that there'll be anything like what she imagines." Her laugh was full of angry satisfaction.

"She's not in it for the money, Mum." Cecile took a brush to her long hair. "She loves him. I don't want to hurt you, but he appears to genuinely love her."

"Gimme a break!" Justine's voice deepened with sarcasm. "Your father can go to hell, for all I care. If he genuinely loved any of the women he's been involved with over the years—"

"But that's it, isn't it, Mum? Your marriage would have been over long ago. He didn't love any of them, but he loves *her*. They need each another. You never did need Dad. Not really. You had Granddad. He's been the rock in all our lives."

"I realize that, Ceci," Justine snapped. "No need to rub it in. I understand she's quite *plain*. A nondescript little thing?"

Cecile knew she was supposed to say, "And stupid to boot!" Instead she said, "She's neither, Mum. She doesn't have your striking good looks or presence, but there's something really attractive about her. She's fresh and wholesome, well scrubbed."

"Good God!" Justine was genuinely appalled. "No wonder she couldn't get a man till now. Well scrubbed? Sounds like she had to hang herself out to dry."

Cecile sat down in a matching chair. "Okay, here's the story. She had an invalid mother to look after. She was devoted to her. Her mother died not so long ago."

Justine thought about that and what it implied. "So with Mum out of the way Howard decides to call our marriage quits?"

"It does look that way," Cecile said, not without sadness.

"And what am I supposed to do—roll under a bus?" Justine inquired bitterly.

"The stats on getting run over by a bus are very low, Mum. Start looking for another husband," Cecile suggested.

"Another husband? What, more of the same?" Justine asked incredulously. "Besides, I'm getting old...older."

"Nonsense. You're in your prime. Bob Connaught might fit the bill nicely."

Justine gave that some thought. "Actually he *does,* now you mention it. You wouldn't mind my remarrying?"

"Whatever makes you happy makes me happy, Mother dear."

"I'm so sorry for behaving badly!" Unfamiliar tears filled Justine's eyes. "I'm not sorry for cutting up your father's clothes. It made me feel really good. He won't be needing all those Italian suits, anyway, now he's taken a golden handshake."

"He worked very hard for it, Mother," Cecile reminded her.

Justine was silent for a few moments. "How about you start calling me Justine?" she suggested.

"Fine, Justine!" It was no good protesting.

"By the way, I forgot to tell you Daddy took care of Stuart and his blabbermouth." Justine smiled as she said it. "Remember Stuart, your ex-fiancé?" she asked waspishly.

"Vaguely." Cecile put down her hairbrush and began to rub some cream into her hands.

"Thought he was going to humiliate us, did he?" Justine shook herself in outrage.

"It's not as though he was in perfect ignorance of what you might do."

"Indeed!" Justine performed a tattoo on the wooden part of the chair with her long fingernails. "Whatever did I see in him? There must have been something?" She frowned as she looked into her daughter's eyes.

"You like people who agree with you at every turn—could that have been it?" Cecile suggested mildly.

"I don't think I'm going to get that from Rolfe," Justine said slyly.

"Rolfe and I aren't an item," Cecile said, determined to

maintain her privacy. Justine couldn't help interfering, she knew. It was her nature.

"Codswallop!" said Justine rudely.

"What a very odd word. I wonder what its derivation is?"

Justine shrugged. "Who cares! It simply means nonsense. I don't blame you if you're not yet ready to totally forgive him. In fact, I suspect you're relishing keeping Rolfe uncertain about you and the whole situation. It's really weird because you'd die if he looked in another woman's direction."

True.

"But then, that special problem has always existed for us, hasn't it?" Justine said soberly. "Are we loved for ourselves, or has it more to do with being the daughter and the granddaughter of the Man with the Midas Touch? I was fairly paranoid as a girl when it came to trust. I know you are, too. It goes with the territory, my darling."

"You think I should trust Rolfe?"

"You're madly in love with him, aren't you? He's saved you from great harm on two separate occasions. Some might say you owe your life to him. That's a big plus in my book."

Cecile looked away. "He's brave. I know that. I'm not so without self-confidence that I don't know he's attracted to me."

"He's conquered you *and* Daddy in a remarkably short time. That's it, isn't it?"

Cecile couldn't answer. Her mother had too much insight into her particular problems. She had trusted Tara, her friend from childhood, but that episode at Malagari when Tara had turned on her had really hurt.

"You're *not* terrified someone else will get him?" Justine

broke into Cecile's ponderings, uncannily on her daughter's wavelength. "What about that little opportunist, Tara?"

"What about Tara?" Cecile asked with false calm, unsurprised her mother had read her mind. Justine did it all the time.

"Don't tell me! You've had a falling out? We are *soooo* sorry," Justine gloated. "She's a devious miss, that one! Warned you, didn't I?"

Cecile shrugged. "She rang me immediately she read about what happened. She sounded genuinely distressed for me."

Justine harrumphed. "Just so long as she doesn't come for a visit. But she'll try. Mark my words. I've always said that girl can get in where the ants can't." She rose majestically to her feet. "I'll say good night, darling. You don't mind if I don't come with you to Malagari, do you?" She didn't wait for an answer, but swept on. "I've never been one for the great outdoors. If I weren't so obviously a Moreland, I'd begin to wonder if I were Daddy's at all."

A sad little smile edged Cecile's mouth. "Are you saying Grandma slept with someone else?" As far as she was concerned, the things that Grandma Frances had gotten up to were mind-blowing.

"Good gracious, Ceci, that's not nice." Justine turned to reprimand her. "Even in fun."

"I apologize. She simply wouldn't have had the time. She seemed to have spent most of it creating great traumas for other people. Daniel and his poor abandoned mother. Rolfe's entire family. No one was spared."

Justine in her gorgeous peach-colored peignoir paused at the door, one elegant hand to her temple. "Please, Ceci, not another word. I can't bear to hear it. Even as a child I knew there was always something going on with my mother. She would have been quite at home with the Borgias. All the secrets, the scandals and the downright lies have come as no surprise to me." Justine opened the door, then turned with a bright conspiratorial smile. "Do you really think Bob Connaught and I are suited?"

However had her parents stayed together long enough to have her? "I think it would work," Cecile said. For all she knew, Bob Connaught, a very nice man, could be abstemious in the sex department, too.

"Perhaps." Justine shrugged. "You know what they say. What's good for the goose is good for the gander."

A COUPLE OF DAYS after Justine's return to Melbourne, Joel joined Cecile in the garden room where she was endeavoring to reply to a stack of Thinking of You cards, to tell her he had given Rolfe, who was back in town, permission to take one of the station helicopters across the ranges to the old Lockhart cattle holding.

"I think it would be a good idea if you went with him," Joel said. "In many ways Rolfe has been alone a long time. He had his mother of course, and his new family, but it's obvious he never forgot his own world. Rolfe has the same connection to the land that you and I have."

"He deceived us, Granddad. That's what I can't accept."

Joel sighed. "At the beginning deception was his only cover. I'll stake my life he isn't a man who normally dealt in deception. I think he hated having to lie to you, but that desire for revenge on the Morelands was deeply entrenched."

"You say, *was,* past tense."

"I think his quest for revenge is now over, my darling.

You're the trained psychologist. Revenge must have filled up the terrible void in his life. But only love can heal a wounded heart. I believe he loves you. You must see it. You must feel it don't you? In its way it's a wonderful redemptive love. It's within your power to lay the ghosts of Rolfe's painful past finally to rest."

ROLFE PUT THE CHOPPER down on the perfectly flat ground that ran away to the ranges at the front of the old homestead. Red desert forever. A world of color. The marvelous contrast of blazing blue skies, fiery earth, ghost gums with their stark white boles, dusty khaki misshapen trees and bushes, great cylindrical clumps of spinifex scorched to a dull gold and looking for all the world like the biggest wheatfield on earth.

Painters would revel in it, he thought. This was his first visit here in over twenty years, and it was as he had fully expected it to be: emotional. But he had to hold his emotions in check, remembering what his grandmother had said to him as a six-year-old when he'd broken his arm: "Brave boys don't cry, Rolfie!"

He'd cried plenty. But always when he was absolutely alone. Tragedy had haunted his life. It was only since he had met Cecile all the pent-up anger and bitterness inside him had all but crumbled to dust. He had thought to get on with his life. Only it wasn't so easy.

A deception of such magnitude!

That's what she had said with such hurt in her eyes. What could he do to win her trust? She felt herself tricked and betrayed. It had been impressed on him enough that heiresses feared not being liked or loved for themselves. It wasn't difficult to understand. Not when people wore masks. At least today she had consented to come with him, although he knew he probably had to thank Joel for that. Joel was turning into the grandfather he had once known.

As they walked toward the single-story homestead, he felt his profound link with it rise up through his very boots. Gradually he became aware of a general *tidiness* about the place. "There's no doubt about him, is there," he murmured.

"Granddad?" she asked.

He nodded, staring about him. "Someone has been here to clean up. Everything is much too neat and tidy for a deserted old homestead."

"That's Granddad for you!" said Cecile slightly discordantly, pausing to take in the old building. "He probably sent a couple of the men over."

"A couple of dozen is more like it." Rolfe lifted his eyes to the purple-hazed ranges that lay in the exact center of the continent. Known collectively as the Macdonnell Ranges, they stood in stark relief against the cloudless sky, among the oldest geological formations on the planet. Extending east to west some hundred miles across the floor of the sandy desert, they were famous for their extraordinary shapes and colors. There was a spectacular gap in the ranges, he remembered. A great chasm of multicolored scalloped layers, rusts, yellows, pinks and creams that impressed itself upon the eye. That was what was so extraordinary about the Red Centre, its stark primal beauty, the inviolability that told you plainly no one could own it.

Close by a flock of white corellas took flight, and he stared after them appreciatively. His head began to fill with childhood memories: riding through canyons and gorges with his grandfather, the sheer cliffs towering to either side;

sparkling water holes and great stretches of *Ginda Ginda* flowers. He remembered the magnificent wedge-tailed eagles that soared on high, the huge flocks of budgerigar that seemed to follow them around. He remembered his father letting him ride pillion on his motorbike as they raced across the iron-red plains. He remembered being allowed to join in the chase for brumbies. Was there ever a time he hadn't loved horses? Most of all he remembered when he was very small, racing out into the open paddocks to be the first one in the family—they let him believe he was, anyway—to sight the miraculous appearance of the zillions of paper daisies that appeared after rains.

Sadly he remembered, too, the man from the bank who traveled all the way to tell his grandfather the bank was repossessing the property. He remembered how he had run away and hid for days after his father and Denjie had carried his grandfather's body home. His grandfather's fatal heart attack had happened when he was driving stray cattle into the holding yards.

He couldn't bear to remember the sound of his grandmother's screaming or his mother's brokenhearted sobbing.

"Everything okay?" Cecile asked, seeing somberness come into his expression.

"Sure. Fine." He recovered immediately.

"Good." Perversely she couldn't bear to see him unhappy. She turned slowly to take it all in, the golden sea of spinifex washing right up against the larkspur ranges. "I like this place." It was tiny by Malagari standards, a mere cottage, but it had definite appeal.

"It's a wonder it hasn't fallen down," Rolfe murmured, thinking at some stage the building and the old sheds would have to be demolished. How had they all fitted in there? he wondered. A comfortable home to him as a boy, now it seemed much too small to have sheltered them all. He couldn't recall a single argument. They were a family. They pulled together. They never fell out. Not a one of them wanted to hurt the other. His grandparents had adored him. His grandfather had always called him "my little mate." There had been a unique warmth and companionship between them that had even exceeded the close bond with his father.

"The ranges look quite different from this side," Cecile was observing, shading her eyes. "Namatjira was such a great artist, so much a part of this desert country. He painted with complete accuracy. I've heard city collectors say the colors are too vivid to be true, but we know differently." She looked about her with obvious pleasure. "It's all the Northern Territory, yet there's a great division between our tropical region north and this so-called arid center. No one who has ever seen our desert gardens could possibly call it arid, could they? Lovely, lovely flowers of every kind and color." She was conscious of his eyes on her. "So very strange and so romantic."

They continued to walk toward the old homestead. It was much too hot standing in the sun. "Didn't the early explorer Ernest Giles want to name Palm Valley after all the beautiful flowers he found there?" Rolfe asked. He'd all but forgotten about that.

Cecile nodded. "In the end the palms were so magnificent he called it Glen of Palms, which later became Palm Valley."

"Nothing has changed at all," he said in deep, reflective tones. "Hard to believe now, but we all lived here. My grandparents. Mum and Dad and me until Dad could get a run of

his own. Uncle Benjie. Granddad was the patriarch. I was remembering we never fell out as a family. We were very
closely knit. We had to depend on one another. Benjie might
have been my uncle, but he was more like a big brother. He
was tall, over six feet, with a lopsided grin and eyes as blue
as my mother's. She's a very beautiful woman. Blond. I inherited my eyes, the shape and color from my dad, but I look
a lot like her. I think that's why Ramon took it so easy on
me—because I resembled my mother. It couldn't have been
my sunny nature. I turned into a savage after my dad was
killed."

Something in his expression brought her close to tears.
"How very sad, Rolfe." So much trauma for a young boy to
contend with. It was no wonder he lived in such pain. "You
never did tell me how you felt when your mother remarried."

He grimaced faintly, drawing her up the short flight of
stone steps that led to the wide veranda. The homestead itself
was set some four feet off the ground by brick pillars. The
veranda wrapped around three sides of the house, protecting
the core of the building from the fierce inland heat. "I acted
like I couldn't care less, but for a long time I hated the situation," Rolfe said. "I couldn't bear to think of my mother
being disloyal to my dad, but I didn't accept Ramon at all.
Not as my mother's husband. Not as my stepfather, although
he adopted me almost immediately."

"And how do you feel about your stepbrother and sister?"

He shrugged. "It's possible one day my stepbrother and I
will be friends. No one could help but love Ramona, though."
There was much affection in his voice.

The entrance portico, Cecile saw, was simple but attractive,
flanked by double timber columns and a fretted timber gable

and spire. The roof was corrugated galvanized iron decorated with rather picturesque roof ventilators to aid the cooling of the homestead. Two pairs of French doors to either side of the front door gave onto the veranda. It was a good example of an early pioneering building, but maintenance had not been a priority of subsequent owners who had all gone broke, her grandfather had told her. Cecile didn't think it would warrant restoration work. Possibly the whole structure would have to be demolished. She wondered how Rolfe would feel about that but didn't like to ask.

"Shall we go in?" She turned to him, her eyes sparkling like cool crystal pools in the heat of the day.

He acted completely on instinct. Effortlessly he swept her high in his arms, staring down into her startled face.

"I didn't realize we'd just been married." She tried to make a joke of it that didn't come off.

"I feel like we belong to each other," he said, his handsome face unsmiling. He pushed the door—it wasn't locked—and carried her into the entrance hall. There he lowered her to the polished timber floor, keeping his arms around her. "Thank you for coming today. I know Joel was behind it."

She laid her hand against the flat of his chest, then turned away.

"Even so I wouldn't have come if I didn't want to. Let's take a look around." She felt she could snap at any moment, yet she spoke calmly enough.

His mouth twisted a little. "The place is called Currawa."

She nodded. "I saw the brass plaque beside the front door." She paused to look up at the original cypress pine ceilings, easily twelve feet high. "Doesn't *currawa* mean the tree—"

"From which gum was obtained to fasten the heads to

native spears," he finished for her. "There are other meanings, such as rocky river. There aren't too many rivers around here, barring the oldest, driest river on earth, the Finke, and the Todd, of course, running through the Alice."

"Did you ever get to see the Henley-on-Todd Regatta?" Cecile asked without thinking. She was referring to the annual bottomless boat race, leg propelled down the dry bed of the river. A day of great fun!

"No," he said, standing quite still watching her, "nor the Alice Springs Rodeo where your uncle Jared was killed and Benjie was held responsible."

She bowed her head. "I'm sorry. I spoke without thinking. Why don't we say a prayer for them?" she said quietly. "The two of us together. Members of two families who suffered."

He came away from the wall, straightened his wide shoulders. "I stopped saying prayers when my dad was killed, Cecile," he said, his voice echoing through the empty house.

TOWARD MIDDAY they sat on the front steps in the shade of the gable and ate their picnic lunch straight from the esky. Nothing fancy. Sandwiches and coffee from the stainless-steel flask, a crisp apple for dessert.

"King's Canyon and Palm Valley aren't far away," Cecile said. "We could do a flyover on the way back. It amazes tourists to find wonderful green oases slap bang in the middle of the desert. Beautiful crystal creeks and gullies."

"Remnants of long, long ago when the Centre was once as lush and green as your tropical North."

"Do you remember the wild bush after rain?" she asked, taking a last bite of her red shiny apple.

"Of course! It's a sight no one could forget. My grandmother used to say to my grandfather—it was for *my* benefit of course— 'The paper daisies will be out by morning, Dad!' That was all I needed. I used to get up so early the sun hadn't even crested the ranges. By the time I reached the first horse paddock the landscape was flooded with golden light. I think I was around six or seven at the time."

"You must have been a very sensitive little boy," Cecile said, unable to keep the tenderness out of her voice. "Sensitive to beauty." She vividly recalled her extraordinary vision of that beautiful little boy who looked just like Rolfe amid a glowing landscape of wildflowers.

"I defy anyone to be insensitive to the sight of the arid red desert transformed overnight into a vast garden," he replied. "Miles and miles of everlastings, the one color to one area, yellow, then pink, then white. I never did figure out why that was so. You'd think the seeds would intermingle. After the showers of winter rain the sand used to be wreathed with trailing stems of Stuart's crimson desert pea, the bellflowers, the foxgloves, the pink parakeelyas. When the scorched spinifex sent up its tall seed-bearing stems, it looked more like we were growing giant fields of wheat than raising cattle. All those years ago and I remember it as vividly as though it were yesterday."

"You want to spend the rest of your life here?" She spoke normally, when she was desperate to know his plans for the future.

"What—here on Currawa?" He reached into the esky and found to his satisfaction a bar of orange-flavored dark chocolate.

She spread her hands. "Well, if not Currawa, this region?"

"I thought I made that clear. It's a *magical* place, Cecile." He broke off a square of chocolate and handed it to her.

"Thank you. This has been a feast." She slipped the rich dark chocolate into her mouth, letting it melt. Chocolate had been considered an aphrodisiac since the time of the Pharaohs.

"I don't intend to work Currawa, if that's what you're trying to find out. I don't intend to sell it, either. Joel's handing me the deed was a symbolic gesture. We both knew that. What I was thinking was at some time in the future turning the site into a tourist destination. A small working station taking in selected guests. It's a hop, step, and a jump to the Alice and from there Uluru, Kata Tjuta and the rest of the desert monuments. Just an idea, a fairly long-term project. What do you think?"

"Have you spoken to Granddad about it?" So many things he talked to her grandfather about. Why not her?

"In due time I'll ask his advice," he said, capturing and holding her gaze. "It's *you* I'm telling first. *You* I wanted to be with me when I returned here. That's the big reason I delayed."

"Then I'm honored," she said, her throat tight. "You've become quite a favorite with Granddad."

Gold flashed in his dark eyes. "Joel and I connected easily. It could have been very different."

"But you took the gamble?" Inside a voice said, *leave this alone*.

"I can't deny that, Cecile," he said, suddenly looking grave. "I was a different person then."

"Is that likely, your changing so quickly?" she asked, unable to resist the challenge.

"I think falling headlong in love changes people pretty smartly," he retaliated. "You say you would have gotten around to breaking off your engagement to Carlson without my coming into your life. I have a little trouble believing that. I think your meeting me changed you overnight."

"You're so sure of yourself." Cecile began to busy herself tidying up.

"How can I not be when I have you in my arms?" he countered, his voice deep in his throat. "Stop that. What are you so afraid of?" He reached out to lock his hand gently around her wrist.

"Let me go, Rolfe." She trembled as she said it.

"Why can't you look at me? I feel like holding your head still."

She stopped what she was doing. "All right, are you listening?" She reacted emotionally. "As soon as you touch me I spin out of control. I don't even know how to put a stop to it. You can't fall madly in love with someone you hardly know."

He laughed softly. "You're not the first person to say that nor the last. Can't you accept a great thing has happened to us?"

She looked away from his eyes. "I can accept something cataclysmic has happened to us, certainly to *me,* Rolfe," she said more quietly, "but I have more difficulty accepting your dramatic change from a man hell-bent on exacting whatever revenge he can on my family to a recent convert. It's like men in jail suddenly finding God."

He stood up and looked down at her. "I think you better stop there."

"So do I." Her heart was going madly. She didn't want to fight with him, but it was happening.

"And you'd better start questioning if you're as much in

love—or lust—or whatever the hell you call it—as you claim to be. Falling in love *is* a time of transformation. I know it if you don't. You might also consider whether you're not the least bit neurotic. The poor little rich girl always condemned to testing people. Is there *anyone* you can trust? Mightn't that mean you haven't sufficient sense of yourself? I love you. I'll shout it out loud. *I love you!* But today, right now, I don't even like you."

Cecile too came to her feet. "Didn't take you long to admit it," she said angrily. "Maybe you have difficulty distinguishing love from hate? I'll never forget the way you were looking at me when I was standing on the balcony at Daniel's wedding. It was so—" She sought for a word. "So…"

"Desiring?" he suggested curtly.

"I was going to say, calculating. I *saw* that, Rolfe. I didn't dream it up."

"So I'm supposed to feel guilty for the rest of my life? Why can't you just let a man be?"

"I'm sorry we started this conversation," she said.

"You brought it up in the first place."

"That's right, blame me." She rushed back up the step, catching the toe of her shoe in a split timber plank. "Damn!" She pitched forward and he caught her.

"Careful," he said. "You are so trouble prone."

She lifted her head, saw the tormenting little smile in his eyes. "Are you after the job of minder?"

"I'm after the job of *husband,*" he said bluntly, getting his arms around her. "Maybe I should keep you here like this until you say yes. My prisoner." He bent his head and kissed her, not stopping until she was making little moaning sounds of surrender.

"I'd be shattered if you ever wanted to leave me," she told him passionately. "Think about it, Rolfe." She hit a hand to his chest. "You *say* you're not going back to Argentina to live, but you might want to at some stage. It happens."

"And you wouldn't come with me?" He rocked her slightly.

"I could say my life is *here*."

"If we married *you* would become my life," he said, looking deep into her eyes. "As I would become yours. You mustn't fear I'll return to Argentina. I've already promised you I won't."

"So what happens now?" Cecile asked, feeling near helpless. "Where is this great tide of feeling going to carry us?"

"Toward the future, Cecile," he said with great confidence. "Not the past. Think how terrible it would be if we parted. Do you really want that?"

No! "I'd never get over you," she said, finally accepting whether it was safe or not, it was true.

"Then you have to believe in me."

THE ANSWER DIDN'T DROP out of the sky. That night Cecile stood at the French doors of her bedroom staring up at the great copper moon of the tropics. This was decision time. She had to make up her mind for good. She wanted Rolfe in her life. Indeed she couldn't bear the thought of life without him. She was a child psychologist. She had studied and treated many kinds of conflicts that arose during the early years of life. As the granddaughter of a very rich man, she had virtually been programmed to look very carefully at the people around her before she offered her trust. Trust had become of paramount importance to her. She had suffered little betrayals over the years any number of times. But being left totally in the dark by the man she had come to love had crushed her. It had precipitated an emotional crisis, but to resolve it she had to get out from under. Rolfe, for his part, had been programmed from a blighted childhood to hate the family who had wreaked such painful trauma on his own. His mother apparently hadn't known the full story, either, but it was certain she, too, hadn't let go of her loathing of the Morelands. Looked at objectively, putting aside her own troublesome fears and anxieties, it was easy to see Rolfe had been made a victim, not once, but many times over. It was characteristic of a man not to want to talk. Men walked away from talk, whereas the need to talk things through, sometimes exhaustively, came naturally to women. She had to take that into consideration. Rolfe had acted on his programming. She had acted on hers.

Their crisis had reached a peak. Resolution had to come from her. Hadn't Rolfe confided with deep emotion that she had offered him redemption? Why doubt him? She understood so much about children and how their experiences formed them. Now she had to turn her clear professional regard on herself and Rolfe. The sins of her grandmother, Frances, could no longer be allowed to visit themselves on her and Rolfe. She was the one who had to take meaningful action.

"You have to believe in me!"

Their happiness together rested on that foundation. She had to start turning herself in another direction. There was no one else like Rolfe for her in the world.

CHAPTER FIFTEEN

THE MONTHS SINCE Daniel and Sandra had left on their honeymoon had flown by on wings. The happy couple were due home in a couple of weeks. Their honeymoon trip—from all accounts glorious—had taken in all the great capital cities of Europe and had been extended when the newlyweds decided they wanted more time to explore the countryside of the various regions.

No sooner had they learned the details of the return flight home than Joel started planning a reunion party.

"Nothing big, around a hundred or so, Ceci. I'm sure Sandra's bridesmaids would like to come. We can organize their tickets. Bea will want to be here. I'll send the jet for her and your mother."

"Don't you think you should give Daniel and Sandra a little time to recover, Granddad?" Cecile asked. "There's such a thing as jet lag." Nevertheless she was as excited as her grandfather Daniel and Sandra were coming home.

Joel looked up from some property development plans he had spread out on the coffee table. "They'll be fine, Ceci. They're young." He dismissed jet lag with a wave of his hand. "Let's see. They'll be home early morning of the Wednesday. We'll plan it for the following Saturday night. What do you think?"

Cecile didn't have the heart to say, "Wait a while!" Her grandfather was living his life as though every day was his last.

"Something else I wanted to talk to you about, my darling. Sit down now. Those flowers are just right." Cecile had been twitching a dried oleander branch around her arrangement of orchids and Asian lilies in a celadon vase.

"I'm sitting." She smiled at him affectionately and began to twiddle her thumbs.

"Serious now." Her grandfather took another sip of his coffee and put it down. "I'm thinking of offering Rolfe much the same job he was doing so wonderfully well for his stepfather. Breeding and schooling fine polo ponies for the international market. That means second in charge to Jock Lindsey at Lagunda. Jock has been with me for donkey years, as you know. He isn't far off retiring. At that time Rolfe would take over. What do you think?"

A faint trembling began in Cecile's hands and spread to her body. "It's a lot to take in, Granddad. Have you discussed it with him?"

Joel shook his head. "Not as yet. I'm sounding you out first."

That made sense. "On the face of it, Granddad, it sounds a perfect solution for both parties," she said quietly, "but I don't really know what Rolfe's plans are."

"Then you'd better find out, my darling," Joel advised her. "Rolfe and I have discussed his idea of turning Currawa into a small working station and tourist destination. He told me he'd already discussed it with you. More and more tourists are visiting the Red Centre. Many like the idea of staying on an Outback station and getting an idea of Outback life. It could work well, handled the right way. But Rolfe's got a wonderful way with horses. He said himself horses are his passion. What could be better than working at Lagunda? His stepfather will be very sorry to lose him, but I'm hoping his loss will be my gain. Of course if you're against it, I know he won't consider it."

"Are you sure of that?"

"Surer than *you* are apparently," he said shrewdly. "Rolfe has been working very hard to restore your trust, my darling."

"I know." She touched her grandfather's hand. "Both of us are working to iron out whatever problems we have left. The process is almost complete, but making that final commitment is a huge decision, Granddad. You weren't happy in your marriage. Neither were my parents. I can't hide the fact I love Rolfe. I don't want to. I want to shout it aloud, but some part of me, down deep, is very sensitive to how marriages, even marriages founded on love, can fail."

"Well, marriage is a big gamble for anyone, Ceci." Joel sighed. "We all pursue happiness but it's very elusive. The thing is, time passes. You can't let your life slip by. You have to take action one way or the other. The failure of your engagement to Carlson was a setback. You're too intelligent to set the stage for another failure. Rolfe is a very different man from Carlson."

Cecile's eyes glittered with the depth of her emotion. "I love him so much, sometimes I'm *afraid* of it." She spoke the simple truth.

Her grandfather leaned back in his chair, deep understanding on his face. "Ah, Ceci," he said. "With love there's always the underlying fear of loss. Fear one party will profoundly change and cease to care. Fear of a third party entering the marriage to rock the boat. Fear of terrible things happening to the loved one. That happened to me with Jared. I started having bad dreams a couple of weeks before he was killed."

"I didn't know that, Granddad." Cecile looked at her grandfather with compassion in her eyes.

"Sometimes I had such a tight feeling in my chest I thought I might have a heart attack, though I was only in my forties, very fit and strong. Still, that's how I felt. Presentiments. Hordes of people have had them. I had an intense passion for Frances at the beginning. God knows why, but it faded fast. I suppose the things that mattered to me didn't matter at all to your grandmother. She only pretended in the early days for my benefit. She told me that herself. We grew apart. I have to accept blame. There was always the pressure of business on me. It wasn't that I was dedicated to making money. That wasn't it. I had *vision*. I wanted to do good things. For the community, for the Territory, for my country."

"You succeeded, Granddad. Have no fear. You're an Outback icon. We're all very proud of you."

"And I'm proud of you, Ceci," said Joel. "And Daniel, my fine grandson. Your mother, you and Daniel are the three most important people in my life. But I have to tell you I thoroughly approve of Rolfe. We get on like a house on fire. At times we seem like family. I sense he's missed a grandfather figure in his life. I'm happy to be it. I would be absolutely delighted to welcome him into the family—which wasn't exactly the case with Stuart."

"Stuart turned on me very quickly," Cecile said, disenchantment in her voice.

Joel shrugged. "Well, one couldn't blame him for being tremendously upset. But he should have stopped there. Of course he was trying to discredit Rolfe in your eyes, but he can't be allowed to put private business on the public agenda. You'll have no trouble there. But getting back to Rolfe, I know I have to wait until you two make a decision regarding your future, but tell me this—could you consider life at Lagunda?"

The reality was she would consider Mars as long as she was with Rolfe. Yet she couldn't commit herself at that moment. "I have to think about it, Granddad. Malagari is my favorite place, but I love Lagunda, too. It's a different world."

"Subtropical, glorious location, the Pacific ocean at your doorstep. Most people would think they'd died and gone to heaven if they lived there."

"I know. But I'm still sorting out a few aspects of my life."

"Of course. As far as Malagari goes, I need Daniel to take over the running of it. He's a born cattleman. But Malagari will always remain the ancestral home. Half goes to you, half to Daniel. I know how much you love it. Lagunda, as you say, is a very different world, lush and green. Would you want to continue your career? It has its dangerous side. That's been brought home to us."

Cecile looked down at her ringless hands. "I trained hard for it, Granddad. I've been able to help a lot of children. That was my aim."

He looked pointedly at her. "You want children yourself?"

She flushed and looked up. "Of course I do. What a question! I love children."

"Sorry. I know you're very different from your mother. Justine always made the excuse that having more children was dangerous. It wasn't true."

"I know. Bea told me."

He clicked his tongue. "Bea got wise to Justine early. She fooled the rest of us for years. In that sense I feel sorry for your father. This other woman, you like her?"

"Yes, I do." It was no shock he knew they'd met. "I believe and I hope she and Dad will be very happy together. Life is too short to be unhappy."

"Absolutely," Joel said. "I can tell you something that would make me enormously happy." His whole face lit up.

"Tell me, it's yours!" Cecile felt a great wave of love.

"That's a promise?" He leaned across the table and put out his hand.

"Yes, if I can." She shook his hand.

"Then make me a great-grandfather someday soon," he begged. "You *and* Daniel. I can tell you now I can't wait."

TWO DAYS LATER Cecile and Rolfe and Joel flew to Queensland, Joel's pilot landing at the Gold Coast airport. From there they rented a car to drive to Lagunda in the beautiful hinterland. Jock and his wife, Valerie, welcomed them warmly. A delicious lunch was waiting, and afterward Cecile, Rolfe and Joel made an inspection of the property—an entire world especially designed for horses—with Jock at the wheel of the 4WD. It was a delightful trip. This was some of the prettiest country in Australia. The blue ranges formed a background for the lush green pastures, there was abundant wildlife, swans, ducks, even a couple of pelicans on a big spring-fed lake just deep enough for a horse to enjoy a dip. There was the tang of salt in the air as the wind blew in from the ocean.

In the white-fenced paddocks was the sweet familiar sight of horses galloping around the perimeter, full of the joy of life, tails and manes flying. Jock stopped from time to time to point out a special horse. Others, each as beautifully groomed as the next, trotted over to the fence to see what was happening and hopefully be petted. There were mothers standing in the paddocks with their foals, a heart-melting sight. The place was filled with incredibly beautiful horses, around three hundred at any given time. Back at the stables they looked in on the latest addition, a foal that had arrived just the previous night. A little colt, he was all legs with a bobtail that he flicked the minute he caught sight of them. Cecile waited long enough to see him cuddle up to his mother to nurse, his little tummy fast filling with milk. A feed, a satisfied sigh, then a nap.

The reason they had come was for Rolfe to make his own inspection, to see what he thought, and from there make a decision as to whether he wanted to take up Joel's offer. He and Jock had hit it off immediately. If they hadn't, there would have been a problem, but both had a relaxed manner and there was the great common bond of the love and deep knowledge of horses.

After the horses came the lengthy discussion on programs, with breeding charts produced. Cecile found herself a little light-headed from the flight, so she returned to the homestead to enjoy a quiet talk with Val. They were old friends, so the time passed quickly.

"Well, what's the verdict?" Joel asked as they drove away a couple of hours later.

"It's a splendid property, Joel," Rolfe, at the wheel, answered. "Jock is a good man. You must value him highly."

"I do, but I happen to know Jock is just about ready to retire. He's well into his sixties now. He and Val have always spoken about traveling. You wouldn't have long to wait to do your own thing."

"I would *want* to," Rolfe said, making that clear. "Some

of my methods are quite different from Jock's. I'm not saying *better,* Jock is obviously doing all the right things, but *different.* You're being incredibly generous to me, Joel. Let me think about this." He caught Cecile's silver eyes in the rear view mirror.

She knew then she held the answer. She had to think no more to give it. Hadn't Rolfe's eyes told her, *"I will always, always love you."*

FIRST LIGHT WOKE HER. No point in lying there. She rose quickly, then fell back on the bed again, shocked by the wave of nausea that rolled through her stomach. She lay back, waiting for the sick feeling to subside. Mercifully it did. She tried to tell herself it was a quick drop in blood pressure. Or maybe she'd caught a bug. She'd been feeling vaguely off color and light-headed for days, without her usual energy. It could have been a bug, but she knew better. Regular as clockwork she had missed her period. She had waited a week for it to make its appearance, but she *knew* it wasn't going to.

She was pregnant.

A blood test would confirm it. She had pretty much invited it. She had been so emotional after her estrangement from Rolfe she had stopped taking the pill. Her love life was a disaster, wasn't it? She had subsequently gone back on the pill, but she'd known at the back of her mind she was putting herself at risk the night Rolfe had rescued her from the abominable Dr. Wheeler.

No protection.

Exquisite timing!

Such a night!

Was it any wonder, then, she would wind up pregnant?

Yet wasn't that what everyone wanted? She lay there with her hand over her eyes, waiting for her stomach to settle. Her mother, her grandfather? The two of them would be wild with joy after they got over the initial shock. She realized that, mingled with her dismay and sense of trepidation, she herself was already thinking ahead to when she would hold her own child in her arms.

It's not you, my darling, my beautiful love child who jumped the gun. It's me! She patted her stomach, talking to the embryo she was certain at that very moment was growing in her womb. *I love you already.*

She would have to tell Rolfe. When? After she had her own diagnosis confirmed by a blood test? She could arrange that quickly enough. On her own reckoning—she fully expected to be proved right—conception had taken place three weeks before. She couldn't bear to wait six weeks to tell him.

Would he turn on her, his voice rising in dismayed accusation? No, Rolfe wouldn't turn on her. That wasn't his way. But how *would* he take it? Would he have a sense of being tricked? As though she, being the mother of his child, would have control? It would certainly bring any plans he might have rapidly forward. He claimed he wanted to marry her, said he wouldn't take up the position on Lagunda without her.

Should she subject him to another test? He had brought her little habit of testing people out in the open, after all. That aspect of her character might continue with certain people but not with Rolfe. She no longer swung back and forth like a pendulum. Her trust in him from this day forth was rock solid.

THE WAVE OF NAUSEA had subsided. This time she stood up more slowly and walked into the bathroom to take a shower.

She pulled her nightgown over her head, then turned to look at her naked body in the mirror. She looked exactly the same. No changes in her breasts. She couldn't have been more slender without being downright thin. Yet it was momentous to think a baby was growing inside her. She rubbed a hand over her flat stomach, circling it gently. How long would it be before anyone saw a difference? Five months, six, maybe into the seventh month? She was taller than average and it was her first child.

She was feeling a lot better now. In fact, she had never felt more womanly.

I'm carrying a baby. Rolfe's baby. I'm the luckiest woman on earth!

MIDMORNING when her grandfather and Rolfe were closeted in the study, discussing God knows what—they'd been in there an hour and a half—Cecile took a call from a Detective Superintendent Bormann from the Melbourne police in connection with the Peter Wheeler case. Cecile listened to what he had to say in absolute silence, thanked him for ringing, then hung up.

She knocked on the study door, then entered the room at her grandfather's response.

"Cecile?" Rolfe was very quick to his feet, her grandfather more slowly, their faces mirror images of concern. "Is everything okay?"

She was aware that Rolfe started toward her. She thought she said his name. She knew she put out her hand to him, but her vision was wavering. It was like lying at the bottom of a murky pool. A dark shape swooped down on her from the surface of the water, gathering her into its cold embrace.

SHE CAME TO within moments. She was lying on the burgundy leather sofa, both legs raised on a cushion.

"One in five people faint at least once in their life," she quoted medical opinion somewhat woozily.

"That's the second time for you. One time too many." Rolfe was sitting beside her, eyeing her anxiously.

"I'll get a doctor." Her grandfather, too, was looking agitated.

"No, Granddad!" she protested. She would be seeing a doctor soon enough. "Please. I'm okay."

"It wouldn't hurt to get one here." Rolfe backed Joel.

"I'm telling you there's nothing wrong with me." She put strength into her voice. "I've had a shock. Peter Wheeler is dead. He was killed in the jail laundry by one of the other inmates. That was a Detective Superintendent Bormann on the phone. He rang to tell me before it got into the papers."

"Good God!" Joel sat down heavily in the nearest club chair. "What a terrible business. He's not the first man guilty of such a heinous crime to come to a violent end in jail."

"He'd been making threats against his wife, as well," Cecile added.

"Don't talk for a moment," Rolfe advised. "Just lie quietly."

"I will if you'll stop fussing." She looked into his eyes. "You're the one who fainted."

"Her color is coming back," Joel said, placing a comforting hand on Rolfe's shoulder.

"I'm still here," Cecile reminded them. "I haven't left the room."

"Behave yourself, Ceci," her grandfather admonished. "It's right for us to worry. You're very precious, you know."

"You might put a trip to the doctor on the agenda," Rolfe suggested. "I know the news was ugly, but a faint?"

"I promise I'll go and have a checkup," she reassured him. "You can come with me, if you like."

"I just might do that," he replied.

"At least Wheeler's death has taken the terror out of his wife's life," Joel mused.

"You're not worried about your part in anything, are you?" Rolfe's dark eyes were still intent on Cecile.

She shook her head. "My job was to save Ellie. Peter Wheeler should have sought help a long long time ago."

"How about if I ring for tea?" Joel suggested the universal fix-it. "I could do with a cup. It's a good thing Rolfe is so quick on his feet. It's a pretty hard floor and you were about to hit it, my girl."

"Rolfe has heaps of assets," she murmured, smiling into his eyes.

"May it be my destiny to be always there to catch you," he said.

IT WAS JOEL and his cronies' card night—a thirty-year fixture when Joel was in residence—so Rolfe suggested he and Cecile go out to dinner.

She dressed very carefully in a white crepe jersey dress, sleeveless with a low V neckline and a fluid skirt. She left her hair long and flowing the way he liked it. At the last moment she added the long string of lustrous South Sea pearls that had been her grandfather's twenty-first birthday present to her. They fitted perfectly inside the V neckline and looked beautiful against her skin. The pearls were so big most people would assume she was wearing lovely costume jewelry and not the real thing. There was some safety in that.

She and Rolfe popped into the card room to say hello, and her grandfather introduced Rolfe to his friends, looking extremely pleased with himself and the world. He was especially chuffed to see Cecile wearing his birthday gift to her. "Pearls can't hide away, my darling. They have to be worn and they're absolutely perfect on you."

"HOW IS IT POSSIBLE you get more beautiful every time I see you?" Rolfe asked as they walked to the car.

She could tell by the light in his eyes that the trouble she had gone to was well worth the effort. "I pay attention to all the little things." She smiled.

"Like perfume." He lifted aside her long gleaming hair, breathing her in while he kissed her neck.

By the time they parked and walked into the Darwin restaurant, the place was almost full. The maître d' saw them to their private table for two. It was out of the way of the main room, just as Cecile liked it. The floor-to-ceiling windows reflected all the light and glitter from the large elegant main room, and they could also enjoy the outside harbor lights, which glittered like a fairyland.

"Champagne?" Rolfe asked, his eyes savoring her. She was beautiful at all times, but tonight she seemed to have extra bloom. "Or would you prefer something else?"

She shook her head, already concerned for the well-being of their baby. "Usually I have champagne," she said sweetly, "but tonight I'm on a diet."

"What?" He drew back in his chair. "What would you have to go on a diet for?"

"The party," she invented. "Daniel's and Sandra's party. I have a beautiful strapless dress I want to get into."

He shook his head, letting his eyes assess her. "I don't believe this."

"I've put on a pound or two," she fibbed.

"Have you really?" His mouth turned down in disbelief. "Well, I'll check that out tonight."

"You're assuming I'm coming back to your apartment?" she challenged

"You're assuming right," he said dryly. "No wonder you fainted if you've put yourself on some silly diet."

She reached over and touched his hand. "I promise I'm eating all the right things. It's just that I'm off alcohol. But you go ahead."

She didn't remember much about what they ate, but she would always recall with great vividness the deep joy and excitement of being with him.

Over dessert he asked curiously. "You're hiding something. What is it?"

She was feeling so incandescent she wasn't surprised it showed. "Why would you say that?" She was going to hold on to her secret a little longer.

"Because I *know* you. There's something you're not telling me."

"Maybe." She smiled at him. "You told me you wouldn't take up Granddad's offer if I didn't want to go to Lagunda. Did you mean it?"

He looked perfectly self-possessed. "I said it, didn't I? You're the only woman who could have that kind of power over me."

"Lucky me!"

He clasped her hand across the table. "Seriously, if you

think you wouldn't be happy on Lagunda, we won't go there. I'll find something else. I'm not without resources. I understand perfectly if you don't want to give up your career. You've worked hard for it and you're obviously very good at it. At the same time I am concerned, like Joel, about the dangerous situations people in your line of work can become involved in."

A shiver passed over her. "Don't remind me. I do get satisfaction out of my work. Having said that, I am prepared to put my career on the back burner for a while."

"What's a while?" he asked, watching her closely.

"Oh, a year or two. And I'm not stopping you from taking up the appointment at Lagunda. You're so good at what *you* do. As I can't bear to be parted from you, I'll go along as well."

"So I should accept?" His focus on her was intent.

"Yes."

"You were testing me?"

She snapped her fingers. "My darling Rolfe, I've moved on from that. Do you want to stay here any longer or are we done?"

For answer he put up his hand to signal the waiter.

IN THE BEDROOM he began to tenderly undress her, removing her beautiful pearls first and laying them on top of a chest of drawers. "So let's check out these extra couple of pounds, shall we?" His voice was a deep sexy purr.

She was down to her underwear, a white bra with fine silk lace and matching delicate lace briefs.

He stood back to allow his eyes to travel all the way over her. "Beautiful, beautiful, beautiful!" He delivered his verdict, moving back to her again and drawing her against his aroused body. "Have you actually checked yourself out in the mirror lately? You don't have an ounce of excess weight on you. Not that I'd mind if you put on a few pounds." He let his hands run down her back to the curves of her taut rounded bottom.

"Maybe I will!"

"Okay by me." He pinched her bottom lightly. "Then I'll have more of you. You are going to marry me, aren't you?" He bent his head, planting kisses all over her face. "We're not going to Lagunda to live in sin as they still say in Argentina."

She started some caressing of her own. "On the contrary I'm going to put pressure on you to marry me. I don't want to wait."

"What about tomorrow afternoon?" He reached behind her back and unclipped her bra, setting her breasts free.

"Great," she said. "Fine with me!" Her breathing was coming faster. She was trembling with pleasure as his hands took the weight of her breasts.

"I'm serious, Cecile." Now his thumbs were circling the nipples, moving from the outside of the rose-pink areola to the tightly furled buds. He began to massage them very gently, watching her face.

"So am I," she moaned.

"Then it has to be sometime very soon. A good thing I've got an engagement ring."

Her eyelids, weighed down with desire, snapped back. "What?"

"I'll just get you comfortable on the bed, then I'll show it to you." He lifted her so quickly, so smoothly, she was lying on the king-size bed before she knew it.

She sat up, amazed, her hair tumbling around her shoulders. "Have you really got a ring for me?"

His back was to her as he opened a drawer in the small desk that occupied a corner of the bedroom. "You didn't really think we were just having an affair, did you?"

She shook her head dazedly. "You are so full of surprises!"

He came back to her, this wonderful man who loved her, and she felt the tears begin to rise to her eyes.

"Open it," he said. "But before you do, tell me what stone you think it is."

She screwed her eyes tight, clutching the small box to her naked breasts. She began to run her fingertips over the polished lid. "It's…it's *not* a diamond."

"It's not a diamond," he confirmed, sinking onto the bed beside her. "I'm not telling you anything else."

Her eyes were still closed. "So it's a ruby, a sapphire or an emerald. It could be a royal purple amethyst, but I don't think so."

She opened her eyes, staring into his face. "If I had blue eyes I'd say a sapphire. I would *love* a fiery pure red ruby, but that's the rarest stone of all. For that matter, I would love an emerald. But I would love and cherish any ring you gave me."

"Perhaps you ought to open it," he said.

"Oh, this is wonderfully exciting!"

"I think so. I've never been engaged before, so you're one up on me."

"Could you puh-lease not mention that!" she begged, aiming a soft slap at him.

"Never again," he promised, making a pretense of defending himself.

"Aaah, Rolfe!" Delight fell over her like a silken net. Inside the box glowing up at her, sat a glorious oval-shaped ruby surrounded by a blaze of diamonds. "Wherever did you get this?"

"In my spare time I was a jewel thief."

"Darling!" She reached up to kiss him. "I can't marry a jewel thief."

"I've changed a lot." He smiled, watching her return to admiring her engagement ring. "Actually it's a long story and fascinating, to boot. How I came by the central stone I mean. I had the ring made to my own design. A few years back I saved a fellow polo player from a potentially fatal fall. Anyway, as it turned out, he was a relative of the Sultan of Brunei."

"Wow! No wonder you galloped after him," she retorted facetiously, turning the boxed ring this way and that to catch the light.

"I'll tell you the full story later," Rolfe said dryly. "Let's put that ring on, shall we?" He took the box from her and extracted the beautiful piece of jewelry. With it in hand, he slid from the side of the bed, kneeling before her like a supplicant to a naked goddess.

"You are my chosen woman out of all the women in the world," he said, taking her hand and raising it to his mouth. "With this ring, Cecile, I swear my everlasting allegiance. I shall love and treasure you until the day I die."

His words struck her ears like heavenly music, and tears of joy started streaming down her cheeks.

"Don't cry, darling. *Please.*" He was torn between laughter and tenderness.

"Hey, that's what women do."

"Right-o, go ahead. I can lick all those tears up." Keeping his eyes on her, he slid the ring over her knuckle to the base of her finger. It came to rest there as if made for her alone. "It looks wonderful on your beautiful hand."

"It *is* wonderful!" She tried to halt the flow of tears, but they continued to stream from her eyes. Maybe her being pregnant had something to do with it? she thought. Pregnancy, fulfillment, happiness. A good strong man who loved her, the father of her child.

"All right!" Rolfe started stripping off his clothes very purposefully. "I know one way to stop those tears. I'm going to get naked, then I'm going to make hot, impassioned love to you and it's going to go on for a long time."

"Well, that's what I'm here for," she said. "Impassioned love *is* your specialty!" She threw herself languorously onto the pillows, holding up her ring to the light. "Hurry, darling," she said. "I'm calling a wedding officiant first thing in the morning."

THEY WERE LYING quietly in the aftermath of truly beautiful sex, still marveling at the miracle of their love.

"How do you feel about babies?" she asked as though sounding him out on his views for their future. She was turned on her side, snuggling into him, her ring hand splayed across his chest. The Bruneian ruby, a splendid pure red, was the perfect symbol of their love.

He took a moment to answer, continuing to wind a raven lock of her hair around his hand. Then very seriously, "I love babies," he said.

* * * * *

"OH, NO!"

The reaction slipped out before Emma Valentine could stop it, for there stood the very man she most wanted to avoid seeing again.

He didn't look any happier to see her.

"Well, come on, get on board," he said gruffly. "I won't bite." One eyebrow rose. "Though I might nibble a little," he added, mostly to amuse himself.

But she wasn't paying any attention to what he was saying. She was staring at him, taking in the royal-blue uniform he was wearing, with gold braid and glistening badges decorating the sleeves, epaulettes and an upright collar. Ribbons and medals covered the breast of the short, fitted jacket. A gold-encrusted sabre hung at his side. And suddenly it was clear to her who this man really was.

She gulped wordlessly. Reaching out, he took her elbow and pulled her aboard. The doors slid closed. And finally she found her tongue.

"You…you're the prince."

He nodded, barely glancing at her. "Yes. Of course."

She raised a hand and covered her mouth for a moment. "I should have known."

"Of course you should have. I don't know why you didn't." He punched the ground-floor button to get the elevator moving again, then turned to look down at her. "A relatively bright five-year-old child would have tumbled to the truth right away."

Her shock faded as her indignation at his tone asserted itself. He might be the prince, but he was still just as annoying as he had been earlier that day.

"A relatively bright five-year-old child without a bump on the head from a badly thrown water polo ball, maybe," she said defensively. She wasn't feeling woozy any longer and she wasn't about to let him bully her, no matter how royal he was. "I was unconscious half the time."

"And just clueless the other half, I guess," he said, looking bemused.

The arrogance of the man was really galling.

"I suppose you think your 'royalness' is so obvious it sort of shimmers around you for all to see?" she challenged. "Or better yet, oozes from your pores like…like sweat on a hot day?"

"Something like that," he acknowledged calmly. "Most people tumble to it pretty quickly. In fact, it's hard to hide even when I want to avoid dealing with it."

"Poor baby," she said, still resenting his manner. "I guess that works better with injured people who are half asleep." Looking at him, she felt a strange emotion she couldn't identify. It was as though she wanted to prove something to him, but she wasn't sure what. "And anyway, you know you did your best to fool me," she added.

His brows knit together as though he really didn't know what she was talking about. "I didn't do a thing."

"You told me your name was Monty."

"It is." He shrugged. "I have a lot of names. Some of them are too rude to be spoken to my face, I'm sure." He glanced at her sideways, his hand on the hilt of his sabre. "Perhaps you're contemplating one of those right now."

You bet I am.

That was what she would like to say. But it suddenly occurred to her that she was supposed to be working for this man. If she wanted to keep the job of coronation chef, maybe she'd better keep her opinions to herself. So she clamped her mouth shut, took a deep breath and looked away, trying hard to calm down.

The elevator ground to a halt and the doors slid open laboriously. She moved to step forward, hoping to make her escape, but his hand shot out again and caught her elbow.

"Wait a minute. *You're* a woman," he said, as though that thought had just presented itself to him.

"That's a rare ability for insight you have there, Your Highness," she snapped before she could stop herself. And then she winced. She was going to have to do better than that if she was going to keep this relationship on an even keel.

But he was ignoring her dig. Nodding, he stared at her with a speculative gleam in his golden eyes. "I've been looking for a woman, but you'll do."

She blanched, stiffening. "I'll do for what?"

He made a head gesture in a direction she knew was opposite of where she was going and his grip tightened on her elbow.

"Come with me," he said abruptly, making it an order.

She dug in her heels, thinking fast. She didn't much like orders. "Wait! I can't. I have to get to the kitchen."

"Not yet. I need you."

"You what?" Her breathless gasp of surprise was soft, but she knew he'd heard it.

"I need you," he said firmly. "Oh, don't look so shocked. I'm not planning to throw you into the hay and have my way with you. I need you for something a bit more mundane than that."

She felt color rushing into her cheeks and she silently begged it to stop. Here she was, formless and stodgy in her chef's whites. No makeup, no stiletto heels. Hardly the picture of the femmes fatales he was undoubtedly used to. The likelihood that he would have any carnal interest in her was remote at best. To have him think she was hysterically defending her virtue was humiliating.

"Well, what if I don't want to go with you?" she said in hopes of deflecting his attention from her blush.

"Too bad."

"What?"

Amusement sparkled in his eyes. He was certainly enjoying this. And that only made her more determined to resist him.

"I'm the prince, remember? And we're in the castle. My orders take precedence. It's that old pesky divine- rights thing."

Her jaw jutted out. Despite her embarrassment, she couldn't let that pass.

"Over my free will? Never!"

Exasperation filled his face.

"Hey, call out the historians. Someone will write a book about you and your courageous principles." His eyes glittered sardonically. "But in the meantime, Emma Valentine, you're coming with me."

SAVE UP TO $30! SIGN UP TODAY!

**The complete guide to your favorite
Harlequin®, Silhouette® and Love Inspired® books.**

✓ Newsletter ABSOLUTELY FREE! No purchase necessary.

✓ Valuable coupons for future purchases of Harlequin,
  Silhouette and Love Inspired books in every issue!

✓ Special excerpts & previews in each issue. Learn about all
  the hottest titles before they arrive in stores.

✓ No hassle—mailed directly to your door!

✓ Comes complete with a handy shopping checklist
  so you won't miss out on any titles.

- -

SIGN ME UP TO RECEIVE INSIDE ROMANCE ABSOLUTELY FREE

(Please print clearly)

**Introducing an exciting appearance
by legendary
New York Times bestselling author**

DIANA PALMER
HEARTBREAKER

He's the ultimate bachelor...
but he may have just met
the one woman to change his ways!

Join the drama in the story of a confirmed
bachelor, an amnesiac beauty and their
unexpected passionate romance.

"Diana Palmer is a mesmerizing storyteller
who captures the essence of what
a romance should be."—*Affaire de Coeur*

---

*Heartbreaker is available from Silhouette Desire
in September 2006.*

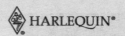
HARLEQUIN®

American **ROMANCE**®

IS PROUD TO PRESENT THREE NEW BOOKS
BY THE BESTSELLING AUTHOR OF THE
COWBOYS BY THE DOZEN MINISERIES

Tina Leonard

The Tulips Saloon

The women of Tulips, Texas—only thirty miles
from Union Junction—have a goal to increase the
population of the tiny town. Whether that means
luring handsome cowboys from far and wide, or
matchmaking among their current residents, these
women will get what they want—even if it means
growing the town one baby (or two!) at a time.

MY BABY, MY BRIDE
September 2006

THE CHRISTMAS TWINS
November 2006

HER SECRET SONS
February 2007

Available wherever Harlequin books are sold.

ANGELS OF THE BIG SKY
by Roz Denny Fox

(#1368)

Widow Marlee Stein returns to Montana with her
young daughter, ready to help out with Cloud Chasers,
the flying service owned by her brother. When Marlee
takes over piloting duties, she finds herself in conflict
with a client, ranger Wylie Ames. Too bad Marlee's
attracted to a man she doesn't even want to like!

On sale September 2006!

THE CLOUD CHASERS—
Life is looking up.

Watch for the second story in Roz Denny Fox's two-
book series THE CLOUD CHASERS, available in
December 2006.

Available wherever books are sold, including most
bookstores, supermarkets, discount stores and drugstores.

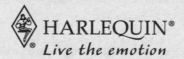

HARLEQUIN®
Live the emotion

COMING NEXT MONTH

#1368 ANGELS OF THE BIG SKY • Roz Denny Fox
The Cloud Chasers
Widow Marlee Stein returns to Montana with her young daughter, ready to help out with Cloud Chasers, the flying service owned by her twin brother, Mick Callen. Because of Mick's surgery, Marlee takes over piloting duties, including mercy flights—and immediately finds herself in conflict with one of his clients, ranger Wylie Ames. Too bad Marlee's so attracted to a man she doesn't even want to *like!*

#1369 MAN FROM MONTANA • Brenda Mott
Single Father
Kara never would've dreamed she'd be a widow so young—or that she could find room in her heart for anyone besides her husband. And then Derrick moved in across the street....

#1370 THE RETURN OF DAVID McKAY • Ann Evans
Heart of the Rockies
David McKay thought he'd seen the last of Broken Yoke when he left for Hollywood—until a pilgrimage into the mountains to scatter his grandfather's ashes forced him to return and face his first love, Adriana D'Angelo. That's when he realized the price he'd paid for his ambition. And how much a second chance at happiness would change his life...

#1371 SMALL-TOWN SECRETS • Margaret Watson
Hometown U.S.A.
It took Gabe Townsend seven years to return to Sturgeon Falls after the fateful car accident. He would never have come back if he hadn't had to. Because he still loved Kendall, and she was his best friend's wife.

#1372 MAKE-BELIEVE COWBOY • Terry McLaughlin
Bright Lights, Big Sky
A widow with a kid and a mountain of debt. A good-looking man everyone *thought* they knew. Meeting for the first time under the wide-open skies of Montana!

#1373 MR. IMPERFECT • Karina Bliss
Going Back
The last will and testament of Kezia's beloved grandmother is the only thing that could drag bad boy Christian Kelly back to the hometown that had brought him only misery....